Death
of an Irish
Druid

The Dublin Driver Mysteries

Dead in Dublin

Death in the Green

Death of an Irish Mummy

Death in Irish Accents

Death by Irish Whiskey

Death of an Irish Druid

Death of an Irish Druid

CATIE MURPHY

Kensington Publishing Corp.
kensingtonbooks.com

PRONUNCIATION GUIDE

Irish words will often trip up English-speaking readers because we try to map English letter sounds and combinations onto a language never intended to use them. The trickier words and names in *Death of an Irish Druid* are pronounced as follows:

a chuisle mo chroí = a cushla muh khree ("pulse of my heart," or "my heart," in Irish)

Abhaile = ahWAHLya

Aisling = Ashling

An Garda Síochána = ahn garda shee oh cawna ("Guardians of the Peace," in Irish)

Banchomarbae = ban corba

Columbkille = columkill

Crann Bethadh = crawn BEHha ("Tree of Life," in Irish)

Naas = Nayss

Niamh = Neev

Seamus = Shaymus

CHAPTER 1

Rafael Williams, Megan "#MurderDriver" Malone's best friend, was not, thank goodness, dead.

He was, however, a huge dork. The moment he came through the arrival doors to see her, he called, "Megan in the *hoooooooouse*!" to the dismay of both Megan and the slender Black woman with him, and to the amusement of everybody else within earshot. Which was several hundred people, at eight fifty in the morning at Dublin International Airport.

Megan put her face in her hands, laughed into them, and lifted her gaze to beam at Raf, who reached across the waist-high barrier to hug her like he couldn't wait an extra four seconds to walk around it. Megan said, "I am so glad to see you, *mi amigo*. You know it's no longer two-thousand-and-whatever-it-was when we still said things like that, right?"

His wife, Sarah, said, "No," wryly. She wasn't tall—not even Megan's height—but she was ballerina-slim and had long limbs that made her seem tall. Her hair was pulled back in very, very dark-blue braids that looped at her nape, and she had an elegant, calm air even after an international flight. Rafael let Megan go, and the two of them came around the barrier before Sarah added, "Raf is convinced that if he's cringe enough, he'll actually come out the other side and be cool again. I don't know how to convince him otherwise."

"That's what I'm here for," Megan said happily. "Your oldest friends are the people to tell you the hard truths. So, I'm Megan," she added, and offered a hand, smiling broadly. "Nice to finally meet you, Sarah."

"Oh, we're doing it that way, are we?" Sarah shook Megan's hand very formally, then pulled her into a hug. "It's about time. I'm so glad to actually put a hug with the face."

"My two best girls." Rafael's perpetual tan was paler than Megan could ever remember seeing it, and he had more gray scattered through his black hair than Megan expected, yet he beamed at the two of them. "I can't believe it's taken this long to get you two in the same place."

"And that we had to end up in Ireland to do it." Sarah gave a slightly dramatic shiver, beneath her long, chocolate-colored wool coat and the bright, lightweight scarves around its collar. "Is it always this cold?"

"In January? Mostly, yes." Megan glanced back at the big windows and sky bridge behind them. Enough clouds rolled across the sky to justify the spatters of rain against the windows, but sunlight glimmered around the horizon, and she figured the odds of rainbows as they exited were fairly high. "Come on, though, you live in San Francisco."

"'The coldest winter I ever spent was a summer in San Francisco,'" Sarah quoted. "I was born in Abuja and haven't been warm since I left at age eight."

"I've turned out to be better at chilly weather than I expected," Megan admitted. "Austin runs at least ten degrees warmer than Ireland at all times, but I don't really miss it. Are we ready? I've got the car in the parking garage."

"We're ready." Rafael hefted two suitcases that moved so easily it was clear they'd packed light on the trip over, presumably in anticipation of packing much more heavily on the way home. Megan offered to take one, and in a true chivalrous fashion, he let her. "Ten degrees, that can't be right, though. It's gotta be more like twenty, at least."

"Celsius," Sarah said in an almost-smug tone. "I told you, everywhere civilized uses it."

"And I've apparently been in Ireland long enough to default to it," Megan said with some surprise. "I never would have thought I would. Oh my god, I'm so glad to see you two again."

"Me again," Raf said. "Her for the first time."

"I have seen Sarah *many* times on vone calls," Megan protested. "It's not my fault I missed the wedding." Which was true: she'd been on active military duty at the time, unable to get leave, and Sarah had been on tour with her ballet company the only time Megan had made it San Francisco before moving to Ireland.

She stopped dead in the sky bridge, distracted from her thoughts by a brilliant arc of colors in the sky. "Oh, look, there *is* a rainbow!"

The other two squealed like they'd never seen one before, and Raf put his suitcase down to fumble for his phone so they could get a selfie. "In the Dublin airport sky bridge," Megan said aloud, grinning. "With the parking garage in the background. So picturesque. Let me take that for you."

She took his phone, snapped a couple of pictures, and then got dragged into a selfie after all, a rainbow shining behind their heads and all three of them smiling like overexcited teenagers. "I'm posting this with the murder driver hashtag," Rafael said gleefully.

"I will *end* you." Megan lunged for his phone and knocked them both into the sky bridge wall, causing a reverberation that made half the travelers in the area glare at them with a mix of scorn and concern.

"He warned me you would revert to being nine," Sarah said with a note of wonder. "I didn't know he meant it literally. Or that it would happen so fast."

"I blame an international flight and having no idea what time it is." Raf wobbled to his feet, made sure Megan was on hers, and stuffed his phone safely in his pocket, where she couldn't get to it. "And I'm not really going to murder-driver-tag it. How are you doing with that, anyway?"

"With murder driving? Great, it's been *weeks* since anybody died on my watch."

Rafael gave her a gentle look, as if she hadn't known he wasn't talking about the actual murder driver thing at all. Or he was, but only in the context of the latest spate of murders having been the final straw for Megan's now-ex-girlfriend. They'd broken up a couple of months earlier, and she wasn't as over it as she thought she should be. "You're not here for me to be all gloom and doom at you for two weeks. I'm fine, really. It's okay."

"We *are* here for you to lean on us," Sarah said as gently as Raf had looked. "That's what friends are for."

"Well, they're also for dragging all over the countryside and showing off everything I've learned living in Ireland, which will be a lot more fun if I'm not mopey. And speaking of which, how are you two feeling after the flight? Do you want to throw yourself into things so you stay awake today and then get sent to bed at a sensible hour, or do you need to collapse for a while?" They were down the escalator by then, walking across into the parking lot for privately hired cars, where Megan was shamelessly taking advantage of her limo-driver status and the car she'd rented from her boss's business for two weeks.

Sarah tightened her coat around herself again, shivering less theatrically this time. "Coffee and then exploring. If I go to sleep now, I'm never going to get onto Irish time, but I need something warm to drink."

"She can say that because she didn't work an eighteen-hour shift right before getting on the plane," Raf mumbled, but nodded agreement anyway. "No, she's right, though. Give me a coffee drip, and I'm good to go."

Megan snorted. "Drip coffee isn't much of a thing in Ireland."

"*Doctor* Williams knows the difference between a coffee drip and drip coffee!" Raf said, mock-offended, and both women laughed. A minute later they were hefting their bags into the back of the limo—actually a Lincoln Town Car, Megan's favorite of the limo service's vehicles—and she was promising that if they could stay awake through forty minutes of approaching-Dublin traffic, she would take them out for the best coffee in the city.

"I have a better idea. I could sleep for forty minutes and *then* have the coffee." Raf put his head against the window and closed his eyes as soon as he got in the car, apparently meaning to do exactly as he'd said. Sarah examined him a moment, then got in the front with Megan and gave her a wicked smile.

"Perfect. You can tell me all his embarrassing childhood secrets while we drive."

From the back seat, Raf said, *"Hey!"* without opening his eyes, and before they'd left the parking lot, he was snoring very, very softly.

Sarah gave him a fond look over her shoulder and murmured, "He really is exhausted. Those long shifts at the hospital are impossible. I don't know how we're going to deal with it if I ever *do* get pregnant. Sometimes I get the impression that being married to an ER doctor is a lot like being a single parent." She made a face. "Which isn't what we came here to talk about, either."

"What was that you were saying about friends being there to lean on?" Megan asked as softly. "Can he move into a private practice? I don't know anything about whether you have to do special training to be a general practitioner if you've been an ER doctor."

"He's been doing the training," Sarah said with a nod. "Which cuts into his home time, too, and it's going slowly because he's trying to study around the ER hours. But he's also got this underlying belief that if he quits, the entire emergency department will actually fall apart. Institutional guilt, or something."

"He was always like that," Megan said. "He was on the student council from seventh grade onward because he couldn't trust anybody else to do the job right. To his amazement, the school didn't collapse when he graduated. Even the student government managed to keep staggering along without him. Remind him of that," she said with a quick smile. "And then he'll make that 'you betrayed me' face at me, and it'll be great."

Sarah grinned. "See, this is exactly why I needed to get together with you and talk without him being on the call, too. You've got almost four decades worth of ammunition to use against him."

"Well, between my ammunition and your feminine wiles, maybe you can make him see reason. He's always wanted to be a dad, though," Megan added quietly. "He'll make the change so he doesn't miss out on that."

"If it happens."

"I have a plan for that," Megan said sagely.

Sarah clapped both hands over her mouth and Megan had to muffle herself to keep a loud laugh from bursting free. "Oh, God, that didn't come out the way I meant it to."

"I hope not! I like you, Megan, but I don't think I need you intimately involved in the job of getting me pregnant!"

Megan waggled her eyebrows. "Just you wait and see."

The plan for coffee was slightly delayed by needing to stop at Megan's house to pick up two small, very excited Jack Russells who were no longer really puppies, even if she still thought of them that way. Dip, the male, whose face looked like it had been dipped in chocolate, fell in love with Sarah immediately and collapsed wriggling on her feet. His sister, Thong, who fortunately didn't have markings to match *her* name, believed she had slightly more dignity than her brother, and thus sat and waited to be noticed—with her tail thumping at a million miles an hour.

Both of them knew the carrier meant a car ride, which was possibly even more exciting than meeting new people. After Sarah had greeted them with enough enthusiasm to prove her instantaneous love, they scurried into the carrier, curled up around each other, and went to sleep almost before Megan got the carrier into the car. Rafael managed to sleep through all of it, even the dogs' hopeful whining when they realized there was someone else for them to meet. They stopped for coffee, and Megan got one for Raf in the thermal mug she kept in the car, knowing it would still be hot when he woke up.

The drive in to Dublin from the airport wasn't a lovely

one—the motorway had a lot of tall concrete walls and comparatively little visible countryside—but once they were on the road to Kildare, the rolling green hills Ireland was famous for spread out ahead of them. Sarah gave a contented sigh. "All right, it *is* beautiful, even if it's cloudy."

"Not too bad," Megan agreed. Even in winter, with many of the fields cut back and gleaming gold instead of green, it *was* a country of gentle greens, misty grays, and washed blues at the sunlit horizons. That specific soft light was frequently depicted in the paintings and photography of Ireland, although Megan herself had a particular fondness for the sudden glowing clarity after a hard rain beat the mist down, and the sun came out as if to prove it could. They drove in silence a few minutes, and when Megan glanced over, Sarah had rested her head against the window and drifted off into a light sleep that lasted the hour long drive to Kildare.

The well was tucked away just outside of Kildare town, part of a quiet heritage centre and small park that had been built around the holy well. Megan, feeling a little guilty about it, woke her guests, who blinked around blearily for a few minutes before being ready to get out of the car. A priest, recognizable by his collar and rosary, if not the rest of his clothes, walked by as they finally crawled out, and offered them a solemn, quiet smile as if not wanting to disturb the air. Megan gave him a smile in return, and the other two waved sleepily, with Rafael trying to arrange his features into something pleasant and ending up yawning until tears came to his eyes. The priest murmured, "Welcome to Ireland," and drove off in a car that didn't look wide enough for his shoulders.

"How'd he know?" Sarah asked around a yawn of her own. "That we're visitors, I mean?"

"Probably because you're yawning your brains out while at a tourist attraction," Megan replied, surprisingly happy. Sarah giggled and yawned again, and Rafael gratefully slurped at his coffee while they woke the dogs and all went trooping past the visitors' centre to the well. There was an air of ancient faith that carried a serenity of its own in the little park, which had touches of the modern in a beautiful bronze statue of Brigid lifting a flame to the sky, and in the rather practical concrete steps around the nearer part of the well. Megan walked up to a lichen-painted stone arch that she assumed was at least several hundred years old and put her hand against it, surprised to feel warmth. For a heartbeat she actually wondered if there was magic going on, but then realized the priest had probably been standing here himself, and a trace of his body heat hadn't yet faded.

"Tell me about Brigid," Sarah said through another yawn. "Oh my God, I've got to wake up."

"I'll make you walk back to town if you're not awake in half an hour," Megan promised, although quietly, finding that, like the priest, she also didn't want to disturb the site with noise. "Brigid was a goddess in the old Irish pantheon. There's kind of a debate about whether there was also a human nun named Brigid, or if Catholicism just adapted her to be one of their saints."

"She's the patron saint of women?"

Rafael crouched on the concrete steps to draw his fingertips through the cold, still water. "Oh, that'll wake you up. Think it's okay to wash my face in the holy well?"

Megan started to answer, but Dip, not at all impressed with human traditions, stuck his nose in the well and took a long, slurping drink that made them all laugh. Thong pranced farther along the green between where the well-feeding stream dipped underground, and a second well some ten meters farther on. "I guess so," Megan said more loudly, and cheerfully. "Besides, maybe it's good luck. She was a goddess of fire and childbirth, and . . . maybe something else. I don't remember." She hesitated. "Well, it's the childbirth thing I brought you here for. If you want to try a little ancient Irish magic, anyway."

Sarah gave her a startled look that turned glassy-eyed, although the tears didn't quite fall. Rafael stood, shaking water off his hands, and came to put his arms around his wife, who cast a glance up to find him giving her a supportive nod. She nodded, too, looking back at Megan. "I think we'd like that. What do we do?"

Megan gestured to five or six low, rounded standing stones that led in a straight line from the stone arch to the second well, which Thong was snuffling her way to. "It's a little silly, but I know people who swear it works. You sit on one of the stones and ask Brigid's intervention to help you get pregnant."

Both of them paused briefly before Rafael gave a

quick laugh. "I assume Sarah does the sitting on the stone. How very . . ."

"Phallic," Megan said with a rueful grin. "I know. But honestly, I *know* people who got pregnant after coming here to ask for Brigid's help, so it can't hurt to try, right?"

"No, it's great." Sarah was still bright-eyed. "What does Raf do?"

He waggled his eyebrows, and Megan hid her face in her hands, like she wasn't forty-three years old, and could still be mortified by sex. He cackled, and she dropped her hands to grin at him. "He goes to the standing stone with you and asks for Brigid's help, too, however you two want to make that work. The rest of what he does is entirely up to you, ideally behind closed doors."

Sarah, almost shining with happiness, stepped out of Rafael's arms to hug Megan. "I don't know if I believe in magic or prayer, but I do know that I really love that you thought of this for us. Thank you." She caught her husband's hand and tugged him toward the standing stones like they were a couple of kids let loose at a playground.

Megan watched them go, then, feeling that it was all something of a private business, whistled for Dip and went to catch up with Thong. The little dog was leaning over an opening in the farther well's low stone wall, her tail wagging as she growled and barked at the water in its depths. Megan called, "Shhh," as quietly as she could, which made about as much difference as she expected it would. She hurried down to the well to reassure Thong that she was only barking at her own reflection.

And then she sat down on the low stone wall and put her head between her knees, trying to fight off dizziness, because there, floating in Saint Brigid's holy well, was a dead man.

CHAPTER 2

After a count of thirty and three very deep breaths, Megan looked again.

Breathing through it, unfortunately, hadn't made there be any less of a body in the well.

It *was*—she thought—a man; the shoulders, where they hung at the surface, were broad, and the shadowed body dipping deeper in the well looked taller than most women. On the other hand, loose, long hair floated across the water, and the body was wearing a loose white dress, wrapped at the waist with some kind of belt and the skirt floating upward. But whatever gender they were, they were definitely dead: Megan and her friends had been poking around the site for at least twenty minutes already. The person in the well had been there awhile.

Thong barked again. Megan picked the little dog up, which seemed to satisfy whatever urge to alert the world that she'd had. She nestled into Megan's arms, warm and cozy.

That was more than Megan could say for herself. This was the second drowning she'd come upon in the past few years, which was a good solid two too many. She closed her eyes one more time, counted to ten, and wondered what she had done in a previous life to keep finding dead people in this one. Maybe her ex was right after all. Maybe Megan *was* somehow cursed, or touched by fate, or otherwise doomed to a Jessica Fletcher–like existence.

When she opened her eyes a second time, it was to find Sarah and Rafael with her gaze. They were at the other end of the standing stones, which were about thigh-high. Sarah sat astride one of them, her back to Megan, and Raf, mostly hidden from Megan's view, knelt in front of her with his arms around her waist. They were both laughing, that shy, nervous giggle people sometimes did when they felt something was both absurd and important. Sarah ducked her head over Raf's, and although Megan couldn't hear them speaking, after a moment the quiet laughter stopped, and they simply held on to one another, an intense, private bond that Megan felt privileged to glimpse.

She ducked her own head over Thong, smiling a little as Thong lifted her nose, bumped it against Megan's chin, then licked her a few times. Dip, perpetually jealous, lay on Megan's feet, and when that didn't get her attention, rolled on his back and wiggled winsomely. She murmured, "Good pupper," and bent to rub his tummy, being careful not to squish Thong. Then, still softly, like she was trying to avoid disturbing her friends, she said, "Come on, pups. Let's go tell the heritage centre what we found. And we can call . . . *shoot*."

The last word came out more vehemently, although she still made sure to keep her voice down. Dip wriggled himself to his feet so vigorously the motion looked like it should have come with a cartoon-sound-effect *sproing!* and looked up at Megan worriedly. "No, it's okay," she told him as she stood with Thong still in her arms. "It's just that I forgot Paul's in Morocco with Niamh until her movie's done shooting. I can't call him. Well, I guess I can, but it won't do any good. Okay, never mind. Just the heritage centre people, then. C'mon."

Sarah glanced up as Megan and the dogs went by— Thong had insisted on being put back down with her brother—and Megan gave her a quick smile, trying to look carefree. They were going to have their day up-ended in just a minute anyway. She didn't see any point in interrupting their commune until she absolutely had to. She made her way back to the heritage centre, pausing to tie the dogs up outside before going in.

A woman of around sixty looked up with a quick smile. "How did you find the well?"

Megan bit her tongue on replying, *"By walking down the path and following the signs,"* which would *not* set things off on the right foot. "It's beautiful," she said instead. "Unfortunately there's . . ."

She found it surprisingly hard to say the words. Usually the first person she talked to after finding a body—and she kind of hated that there was a *usually* she could apply to this situation—was Detective Paul Bourke, who at least dealt with bodies as part of his line of work. Telling some poor woman at a heritage centre that there was a dead man in her well was an entirely different prospect.

The poor woman's eyebrows had risen to create an ocean of gentle wrinkles in her forehead. She was white Irish, her thick hair graying and her pale eyes concerned behind a pair of heavy glasses. Everything about her was a little worried, as if that was her fundamental nature. "Yes? Oh, dear, what's gone wrong? Did your dog do his business in the park?"

"What? No! And I would have cleaned up if they had! No, it's—has anyone else been here today?" Megan asked unhappily. "I saw a priest leaving?"

"That would be Father Colman," the woman said decisively. "He's here every morning, rain or shine, to do his devotionals. He says Brigid speaks to his heart, and through her, he's closer to God. Besides him, there's not that many people here early. It's the time of year, you know, it's quiet. In another few weeks, there'll be pilgrims on and around St. Brigid's Day—that's the first of February, also known as Imbolc, the first day of spring in Ireland—" She fell into a happy lecture about things Megan already knew, despite the Texan accent that suggested she wouldn't.

"I'm sorry—I know—I live here—" Megan stuttered out the interruption apologetically, and let herself go right on blurting phrases until the important one came out: "There's a body in the well."

Then she stepped forward to catch the woman's elbow as all the color rushed away from her face and her knees buckled. "I'm sorry. Please, let me help you sit, and put your head between your knees for a moment. Take a few deep breaths." She guided the woman to a bench in the visitors' centre, then sat beside her, holding her hand until her color improved. "What's your name again? I don't know if I caught it."

"Margaret," the woman croaked.

"Oh, I like that name. I'm Megan. I guess my name started as a derivative of Margaret, way back when."

Margaret made a noncommittal sound. "It's sure to be Seamus Nolan in the well."

"Shay—" Megan broke off after the first syllable, head jerking up like she'd be able to see the body in the well through the visitor centre walls. "The *lord*? The Irish Druid? That Seamus Nolan? I guess that explains the robe," she added, more or less to herself.

Margaret nodded weakly and dropped her head toward her knees again. "He's a regular, like. He comes around two or three times a month, always early in the morning. Sometimes before we're open, even, but it's not like we don't know the man. He's welcome whenever he drops by. I saw his bicycle out in the parking lot this morning, but it wasn't there when I went out to get my phone from the car. I'm always after forgetting it. Jesus, it can't be. What do I do? What do *we* do?"

"Call the police," Megan said gently. "I can ring them, if you want. I found the body, after all." She winced as she made the offer, and winced again at the gratitude in Margaret's voice as she looked up.

"Would you? Thank you. I wouldn't know what to say. I can't even say it to myself. Seamus was such a nice man!"

"Why don't you get yourself a cup of tea while I ring the guards?" Megan rose and walked a few steps away, as if the call somehow needed privacy, and dialed 999, the general emergency number for Ireland. Someone picked up after a couple of rings and asked for the address immediately. She said, "St. Brigid's Well, in Kildare," like that was a commonly accepted address, and added, "There's a body in the well."

A brief, sharp pause came over the line before the woman on the other end said, "Are you sure they're dead?"

There was a joke along those lines, a joke that Megan had read was the "funniest in the world" because it translated successfully into so many cultures. She bit her tongue hard on trying to make it work— that would involve running back out to the well and holding the body under another few minutes—and just said, "I am, yes. The only other person I saw here left as we were arriving, and that was at least twenty minutes ago."

"Ah, sweet Jaysus," Margaret whispered, ghost-like. "Father Colman couldn't have done it, could he, now? Never, a man of the cloth like that, and a good man too."

Megan nodded to indicate she'd heard, and the now-grim-voiced dispatcher informed her that emergency services were on their way. She hung up, and Margaret wailed, "Ah, Jesus," in a low, desperate cry before sit-

ting down again, her attempt at tea forgotten. "I might
have rescued him, if I'd known!"

"Probably not." Megan went to finish the tea, brewing a strong cup and bringing it to her. "Did you even
see him today?"

Margaret shook her head miserably. "Just his bicycle. And then it was gone." She paled dramatically
again. "Someone stole a dead man's bicycle? Did Father
Colman steal a dead man's bicycle?"

"No," Megan said with a fair amount of certainty.
"There wasn't a bike in the parking lot when we arrived, and we saw the Father leaving. He didn't put one
in his trunk. Boot. I don't think he could have. His car
was practically smaller than he was."

"Oh, he loves that little car of his," Margaret said,
distracted. "But you can't put a thing in it, no, not besides the weekly shop. But then someone *did* take a
dead man's bicycle!"

That wasn't impossible; bicycle thieves seemed to
be a perennial problem. Megan considered the possibility that it just wasn't Seamus Nolan in the well at all.
Maybe he'd been there, shoved someone else in, and
ridden off on his bike, happy as a lark. It didn't sound
much like what she knew of the environmentalist viscount, but since what she knew about him almost ended
with an awareness that he existed, that was meaning-
less. That, and the fact that people did things all the
time that even their closest friends thought of as un-
characteristic. "The guards will figure out what's happened," she promised Margaret.

Laughter and fond chat with the dogs sounded just outside the door. A moment later, Raf and Sarah, both looking slightly damp—it had evidently started to mist heavily, if not quite rain—stepped into the visitors' centre, both of them bright with smiles and their arms around each other's waists, which made navigating the door a little difficult.

Rafael's smile fell away almost instantly as he saw Megan, though, and while he didn't let go of his wife, his voice turned serious and concerned. "What's wrong, Megs?"

Margaret wailed, "Seamus Nolan is dead in the well!" before Megan even had time to draw breath.

Megan had never seen Raf at work, but she recognized the professional demeanor that instantly snapped into place. He nearly vibrated with intensity, thinking hard and clearly a heartbeat away from rushing out of the visitors' centre to see if there was anything he could do to assist. "We didn't see anyone . . . ?"

"The other part of the well, the round one at the far end of the park," Megan said. "It's what Thong was barking about. I didn't want to disturb you two with it until you were done out there."

Sarah's hand covered her mouth. "Oh my God. I— oh, no. Are you sure he's dead?"

The terrible joke rose in Megan's mind again, and she smashed it down a second time, nodding. "I didn't pull him out, but . . . yes."

"Why didn't you?" Margaret's voice broke, and it occurred to Megan that she'd actually known the dead man. This was a personal loss to her, no matter how lightly acquainted they might have been. "You might've saved him, you could—"

"He'd been in the water since before we arrived," Megan repeated, lifting her voice a little to be heard over Margaret's mounting distress. "Believe me, ma'am, I've gone into the water after a man I thought might still be alive before. If I'd thought he might have been, I'd have tried. But I didn't see how there could be a chance of it, and in that case it's better to let the professionals do their jobs."

"You're not young enough to *ma'am* me," Margaret snapped. That, Megan thought, was better than rising hysteria.

"I'm sorry," she said as evenly as she could. "I fall back on formality when things get tense. Margaret, my friend here is a doctor. When the paramedics arrive, if they want his professional opinion, I'm sure he'll be able to set your mind at ease regarding what any of us might have been able to do."

"You're a doctor?" Margaret's voice went fluttery with relief. "Oh, thank God, you'll know what to do, then. What do we do, Doctor?"

"We wait for the paramedics and any other emergency services to arrive, ma'am. Megan is right. Even in extreme cases of cold-water-drowning survival, you're usually looking at a few minutes of submersion, not half an hour or more. And the water here isn't that cold," he added almost apologetically. "Those cases are almost exclusively situations where people have broken through the icy surface of a lake. I'm very sorry, ma'am."

Margaret didn't object to *him* calling her "ma'am," Megan noticed. It was wonderful, what being a man and a doctor could accomplish. But at least Margaret calmed a little, no longer struggling with the conviction that they could have done something. She noticed her tea and took it in both hands, hunching over it and looking twenty years older than she had when Megan came in with the bad news.

"Who is he?" Sarah asked quietly. "She knew his name?"

Megan moved a little farther away, like the extra five feet would cushion Margaret from her answer. "She thinks it's Seamus Nolan. He's some kind of minor nobility. A title left over from when Britain occupied Ireland. His family's held a huge chunk of land in Ireland for centuries. There's a lot of political ill will around that, obviously, but he's an avid environmentalist— they call him the 'Irish Druid' in the papers, and I guess maybe he's actually some kind of druidic practitioner, but even if he wasn't, the Irish can't resist taking the piss out of . . . well, basically anybody."

"Taking the piss out of . . . ?" Sarah looked dubious.

"Teasing. Sometimes good-naturedly, sometimes not. A landed gentleman with environmentalist tendencies would generally be more on the 'not' side of that, here. Anyway, Margaret says he comes here two or three times a month, and she saw his bike out front when she arrived today, so it's probably him."

"How does she know it's his bike?" Raf murmured.

"I don't know, Raf, maybe it says 'Irish Druid' on the license plate. Or maybe she's just seen it dozens of times."

"Irish bicycles have license plates?" Sarah asked, startled.

"No, now *I'm* taking the piss!"

Despite the circumstances, Raf flashed a bright grin. "So, this is what life as the murder driver is like."

Megan groaned. "I'm supposed to be on holiday, not dragging you two into this kind of horrible mess. This is exactly why Jelena broke up with me!"

"Well, I'm not going to break up with you," Raf promised. "And come on, Megs, given the past few years of your life, I'm not gonna lie, I would've been kinda disappointed if we didn't get a murder on our vacation."

"I wouldn't have been!" Sarah and Megan both chorused, although Sarah looked like she might have been trying to be supportive rather than truthful. Defensively, she added, "No, really, I wouldn't have been. But maybe I'm also not entirely surprised or . . ."

"Disappointed?" Raf asked, and a trace of amused guilt crept across Sarah's high-cheekboned face.

Tires sounded in the parking lot, and an engine was killed before a pair of guards came into the visitors' centre. One was young, male, ruddy-skinned, and uniformed. The other wore a plainclothes suit that looked like it had been slept in, and hadn't fit particularly well before that. The man inside that suit, in his late fifties or a bit older, was short, tanned, and not nearly as rumpled as his clothing, with a crisp haircut, strong jaw, and decisive pale eyes. He looked absolutely nothing like Columbo, but Megan's mind leaped to the TV detective anyway.

His expression also blackened as he laid eyes on Megan. "Bloody *hell*. What the feck have I done to deserve a murder driver case?"

CHAPTER 3

A sense of dread almost as strong as the detective's expression rose in Megan's belly. She knew An Garda Síochána—the police force, more poetically rendered in Irish as "the guardians of the peace"—didn't like her, but it hadn't occurred to her that she might be known outside of Dublin. It *especially* hadn't occurred to her that she might be so well-known that a random garda would recognize her on sight. Trying to hide her surprise, she said, "You have the advantage of me, Detective Garda."

She almost never referred to Paul Bourke by the correct title: she just called him "Detective," if she used his rank at all. He forgave it as an American idiosyncrasy, but nothing about this detective suggested he would appreciate a casual American approach to anything. On the other hand, the kid next to him widened his eyes with something close to glee, and she thought he wouldn't be buying any pints tonight, not with the story of meeting the murder driver as his gossip to trade.

The detective curled his lip, an ugly, bulging sneer that visibly displayed how he stuck his tongue up against the front of his eyetooth to really emphasize the expression. "I expect I do, yeh. Where's this body? Don't feckin' tell me it was you that found it."

"It was," Margaret blurted. "What do you mean, murder driver? My *God*, did she kill him? Oh my God, what's going on? Am I in danger?" She backed away to behind the reception desk, her voice trembling with tears.

The detective's lip curled further in a struggle between the obvious desire to give Megan as little information about anything, including himself, as possible, and the sullen awareness that he ought to follow at least a few social niceties in this situation. With an effort, he cleared his expression to merely gruff, and turned his attention to Margaret. "You're not in any danger, pet. This wasn't just a thorn in the gardaí's side, nothing to worry your pretty head about. I'm Detective Sergeant Patrick Doyle. This is Garda Farrell. We'll get this sorted out quick enough for you to be home for tea. Why don't you show me where the body is?"

Margaret wailed and thrust a shaking finger toward Megan. "She found it. She'll show you."

Doyle's face darkened again, but before he could settle into full curmudgeon, Rafael spoke up. "Excuse me, Detective Sergeant. I'm Doctor Williams. If there's anything I can do to be of assistance, please, let me offer my services."

Megan could have kissed him, which was not an impulse she'd had since an ill-fated attempt at dating in their teens. Doyle muttered, "A doctor is it," as if intrigued against his will, and jerked his chin toward the door. "Let's go see it, then. You're American?"

"I am. My wife and I are here on vacation." Raf gave one of the dazzling grins that used to get him out of trouble when they were kids. "No, I've got that wrong, don't I? We're here on *holiday*."

Somewhat to Megan's amazement, Doyle actually chuckled and gestured for Rafael to precede him out the door. Garda Farrell followed, and Sarah gave Megan a quick glance to verify that they were all pretending Raf and Sarah's presence at the holy well was completely separate from Megan's. Megan figured Doyle would be livid when he figured it out, but she was willing to go along with it until then. Rafael had not, after all, *lied* about anything.

She trailed out after them, holding back a step or two while Sarah caught up with Raf and took his hand, emphasizing the illusion that they were a couple and Megan wasn't part of their group. Rafael was saying, "We were at the near end of the well when she found the body," which, again, was perfectly true. "She was very calm."

"Well, she would be," Doyle muttered. "The woman's cursed, or a serial killer."

"What do you mean? I thought women were hardly ever serial killers," Sarah said, sounding genuinely astonished.

A combination of offense and amusement flew

through Megan as Doyle growled, "Or they don't get caught. She works for a car hire service in Dublin, and she's been turning up dead bodies for years. The whole of An Garda Síochána knows about her. You," he barked at Megan as they approached the well where the body was. "Murder driver. Tell me what happened."

"Megan," Megan said mildly. "Or Ms. Malone, if you prefer. These two were at the near end of the well, and my dog"—she nodded back toward the visitors' centre, where she'd left the dogs tied up—"ran down to this end and started barking, so I followed her to see what she was fussing about. That's when I saw the body. I went back to the visitors' centre, told Margaret, and rang 999."

Doyle glared at her. "You didn't try fishing him out?"

"No, sir."

"Why not? He might have still been alive!"

"I'd been here for at least twenty minutes, sir," Megan replied steadily. "He wasn't on the grounds when I got here. I thought it was very, very unlikely he was alive, and that the gardaí would prefer I didn't tamper with the . . ." Her mind jumped to the word *evidence*, which had implications she was trying to avoid, but for a few seconds she couldn't think of the word she did want. "Scene," she finally managed. "I do have some sense of my reputation, Detective Garda. I didn't want to end up complicating anything any more than my presence already does."

"I'd like to concur that the likelihood of the victim's survival was very low at that point," Rafael said, still in the serious doctor tone Megan was largely unfamiliar with. "We had a similar discussion with the poor woman at the visitors' centre, but having been here twenty or more minutes ourselves, I have to agree that the victim had gone into the water before our arrival. Furthermore, given that we heard and saw no sign of struggle in the water, it seems likely they were dead before we arrived."

Megan almost felt sorry for the detective, who simultaneously couldn't argue with Megan's logic, didn't want to argue with the doctor on the scene, and very, very obviously wasn't prepared to give Megan a single inch on the possibility of having done something right. His younger partner, who thus far hadn't said a word, was drinking it all in with wide blue eyes and ears that could only have been more perked up if he'd actually been a dog.

Before Doyle could formulate any meaningful complaint—because he certainly wasn't going to compliment Megan on making good choices—the rest of the emergency services team arrived. Paramedics jumped out of an ambulance, unfolding a stretcher as they came toward the well. A fire truck released a number of uniformed firefighters in their wake, and two more police vehicles pulled up a moment later. The gentle serenity of the park was suddenly obliterated as voices rose, calling instructions and asking questions, but the main thrust of the first activity was getting the body out of the well.

Megan, watching two people send looped cables on long poles into the water to slide them under the dead

man's arms with skilled ease, was just as glad she hadn't
tried pulling the man out on her own. The best-case
scenario would have involved lying on her belly halfway in the well herself, and the worst would have ended
up with her treading water and waiting for rescue too.

And there was really no doubt he was dead, when he
came out of the water. He hadn't been in nearly long
enough to bloat, but there was no color in his hands or
face, nor any pulse when it was taken by the paramedics. They still began a treatment for cold-water survival, which Megan understood was, at its core, "warm
the body up and see what happens, just in case." Rafael
cast her a glance that suggested he didn't think it would
have any effect, but he also spoke with the paramedics
about what he knew while Detective Sergeant Doyle
stomped around like he wanted people to interview,
but also didn't want to talk to Megan.

Which was fine with her. She'd already told him
what she knew, although she'd forgotten to mention
that Margaret had said Seamus Nolan's bicycle had
been out front earlier, and wasn't there anymore.

She was fairly certain the man in the well was, indeed, Nolan. Since Doyle didn't want to talk to her, she
got out her phone and looked up the name, along with
"Irish Druid," because neither Seamus nor Nolan was
an uncommon name in Ireland.

The first headline that came up highlighted his controversial environmental activities, and the second, a
similar story, had a picture running alongside it. Megan,
clicking through to get the whole picture, took a quick
glance at the body, but didn't really need the verifica-

tion. The man in the photo was rangy, with long, thinning red hair, and was wearing a knee-length white robe that had—unexpectedly—a long wooden rosary over it. In the picture, he wore a priest-ish rope belt, actually quite beautiful in greens and golds, with a fringe that stuck lightly to his robes.

He was also wearing jeans and hiking boots. The entire combination made for a delightfully weird vibe that would either make people want to talk to him immediately, or put them off him entirely.

Now that he was out of the water, Megan could see the soaked-through belt was probably the same one, although his rosary beads were missing. His leather hiking boots were so waterlogged she was surprised they hadn't dragged him deeper into the well. She glanced back at her phone, skimming the article, which highlighted his extraordinary backstory and the success he'd seen thus far in rewilding his family's massive estate without touching much on the more controversial aspects of his life, like the fact that he *owned* a three-thousand-acre estate that British landlords had taken from the people who'd lived and worked on that land for centuries.

She switched back to the search results and read the first article, which was much more focused on that than his rewilding efforts. A few others were more even-handed. Megan put the phone back in her pocket, wondering what Nolan himself had thought of inheriting land stolen from the poor. It was a little late to ask now.

Garda Farrell, silent partner to the grumpy detective, went back to the visitors' centre and returned a few minutes later with a visibly distraught Margaret, who identified Nolan, then fled the scene weeping. Doyle scowled after her, and at the emergency team in general. "We knew it was him. There's no reason to be putting her through that."

"She's the only one who knew him personally," the younger garda said with quiet determination. "A first-hand identification is better than the lot of us agreeing that it's definitely him, when we wouldn't have ever seen or spoken to him ourselves."

"Don't teach your grandmother to suck eggs."

Farrell pursed his lips and looked down, but didn't back off on his opinion. Megan thought working with Doyle must be a constant test of the younger garda's patience, but presumably the detective's experience was well worth learning from. As she watched, the para-medics heaved Nolan's body onto the stretcher and re-turned to the ambulance, still administering oxygen. Doyle stomped after them.

It took everything Megan had not to chase them and ask Doyle what he thought of the whole situation. Farrell, trailing behind his partner, caught her eye, glanced after Doyle, and returned his gaze to hers with a crooked grin before veering toward her. "Have ye anything you'd like to say on the whole nasty matter, Ms. Malone?"

"Margaret there in the visitors' centre said Nolan's bicycle was here earlier this morning, but it's gone again now," Megan said promptly. "And there was a priest here earlier, a Father Colman. Just in case she doesn't mention it when Detective Garda Doyle talks with her."

"If he talks with her," Farrell replied. "But you're telling me this because you think he won't, aren't ye?"

"I wouldn't presume." She had, in fact, very carefully *not* presumed. "I just thought someone should know."

"Very good." Farrell hesitated, then, like a teen meeting their favorite pop star, blurted, "I know it's mental, Ms. Malone, but could I get a selfie with ye?"

Megan couldn't help a loud, startled laugh. "Oh my God. Really? I'm not Niamh O'Sullivan, you know."

The young garda's eyes sparkled. "Not that I don't fancy her, but you rank, among the gardaí. I won't post it to social media, I swear, or it'd be my head Doyle would have, but *could* I?"

"You'd better not post it online! But . . . I guess? Okay?" Megan offered a bemused smile to his phone camera when he angled it for the picture, and chuckled when he turned it to show her the results. "I've seen worse. I hope it gets you 'cool kid' points, or whatever it is you're aiming for at the station."

Farrell grinned brilliantly. "It will so. Thanks very much, you're a hell of a woman for just one woman, ta!" He hurried after Doyle, clearly not wanting to be caught gossiping with the murder driver, but chuffed to have done so all the same. Megan, shaking her head, followed at a more sedate pace, which let Rafael and Sarah fall into step with her for a minute or two.

"Don't hang out with me," she warned. "Right now Doyle likes you."

"I just wanted to make sure you're all right," Raf murmured.

"Oh, grand, this happens to me all the time, you know." Even Megan could tell her humor fell a little flat, but she shrugged it off. "I'm okay. Go make sure somebody tells Doyle about Nolan's bike."

"You are *extremely* calm," Sarah breathed. "I don't know how you do it."

"Practice," Megan said wryly. "Go on now." She slowed even more, lingering at the part of the well nearer the visitors' centre, and the other two pulled ahead like they hadn't been talking. After a minute or two, she decided she'd dawdled long enough, and headed back to the centre, only to meet Detective Sergeant Doyle surging out the door as she approached.

His expression darkened the moment he saw her, which didn't seem entirely fair. On the other hand, if he was simply furious she existed, she might as well push it a little. "I know it's not my business, Detective Sergeant—"

"You're damn right it isn't," Doyle growled. "You and your murder driver nonsense are bad for the whole country. The unlucky bastard fell in the bloody well. There's a knot on his head the size of the county, and blood on the lip of the well. That's all there is to it."

"But his bicycle—"

Exasperation filled Doyle's strong features. "Will turn up robbed by some young gobshite, or not turn up at all because the gobshite's a bit brighter than usual. Yer wan in there says he never locked it up. Trusting to a fault, says she. Rich as Midas, says I, and able to buy himself all the bloody bikes in Ireland if the one he's using goes missing."

Megan inhaled half a sharp breath, then let it go with a short nod. "I'm sure you're right. Sorry for bothering you, Detective Sergeant." She backed off almost literally, and the detective stalked back toward the well with Garda Farrell once more following him like a lost puppy. He cast her one semi-guilty glance when he was certain Doyle wasn't looking, but she didn't really blame him for not pushing anything with his superior. He'd get into a whole different kind of trouble than she would.

She went to kneel by her dogs as the guards moved down the park. Thong, lying on her belly with her legs stretched straight in back and in front of her like a stuffed animal, cracked one eye open. Dip, either more agitated or more vigilant, had been sitting at alert the whole time people had been coming and going, and now leaned against her knee with an alarmed whine. She rubbed his head, murmuring, "It's okay, pup. All the excitement is pretty much over now."

"Is it?" Rafael, leaving Sarah in the visitors' centre for a moment, glanced over his shoulder to make sure the door had closed behind him before he said, "You're satisfied that it was an accident?"

"Are you?"

"It could have been," Raf admitted cautiously.

"Yeah. It could have been. But Detective Sergeant Doyle over there has decided it *was*, so . . ." Megan shrugged and stood so she could untie the dogs' leads, then gave her friend a thin smile. "So I guess I'm investigating another murder."

CHAPTER 4

Rafael all but bounced on the balls of his feet like a six-year-old. "Great. Where do we start?"

"*We* don't start anywhere. Except . . ." Megan could kick herself for involving her friends at all, but since Raf was there, and since he *was* a doctor, she gritted her teeth, grimaced, and let herself ask, "Did he really have a knot on his head? Any chance that was what killed him?"

"There was water in his lungs when they started CPR. There's really no chance he still was alive," he added, as if Megan had been worried about it. "So the blow to the head didn't kill him, no, or he wouldn't have inhaled in the well. But he looks like he's in pretty good shape, so if he'd just fallen in without hitting his head, he probably wouldn't have died of it. At the very least, he should have been able to turn around and hang his arm over the low side of the well and yell for help. If he was conscious, I mean."

"So he wasn't."

"But drowning doesn't look like drowning, either," Sarah said as she came out of the visitors' centre in time to hear the last part of that.

Megan blinked at her. "It what?"

"It doesn't look like drowning, not the way we see it in movies." She demonstrated, waving her arms, pretending to splash, and miming yelling and gasping before lowering her arms again. "That's aquatic distress. When people are really drowning, they can't wave or call for help, almost never. The instinct is to spread your arms against the top of the water, trying to push yourself up so your head is above the water, but you're not splashing when you do that."

"And their mouths barely stay above the water. People don't kick or lie down in the water when they're really drowning." Rafael looked troubled, brown eyes dark and sad. "Basically you stay more or less upright, not kicking, pushing on the water, taking sips of air as you sink straight down. Part of the reason so many people, kids especially, die of drowning is that our cultural idea of what it looks like is just completely wrong, so people *watch* kids drown without even realizing that's what they're seeing. It usually takes less than a minute."

"Why didn't I know that? Why do *you* know it?" Megan asked, horrified, although she knew the answer to the second question: Rafael was a doctor, and Sarah was married to one.

He inhaled, like just talking about it had made breathing more difficult. "So the point is, if he was in distress, he might have yelled or splashed, but if he was *drowning*, even if he hadn't hit his head, he wouldn't have been able to. But unless he couldn't swim at all, I would have expected a man of his age and apparent fitness level to have been able to grab the edge of the well—unless there were extenuating circumstances." He gestured at his own forehead. "Like having hit his head."

"Is that low step slippery?" Megan turned to look down the park, where the gardaí had set up police ribbon and were in low, intense discussion with each other. "I don't know, maybe he *is* taking it seriously. But I'm not going to find out if the step is slippery with him there, either. He'll chase me off."

"I could go find out," Rafael said a little eagerly. Sarah elbowed him, and he looked injured. "What? I have medical expertise that could be of use!"

"In finding out if a step is slippery?"

"In solving a murder," Raf said cheerfully. "Come on, don't lie, you're a *little* bit thrilled we get to be in on a murder driver case."

"I would be much happier if we weren't," Sarah replied sourly. Then, in a relenting mutter, she added, "It's kind of cool. Awful. But cool."

"Well, fine, go see if the step is slippery, since I can't." Megan took a few steps with the dogs, who immediately pulled toward the activity at the far end of the heritage park. "If only you two were ginormous, I could pretend you were just hauling me around and I had no control over you, but you barely weigh thirty pounds between the two of you."

"Besides," Sarah said as she and Rafael headed toward the other end of the park, "if you had two ginormous pulling dogs you couldn't control, Detective Sergeant Doyle up there would probably ticket you for being a bad pet owner."

Megan mumbled agreement and took the dogs around the heritage centre the long way so she wouldn't be too obviously watching what was going on. "Because," she breathed to the terriers, "it turns out I really resent a detective who thinks I shouldn't be involved. Not that Detective Bourke thinks I should be involved. He's just used to me by now." And once, when he couldn't take a case himself, Paul Bourke had actually encouraged Megan to look into it. She didn't say that aloud, in case Doyle could somehow hear a whisper across two hundred feet of space and a quietly babbling brook.

Dip wagged his tail like he'd understood everything she'd said, then strained at the leash, still trying to go back to where all the action was. "Nope, pup, we've got to be cool. Raf and Sarah will give us all the deets when they come back."

Thong twitched a furry eyebrow, and Megan mumbled, "Yeah, okay, I can't believe I said 'deets,' either. Although, honestly, I don't know if that's an Irish thing or something people a generation younger than me say. Or used to say. Oh, God, I'm old and out of fashion."

Both the dogs stared at her like she'd lost her mind. Megan, grinning sheepishly, took some treats out of her pocket and offered them to the animals, who immediately forgave her for being old and unfashionable. Dip lay down to gnaw on his with more careful attention than it deserved, while Thong wolfed hers and thumped her tail hopefully, looking for more. "No, just because you were the greedy one this time doesn't mean you get another, any more than Dip does when he gulps his. C'mon, pup, finish up and let's go for a walk!"

She put enthusiasm into her voice for the last few words, and Dip swallowed the rest of his treat whole before leaping to his feet and making a mad dash toward the edge of the parking lot. Megan laughed and ran a few steps as he reached the end of the leash, and the two little dogs bounced ahead of her as far as they could, sniffing and running back and forth. "Up the road a ways," she promised them. "I know you need to stretch your legs."

They stretched and stuck their noses in the brush along the side of the road, rustling into it and coming out with sticks, while she walked along behind them, leash in one hand and her phone in the other as she first checked the time in Morocco—only an hour ahead of Ireland—and then texted her group chat with Paul and Niamh: *guess what happened.*

Paul responded almost immediately with *Megan, no,* and Niamh came in a moment later with, *Megan yes!* followed by, *Not that it's grand if you're finding more bodies, but I like to be encouraging,* and then, . . . *you didn't find another body, did you?*

Megan sent back a grimace. A couple seconds later, the screen lit up with a video phone call—*vone call,* as Niamh styled it, in an attempt to break away from all the app-specific names for video calls—and both of them crowded into one screen when Megan answered.

Paul, incredibly fair-skinned with golden undertones and red hair, was now sunburn pink: he'd clearly been outside too much, without enough sunblock. Niamh, on the other hand, had her cascade of dark brown curls, highlighted with gold, piled atop her head and falling in appealing ringlets around a heart-shaped brown face and enormous dark eyes touched with makeup that made her glow. She gasped, "You never did. *Another* body?" before her eyebrows drew down and she leaned into pure country Irish with her accent. "Where the divil are you?"

"On a roadside in Kildare. You look fabulous."

"Never mind me, I'm always fabulous. What happened?"

Megan and Paul both laughed, and he kissed Niamh's cheek. "You *are* always fabulous."

"But what *happened*?" They were apparently both lying belly-down on a hotel bed: Megan saw Niamh's toes rise above her head as she kicked impatiently, demanding an answer.

"My friends Raf and Sarah got here this morning, and we came out to Kildare to visit the holy well, like I told you we were going to?"

"*And*?" Niamh kicked again, and Paul did a weird squirm that got an offended look from his actress girlfriend, leaving Megan to suspect he'd gotten kicked, and had put his leg over hers to keep her from doing it again.

"And I found Seamus Nolan in the well," Megan said with a sigh. "I mean, technically, Thong found him, but—"

Most of that went unheard as the other two raised their voices, questions running over each other: *Seamus Nolan, the Seamus Nolan, you mean the Irish Druid, how did he die, what did you do, are you sure he was dead*, until they'd gotten past the initial shock and stopped talking at the same time. Niamh nudged Paul, who pulled back from the details and asked something else. "Are you okay? Are your friends?"

"Raf is weirdly chuffed, and I could kind of kick him, but I also kind of get it. Sarah's less thrilled, but yeah, they're okay."

"And you?" Niamh asked again, more quietly. "This can't be what you wanted, after . . ."

"After getting dumped for being a dead body magnet? No. Not that I'm bitter." Megan wasn't exactly sure she *was* bitter, although the breakup still hurt. She was something, though, and trying to put a name to it was exhausting. It led to her dwelling and moping, which didn't help anything. "I don't know. I'm fine? I mean, it would almost be worse if I never found another dead body again, right?"

The two crowded onto the phone screen exchanged glances, and Megan groaned. "Come on, you know what I mean. If Jelena broke up with me because I kept being a Miss Marple and then I never came across another body again after the breakup, then that whole relationship would have ended for nothing, and that . . . is worse." Not even she thought she'd exactly brought the argument home, although she felt it was basically true.

Niamh, bless her, nodded sympathetically. "No, that

makes sense. Getting involved in another murder—it *is* a murder, right?—at least means you were both right about how your life wasn't going to change in that regard, or . . ." She made a face as if finding it difficult to express her thoughts aloud, which made Megan wave a hand sharply, like she was saying, *See?! It's hard to explain!*

Unfortunately, that hand was holding the dogs' leads, and one of them gave an offended yelp as she yanked them away from whatever they were sniffing at. Megan said, "Sorry, pup," automatically, and a Jack Russell suddenly bounced into the screen, climbing on top of the two people on the bed. "Oh, Abhaile! Hello, sweetie."

The little dog shoved her head between Paul and Niamh's, licked them both, then wriggled her whole body past them and disappeared out of the screen again. She was Dip and Thong's mother, adopted by Paul in the aftermath of his first encounter with Megan. "I wasn't sure if you'd been able to bring her with you. How's she dealing with the heat?"

"Ireland is rabies-free, so it wasn't too hard. And she's better than I am." Paul reached off the edge of the bed to fuss with the dog. "She has the sense to stay out of the sun. Did you call the guards?"

Megan stared at him. "Of course I called the guards." She paused. "I did think of calling you first, I admit, but you're in Morocco, so . . ." They traded a small grin before Megan pointed her chin at Niamh, like that made a difference on a vone call. "How's filming going?"

"Actually brilliant! The director has kids, so she's like, 'I go home at the end of an eight-hour shift, so let's get it right,' and it's brilliant. Everybody's actually gotten enough sleep, and the crew don't look like zombies."

"Which is a shame, because it's a zombie movie," Paul said, deadpan. Niamh made a shocked and insulted sound, then laughed and bumped her shoulder against his. "You're a funny man, Paul Bourke."

"It's a good thing, because God knows you don't want me for my beauty."

Niamh and Megan both said, "Hey!" and Niamh shouldered him again. "No dissing on my man. Against the rules."

"Or my friend," Megan said with a sniff.

"She's working with two of the most beautiful humans I've ever seen," Paul said a bit morosely. "And they're working with *the* most beautiful human I've ever seen. It rather puts one in one's place."

"Hnnh. Good thing you're funny, then," Niamh said, and despite having started it, Paul managed to look offended. Megan laughed at both of them, and Niamh's attention came back to her. "Is it really Seamus Nolan, then?"

"The heritage centre attendant verified it," she said with a nod. "Not that any of us really doubted it when he came out of the water. Did you know him?"

"I've met him a few times at parties. Odd duck, that one, but his heart seemed in the right place. He brought his daughter around to meet me once, years ago, before I got noticed outside of Ireland. She was still beside herself. There's a video clip somewhere of me coaxing her to my side, the wee chicken." Her tone was fond, which made Megan laugh again.

"I will never successfully explain to people in the States that 'wee chicken' is a nice thing to say."

"Ah, c'mere to me, my wee chicken!" Niamh said in another obligingly broad accent. "Sure and I might've said 'wee darling' to an American, but she's an Irish lass through and through. No, he was a nice man, though, from what I saw of him. Had he enemies?"

"He was wealthy Anglo-Irish nobility who inherited a landlord estate and went all conservationist instead of all conservative with it," Megan said dryly. "I assume he had enemies out the wazoo."

The two Irish people she was talking to contemplated her solemnly while the dogs, impatient that she wasn't moving much, put in a concerted effort to pull her farther down the road. "It's not that I don't know what you mean," Paul said eventually, as she stumbled along in the growing dark. "It's just that I'm not sure I've ever heard anyone say 'wazoo' before."

"Stick with me, kid," Megan said in her best Bogart impression, which was not only terrible, but she suspected also the wrong person to be channelling for that line. On the other hand, she couldn't think of who else might have said it, so she carried on, adding, "You'll hear more than you ever wanted to know," which at least got a laugh out of the two friends on her phone. "Okay, no—Dip, Thong, it's late, or at least, it's dark, this is a country road, let's go back before we get killed."

"You're not investigating?" Niamh asked, surprised.

"Weirdly, the random detective in Kildare didn't want the murder driver—and he knew who I was, Paul! What's An Garda Síochána doing, sending around my mug shot?—interfering with his case." Megan paused judiciously. "So I left Raf and Sarah to get all the dirt, because he didn't know they were with me."

Paul laughed twice, drawing breath in between to answer and then losing it again. "An Garda Síochána doesn't need to send around your mug shot, Megan. You've been in the papers. And I'm going to pretend I didn't hear that you were now recruiting accomplices into doing your dirty work. That's got to be illegal in some way."

Niamh, indignant, said, "Whose side are you on here?" to Paul, who spread a hand, indicating that at this point, he didn't know.

"Anyway—Dip, no, come on, buddy, I don't want to crawl through the hedgerow—excuse me, my dog is pulling me into a ditch—" Megan tugged on the leash, reluctant to actually haul the little dogs backward, even if the leads attached to chest harnesses, not their collars. "Oh, for God's sake. How does he get himself wrapped around everything? I have to hang up and untangle my dog."

"No, just put us in your pocket and take us out again when you've got him. I want to meet Rafael and Sarah." Niamh blinked hopefully, and Megan laughed.

"That's not fair. You're a movie star. They'd murder *me* if they knew I'd been like, 'Oh, no, Imma hang up on you and not introduce you to my friends.'"

"I am not above using my wiles, my fame, and my . . ."

Niamh kept talking from Megan's jeans as she put the phone in her back pocket and crawled after Dip and Thong, who had managed to wind themselves in opposite directions around the gnarly base of a prickly gorse hedge.

"You are horrible little animals." Megan got a hand on Dip's collar, unsnapped his lead from the harness, tucked him under her arm, and untangled it with the other hand. "And my hair is going to get stuck in this stuff and then we'll all be here forever." She got him unwound, clipped him back in, and tried to do the same with Thong, except the wretched beast surged forward the moment her lead was unfastened. Megan yelled, throwing herself forward on her belly, eyes clenched so none of the scratchy leaves and sharp branches would stab her. She caught Thong's harness with her fingertips, stretched a little more, and curled her hand around the harness enough that the little dog wasn't going to escape. "Awful, *awful* dog! No! Bad!"

Thong drooped pathetically enough that Megan would have felt guilty if she wasn't lying hip-deep in a hedge at the side of the road with pointy, bristly leaves jabbing her entire upper body. At least it smelled nice. The gorse wasn't in full bloom yet, but the bright yellow flowers were some of the nicest-scented flowers she'd ever encountered. She rather believed they smelled like honeysuckle. She'd never actually encountered honeysuckle that she was aware of, but if it didn't smell like gorse, it should.

Dip climbed up on her back to look over her head at Thong. Megan could feel his tail wagging. They were both so *cheerful*, she thought furiously. "Down.

Down, Dip, I need to scoot back so I can unwrap Thong's lead . . ."

There had been room going in. There should have been room going out, but somehow there wasn't. Niamh, from her back pocket, said, "What's going on? Your arse is dark," which at least made Megan laugh and lift her voice to answer.

"I imagine so, yeah. Thong tried to get away." She squirmed onto her side so she could unwrap Thong's lead without letting the little dog go, and yelped as her hair got caught. "I'm going to need a chainsaw to get out of here. Ow." More quietly, she said, "Okay, dog lead first, then I can use my other hand to untangle my hair, why am I not wearing a hat . . ." and did as she narrated, finally managing to clip Thong's lead back in place. By then both dogs were trying to get out of the hedge. "You could have stayed out in the first place!"

"This is fascinating," her back pocket said in a dry male voice, "but maybe you could call us back?"

"Oh, sure, abandon me in my hour of need. Besides, I tried hanging up on you in the first place! Now you're stuck with this!" Megan wrapped the leash around her arm so she could use both hands to try to untangle her hair, then took the phone out of her pocket, turned the torch on, and put it on the ground next to her so she could see what she was doing.

The snarl of hair was genuinely impressive. Cutting it out would be easier, if she had anything to cut *with*. Niamh said, "At least turn the camera around so we can see what's going on," and Megan picked up the phone to bug her eyes at them.

"You want to see the underside of a hedge?"

Both of their eyes widened, and Niamh pressed her lips together. "Oh, dear. You're really stuck, chicken."

"I hadn't noticed!" Megan angled the phone so they could see what she was doing and shout instructions that didn't help at all. "You know, it might be more helpful if you'd stop giggling!"

"Not a chance," Paul reported without audible apology in his voice. "Oh, there, you've nearly got it, move to the left—your left—there!"

Her hair came free with a yank that knocked her phone over and left a hank dangling from the thorny leaves. "Oh, good," Niamh said from the ground, "an exciting view of leaves in the dark."

"I *told* you you were weird for wanting to see the underside of a hedge!"

"No, g'wan now, though." Paul's voice changed, concerned. "What's that above you?"

"You want me to—" Megan gurgled, covered her hair with her hands as best she could so she wouldn't get tangled again, and twisted onto her back to look up at the harsh shadows created by the phone's LED torch. Something glinted up there, and she groaned. "It's probably a candy wrapper, Paul, it's . . ."

"Too big," he said. "Move the brambles. And be careful."

Megan, muttering, pushed a handful of branches aside, and the glitter turned into the fender of a bicycle falling toward her head.

CHAPTER 5

Megan yelled and thrust a hand up, hoping to catch the bike before it smashed into her face. After dropping a hand span or so, branches and brambles caught it instead, but Megan cowered where she was, heart hammering hard enough to make her nauseous. When that began to pass, she shuddered from the bones out, then began to properly shiver. Damp ground, the spike of alarm, and the dropping temperature were not a great combination. She said, "Okay," hoarsely to both the bike and the dogs, got her phone, took some pictures of the bike, and muttered, "Let's get out of here."

Much to the dogs' delight, she scooted out of the hedge on her back like an inchworm, eyeing the bicycle warily. It slipped another half foot or more, the wheel and fender looming very large even if she was mostly out from under it by then, and she scrambled to her feet outside the hedge, her whole body trembling with adrenaline.

"Well," Niamh said brightly, startling her, "do we think that's yer man's bike?"

"I think it was really well shoved into the hedge." Megan sounded shaky to her own ears. "Could be somebody's bike that some brat threw in there ages ago, but . . . I'll bring it to Detective Sergeant Doyle's attention. Just in case. Look, lads, it's dark here, and I want to pay attention to the road while I'm walking back. I'll call you later so you can see Sarah and Rafael, okay? Which is what I should have said ten minutes ago when I was climbing into the hedge."

"But then we wouldn't have been able to help you untangle your hair," Niamh said. "Or find a *clue.*"

"Assuming it is a clue. All right, I love you both, I'll talk to you later. Have fun in Morocco, and use some after-sun on that burn, Paul."

"I already have," he said grimly. "You should've seen me before." They hung up, and Megan left her torch on to follow the road back to the visitors' centre. The hard white light bounced off glass up high at the side of the road, making her squint and drop her gaze. At least there wasn't much traffic, although one of the fire trucks left as she approached the driveway.

Rafael and Sarah were sitting on the hood of her car when she got to the parking lot, although they both hopped down in alarm as she came into sight. "Jesus, Megs, what happened to you?"

"I lost a fight with a hedge." Megan tried to pat her hair back into place. "And I should have left the car unlocked so you didn't have to sit out here in the cold. Everything okay?"

"Doyle chased us off, that's all. The step isn't slippery," Sarah reported. "He was a tall man, so he could have tripped on its edge and hit his head on the far side, if he was hurrying toward it, maybe. That seems to be the detective's theory, anyway."

Megan made a face. "I'm maybe about to go blow a hole in that theory. I found a bicycle in the hedge. It was too dark to see what color it was, but I took a picture. Is Margaret still here? Maybe she could identify it."

"Doyle sent her home," Raf admitted. "Poor thing was shaking like a leaf."

"Most people do, when confronted with sudden death," Sarah informed him. "You and Megan are weird."

"I have an excuse. I'm a doctor. Megan, though, is weird."

"Megan," Megan reminded him, "was in the army for twenty years, and did basic medic training. Anyway, I'm going to go talk to Doyle about the bike. You two want to stay here, to keep us separate in his mind?"

"He's a detective," Sarah said. "Don't you think he's noticed there's only one car left, and three Americans?"

"I honestly don't know." Megan handed Raf the dogs' leashes, said, "Don't let them pull you into a hedge," and walked down the dark holy well pathway to meet Doyle on the near side of the police tape.

He gave her a long, uninviting look, and when that didn't scare her off, sighed. "What?"

"I took my dogs for a walk and found a bicycle in the hedge just up the road from here. I thought you might want to know."

The uninviting look turned to a level stare. "And why would I want to know that, missy?"

Outright fury flared through Megan, heating her chest and face. It was several seconds before she trusted herself to say, in a steady tone, "Detective Sergeant Doyle, I appreciate that you resent my presence here under these circumstances, but I found something that I thought might be of interest to your investigation and am reporting it to you, which is as cooperative as I know how to be. There is no call to be condescending and rude."

If the man had an ounce of shame in him, she hadn't found the way to make him show it. "I'll decide my own self what's of interest to my investigation and what isn't, and a bloody bicycle in a bloody hedge is as common as Sundays in this country."

They weren't very far from the well Nolan had drowned in. Megan bet if she gave Doyle a really good shove, he'd go in. For the space of a deep breath, she allowed herself to consider it, even if the consequences wouldn't be worth the brief joy of the action. Still, thinking about it made her feel a little better. "Well, then, I'll get out of your hair. Good evening, Detective."

Shoulders stiff and blood still boiling, she marched back to her friends, announced, "I'm a 'missy' who has been dismissed," and watched Rafael's eyes widen.

"Does he still have all his teeth?"

Megan smiled with all of hers. "Not in my imagination. Everybody in the car. I'm going to go climb back into that hedge and take as many pictures as I can, and if you don't mind staying in Kildare tonight instead of going back to Dublin, we can ring Niamh and Paul—"

"Yes, let's do that," Sarah said eagerly, then looked sheepish. "I mean, um . . ."

Rafael smiled at her fondly. "You mean exactly that. I think she's right, though, Megs. And not just because I want to lay my own actual eyes on the marvelous Niamh O'Sullivan."

"It's not actually seeing her any more closely than you would on a movie screen," Megan pointed out. "And she'll be much smaller."

"It's definitely seeing her closer than on a movie screen," he disagreed. "That's a performance. I assume she won't be putting on a performance when you call her."

"I dunno, she might want to impress my friends." They were on the road by then, banter keeping the two American visitors awake on the short, but dark drive back to the hotel. Sarah, with the air of a woman who knew she was reaching the end of her energy for the day, suggested room service so they could call Morocco and eat at the same time, and once they'd parked at the hotel, Megan texted to see if Niamh and Paul were available.

Niamh voned before they were even inside the building, voice and eyes sparking with interest. "Have you solved it yet?"

"No, but I said I'd call back with Sarah and Rafael. You two have a minute? Where's Paul?"

"He's walking Abhaile. He'll be back in two minutes."

"Is that a real two minutes or an Irish two minutes? Hang on, we're going in the lift, we might get cut off." Megan held the elevator door for Raf and Sarah as they tried not to peer at her phone with *too*-obvious interest. "Hang on," she said to them, too. "I didn't think Niamh would ring right away."

Niamh's voice, indignant, said, "Sure and av carse I did!" in her broadest Irish accent again, then froze as the lift doors closed. It gave Sarah and Raf enough time to actually squeal, stomp their feet with excitement, and more or less compose themselves again before they were out of the lift and into the hall, unlocking their room door.

Megan held the phone up so the camera was on them as they went into the room. "Niamh, please meet *mi amigo mejor*, Rafael Williams, and his incredible wife, Sarah. Guys, this is my friend Niamh O'Sullivan."

"I've seen you dance," Niamh said to Sarah. "Not in person, but I've watched all of your company's performances that are available online. You're astonishing."

Sarah's jaw fell open before the most baffled, brilliant smile Megan had ever seen crossed her face. "Thank you. Oh my God. I can't believe you've watched any of it."

"Megan *loves* you two," Niamh said. "Of course I've watched."

Rafael, with a huge grin of his own, said, "Okay, you can keep her, she's amazing," to Megan, who beamed at him while they tried to arrange themselves into a huddle where they could all see, and be seen on, the screen.

Paul came back into their hotel room with Abhaile, and the introductions happened all over again, then devolved into five people often trying to talk at once, sharing stories and laughter. After a few minutes, Megan handed the phone to Raf and got the room service menu, then put an order in without consulting the others. A burst of giggles and guilty looks from Sarah and Rafael suggested Niamh had told a story on her, which made Megan laugh.

"I'm not ordering you dinner, just for that."

"You're not ordering Niamh dinner anyway!" Paul yelled, loudly and clearly enough to be heard from her side of the room.

Megan snapped her fingers in mock dismay, and came back to the phone to smile at the two in Morocco. "Next time I'm doing this on a computer so we're not so crowded."

"But then I wouldn't have gotten the cutest screenshot in the world," Niamh protested. "Look, lads, I hate to break off the beginning of a beautiful friendship, but I've got an early morning call, and if I don't get my beauty sleep—"

"Then you'll still be the most beautiful person I've ever seen," Paul said.

"Yes, but makeup will be annoyed with me." Niamh blew a kiss and disappeared from the screen, leaving Paul to gaze after her besottedly, then shake himself and look back at the screen.

"Your guests are falling asleep on the call, Megan. I'd say she doesn't do this to people all the time," he said to Rafael and Sarah, "buuuut . . ."

"Oh, be quiet. Besides, I have nothing exciting planned for tomorrow." Megan watched her own tiny face squint guiltily in the corner of the call as Paul raised a skeptical eyebrow. "Oh, all right, it's true. We do have to get off the call, because we have to eat, and then tomorrow I'm going to dig around and see what's what about Seamus Nolan in these parts."

"There she is," Paul said wryly. "Don't let her get into too much trouble, all right? It was good to meet you." He signed off, and Sarah and Raf made it two or three whole seconds before shrieking and throwing their arms around each other in fannish excitement. Megan laughed out loud, hugged them both, and went to get the door when room service knocked.

Irish Druid Dies in Tragic Accident! was what was what, according to the headlines the next morning. Megan, stiff and sore from crawling around in hedges, read half a dozen articles that all said more or less the same thing: Nolan, survived by his daughter, Aisling; uncle Adam; and an ex-wife whose name didn't merit a mention, was a well-known and beloved visitor at St. Brigid's holy well, where he had met a tragic end in the early hours of Monday morning when no one else was on-site. He'd been declared dead at the Naas General Hospital after attempts at revival had failed, and funeral arrangements were to be announced for the weekend.

"It's *possible*," Megan said through her teeth over the hotel breakfast, "but it doesn't account for the missing bicycle, whether it's the one I found in the hedge or not."

"Maybe Margaret was wrong? She didn't see a bike? Or are there, what do you call it—" Rafael and Sarah were both leaning heavily into their own hands between bites of breakfast, jet lag having clearly knocked them for a loop. Raf picked up his fork to spin it in a circle like it would help him remember the words. "Security cameras."

"CCTV footage?" Megan offered.

Raf pointed the fork at her triumphantly. "Yeah, that. So there might be footage of somebody stealing the bike, but the detective's got to know that and have checked up on it, right? And if someone did, isn't that evidence of foul play? And he wouldn't hide that, would he? So maybe it really was just an accident."

"I don't know if he'd hide it. I do know accidents take a lot less paperwork than murders," Megan said grumpily. "And it's a small country with a lot of old-boys-club, doing-right-by-each-other nonsense. Who knows who might have leaned on Doyle."

Sarah, who had given up on eating and was looking blearily at her phone, said, "How do you say his daughter's name? Eye-sling? That can't be right. Ice-ling?"

"I don't know how she says it specifically, but it's usually Ashling, Ashlin, or Ashleen."

"That's a lot of pronunciations for one name."

"Try Saoirse on for size," Megan said with a brief smile. "Sur-sha, Seer-sha, Soar-cha, Sir-sha, and probably two others I don't know about. Anyway, I don't like it."

"Saoirse? I think it's pretty."

Megan laughed, and Sarah blinked at her before making a face. "Oh. You mean writing Nolan's death off as an accident. Sorry. It was a—"

"Long trip yesterday," Rafael interrupted, which, from Sarah's slowly lifted eyebrows, hadn't been what she was going to say.

Megan's own eyebrows rose, and she was about to ask, "Late night?" which would have made sense, given jet lag. Then she remembered the two of them had partaken in a sort of fertility ritual before Nolan's body had been found, and a whole different reason for a late night became obvious. She decided she'd better focus on her breakfast until the urge to grin like an idiot had passed, which took slightly longer than she expected it to. She looked up once to find Rafael giving her a gimlet stare that did absolutely nothing to help her fight off the grin. With as much dignity as she could muster, she said, "I'm not twelve, you know."

Rafael snorted, and Sarah looked between them with the expression of a woman who understood that she probably didn't want to know. Megan, in an attempt to take mercy on her, said, "I'm gonna take the dogs for a walk, and then are you two up for going back to the heritage centre? I want to ask Margaret if she recognizes the bike in the hedge."

"You're not going to leave it alone, are you?" Raf looked hopeful.

"Nope. I'm not. If I can satisfy myself that Doyle's right, then fine, but if he's wrong, I'm not gonna let somebody get away with murder if I can help it." The determination underlying the words bothered Megan, although she couldn't say why. She'd felt the same way every time she'd come across a body, but this seemed more urgent than usual somehow.

Maybe it was just that in her usual experience, the detective on the case didn't seem in such a hurry to write it off as a random accident. She got her phone and texted Paul with *I don't appreciate you enough*, then stood to pay for breakfast over her friends' objections, and to go walk the dogs.

"We'll catch up," Raf promised. "We're just not eating very fast today."

"No hurry. I know where to find you." Megan went upstairs for the dogs, who had been out once already, but not for a proper walk. Once on their leads, she took them down by the river, trying *not* to obsess over what little she knew of Seamus Nolan's life and unexpected death. It didn't work, but at least the dogs were able to stretch their legs, and she caught the last bit of a late Irish sunrise over the dripping black fingers of winter-bare trees. Given the clouds just above the horizon, it was probably the only time she'd see the sun that day. Ireland was not, in her opinion, putting its best foot forward for her visitors.

Of course, they *had* opted to come in January. And in theory, their visit was more about seeing Megan than the idyllic beauties of the auld country, but she would have liked to have shown off those fine misty mornings and soft afternoons, rather than given them an up-close-and-personal view of the Murder Driver's life. "All right, pups. Let's go back to the hotel. I'm used to being in a car, not walking around on the moors, not that Ireland has moors that I know about. On the burren. Except that's in the West, I guess. Never mind."

The dogs clearly had no intention of minding. They were used to Megan talking to them so she could pretend she wasn't talking out loud to herself, and they were hardly experts on Irish landscapes anyway. It would have been unlikely for them to offer an opinion. "Although I'd be rich," she informed them on their way back to the hotel. "So if you'd *like* to have opinions on things. Or rather, having opinions expressed in human language, since you're quite capable of expressing them in dog terms. But human language is where the money is."

Thong sat down and stared at her until she was quite certain Megan was done, then rose and walked toward the hotel at such a sedate pace that it seemed like commentary on Megan's monologue. "*See,*" Megan hissed, "I *said* you had opinions on things."

Raf and Sarah, although still visibly sleepy, were ready to go when they got back. The five of them, humans and dogs alike, piled into the car for the short drive to the heritage centre, where dozens of cars and even more people were in attendance. Megan killed the engine, and the three people in the car hesitated a moment, taking in the crush of people and activity after yesterday's mostly serene visit to the holy well.

"Well," Rafael said after a pause, "if they all leave tips, it'll be good for the heritage centre's bottom line . . ."

"The awful thing is, I was thinking something similar," Megan admitted as they got out of the car. "I just hope we can get a minute to talk to Margaret. Oh, God, there's *media* here. I'm going to have to put a paper bag over my head."

There were at least three radio station vans and a larger local news bus with a full crew setting up lights, presumably for some kind of major segment to be featured on Six One, the news report broadcast at 6:01 p.m. every evening. Most of the reporters probably wouldn't recognize her—the only person who definitely would was a sportscaster, who, thank goodness, had no reason to be on-site for this kind of story—but Megan left the dogs in the car and slunk along between Sarah and Rafael anyway.

The heritage centre itself, which had been virtually abandoned the day before, was now filled with people, all of them talking quickly and loudly to one another. The sound bounced off the ceiling, making the small building oppressive. Megan exchanged glances with her friends, and the three of them edged their way toward the reception desk as quickly as they could.

A harried-looking young woman with pale eyes and pink lipstick she had half-chewed off gave them an unconvincing smile. "If you're here to see the well, I'm afraid a great deal of it has been cordoned off. If you're here for the goss . . . She waved a hand at the crowd. "None of them know a thing, and neither do I, but that hasn't stopped them shouting about it."

"We were wondering if Margaret was around, actually?" Megan kept her voice down and leaned in, not wanting the rest of the room to overhead.

Pure pity washed across the young volunteer's face. "No, the poor love, she's that shaken, she is. At home in bed. There were Americans here yesterday that found the body, and she had to deal with them as well as the rest of it."

Rafael coughed, and Megan tried hard to look surprised and sympathetic, although she wanted to gurgle with frustration. Asking about the bicycle she'd found in the hedge seemed extremely difficult, now that she'd been sort-of-pegged as a problem.

To her surprise, Sarah nudged her aside and smiled with genuine sympathy at the girl. "You must be shaken, yourself. I was here yesterday, too, and saw a little of the fuss. Poor Margaret said the unfortunate man came here often?"

Her accent had changed completely, from American to her native Nigerian one. Rafael turned his head, hiding a grin, and nearly lost control of it anyway as he caught sight of Megan's expression. She'd heard Sarah speak Yoruba, and although she *knew* that English was one of Nigeria's official languages, she hadn't ever put that together with the idea that Sarah's original accent probably wasn't American.

It certainly put the young desk attendant at ease, though. There were tens of thousands of African immigrants to Ireland; the idea that this random Black woman who sounded Nigerian might also be one of the Americans who'd visited yesterday wouldn't ever occur to the girl. She smiled at Sarah and nodded. "Rode his bike over all the time, he did. But I suppose he must have walked yesterday? Oh, Jesus, I wonder if I should mention anything about it to the guards . . ."

Sarah's eyebrows furled with worry. "I did think I saw a bicycle in the hedge as I drove in today. Red, with panniers?"

"Ah no, it was green, dark green, and the cheeky man had a wee little Irish flag off the seat of the bike, on a pole like, so it waved in the air above his head."

"Ah." Sarah pressed her hand against her chest in evident relief. "Not the one I saw, then. I'd meant to go and have a moment with Saint Brigid at the well, but it might be better if I came back next week, do you think? I know her holy day is coming up, but I like the privacy instead of the crowd. Isn't that silly?"

"Not at all," the girl said warmly. "I'd say it'll be mental around here for days, and then it'll pick up for the holy day. You might want to wait two weeks? I'll look forward to seeing you again."

"Bless you." Sarah smiled and swept off, leaving the young woman to focus on Megan again.

"I'm sorry, what were we talking about?"

"Nothing important," Megan promised. "I hope this all comes to a peaceful resolution for you. Thanks for your time." She left, making sure not to catch up with Sarah until they were all out the door. "That was amazing, Sarah. Thank you. She wasn't going to tell me anything."

"If we *must* solve a mystery on vacation, I want to at

least do my part." Sarah's Nigerian accent lingered the same way her smile did. "Could you tell what color the bicycle last night was?"

"Dark, but . . ." Megan pulled her phone from her pocket to look at the pictures as her friends crowded around. "I don't know. It *is* dark, but it could be blue or black or green."

"Well, let's go look again." Raf took her phone and expanded some of the pictures as they walked back through the parking lot. "You didn't get any good pictures of its back end, but there might be a broken flagpole there, is that it?"

"Oh, I'm sorry for not taking award-winning photographs in the dark with a camera phone with two dogs climbing on me and a bicycle falling toward my head!"

"Yeah." Rafael grinned at her. "What were you thinking?"

"I can't believe you married him," Megan said to Sarah.

"I can't believe you didn't."

Raf and Megan both said, "Augh, no!" Sarah actually cackled as they left the parking lot for the narrow road, walking along its edge and making apologetic faces at the cars that drove by. The place Megan had climbed into the hedge was remarkably obvious, when they found it: it looked like she'd gone at it with a hatchet instead of her face and a couple of small dogs. "Do I have to go back in? Sarah's smaller."

Sarah's eyes widened in mock distress. "I interrogated the girl at the visitors' centre. You get to go into the hedge."

Megan muttered, "Rats," and crawled in as Raf said, "Why'd it have to be rats?" in the background. A brief argument ensued about whether the quote was rats or snakes, until Megan, having gotten halfway through the hedge, interrupted with, "Uh, guys?"

"Yeah?" Rafael's voice sharpened, all attention, much like he'd sounded when being professional before. "Are you all right?"

"I'm fine," Megan said slowly. "But the bicycle is gone."

CHAPTER 6

Once Megan crawled out, Rafael crawled into the hedge after all, as if she had somehow missed an entire bicycle hanging from the prickly branches. He exited covered in short, pointy leaves and smelling faintly of probably-not-honeysuckle, just as Megan herself was and did. His expression matched hers, too. "Did we go into the wrong place?"

"No." Megan nodded at the soft dirt, where small dog prints were mostly squished out of existence, but still proved that was where they'd been. "Besides, you can look up and down the hedge for forty yards and see there's nowhere else somebody's been wrangling with it."

"Can one 'wrangle' a bush?" Sarah asked thoughtfully. "Does wrangling not require two active participants?"

Megan and Rafael looked at each other, at themselves, and at Sarah, who took a moment to examine their bedraggled state. "I see your point."

"Who would take the bike?" Megan rubbed her eyes, winced at the sap and goo she smeared on her face doing so, and tried to rub it off again with her wrist. "Ow. Back to the car, I need wet wipes."

"The murderer," Rafael suggested as they worked their way back down the road. "Assuming there is one."

"The detective," Sarah said. "So he wouldn't have to investigate the murder, if there was one."

"Or some ambitious kid who saw it once it was day-light, and decided he could make a few quid selling it," Megan finished with a sigh. "Usually you could, what's it called, razor it, but I think all three of those seem fairly likely."

"Occam's razor," Raf offered.

Megan pointed at him and nodded. "Right, that. You know with other people I have to actually think of my own words?"

"The advantages of ancient friendship."

"We're not that old!"

Sarah laughed. "This is even better than listening to you two on the vone calls. I'm so glad I got to come to Ireland and meet you in person, Megan."

An unexpected swell of sentiment made Megan's throat tighten and her nose sting. "Even with the mur-der driver nonsense?"

"Even with it," Sarah promised. "I'd give you a hug, but you're covered in sap and dirt. *That* wasn't here be-fore, was it?"

That was a MINI Cooper, new enough to look straight off the lot except it was shining electric pink that deepened to purple in the shadows. There was no way it had come off the line with that paint job. If they'd been in a country with vanity plates, Megan was sure its plates would have proclaimed the vehicle's name with as much exuberance as the paint job exhibited. "No," she said, unable to hide the admiration in her tone. "No, it wasn't, because I would have gone over and given it a hug."

Raf caught her by the collar, pulling her back as she started to make good on that threat. Megan grinned at him while Sarah whistled. "Boy, if he'd done that to me . . ."

"If anybody *else* had done it to me," Megan agreed. "But it's our thing. We used to make a big fuss about steering each other away from stuff we'd waste a lot of time or money on, when we were teenagers. I'd collar him and drag him out of gaming stores, and he'd pull me out of bookstores, mostly."

"And the first time I did it, without thinking about it, to somebody who *wasn't* Megan, I learned my lesson," Rafael said. "I think my ancestors learned my lesson retroactively, and my progeny . . . proactively?" He squinted, trying to decide if that was the right way to phrase it as Megan went ahead and approached the hot-pink MINI. It was the newest model, an electric vehicle, and clearly belonged to someone who didn't mind being noticed.

"I love it," she announced. "I wonder who it belongs to. I'd like to meet them."

"Me," a young woman said from behind her. "And I never should have driven it here. Sorry." The girl, who looked about seventeen, stepped past her and got into the car, followed by a small horde of reporters who weren't quite running after her. One of them yelled, "Miss Nolan, wait, Miss Nolan—" as the girl closed the car door, and sudden understanding flashed through Megan.

Without thinking, she stepped directly in front of the car door, putting herself between the girl, who had to be Seamus Nolan's daughter, and the media who wanted to talk to her. She cast a quick look over her shoulder, said, "Go on, get out of here if you need to," in case the girl could hear her, and shot the Williamses a grateful look as they joined her in putting themselves between the teenager and the reporters.

"Sorry, look, you're in the way," said the guy who'd shouted after Aisling Nolan. He had a pleasant, mellow radio voice, and a large, intimidating presence that didn't go with the voice at all. "I've a right to talk to that young woman—"

"Don't be silly. She's in mourning, and you're haranguing her. G'wan with ye." Megan's accent went from pure Texas to inner-city Dub without her personal control over the matter, and for a moment she thought of her boss at Leprechaun Limos, whom she'd almost certainly gotten the latter accent from.

It took the reporter off-guard for a heartbeat, enough time for Miss Nolan to turn her vehicle on and begin to back up. Then the reporter's face darkened in a combination of annoyance and recognition. "You're Megan Malone, aren't you? The murder driver? I've heard you've a soft spot for the young wans, always trying to help them out of a spot of trouble. What're you doing here?" His interest in Aisling suddenly fell away as the other reporters converged. "Was it you that found the body? Go live," he said to somebody, and then, in a smooth, professional voice, said, "This is Peader Haughey, and I'm here at Saint Brigid's holy well in Kildare with Megan Malone, known across Ireland as the 'murder driver,' and it looks like Ms. Malone has found herself in another incident. Ms. Malone, would you like to tell our listeners how you got involved Seamus Nolan's unfortunate death?"

The impulse to actually answer went to war with having no idea what to say, which kept Megan's tongue tied just long enough to remember Niamh's advice: *Never talk to them without clearing it with your publicist first.* Never mind that Megan didn't have a publicist. Niamh had, in fact, volunteered her own several times, just in case Megan really needed one. She was beginning to think she might.

For now, though, she could, and did, manage a, "No comment," as she tried to back away. Aisling Nolan's car was still sort of in the way, because there were too many people for the young woman to simply drive through. Megan sidled along the MINI's hot-pink side, trying to aim for her own vehicle, and yelped with surprise as the MINI's passenger door suddenly popped open.

"C'mon then," Aisling said from inside, and Megan, having no better escape route, fell in.

She caught one brief glimpse of Rafael and Sarah's bemused expressions as Aisling reached across her to pull the door shut and locked them. The Williamses exchanged a quick look before Raf jerked his chin, first toward Megan, like he was telling her to go ahead and leave, and then toward the Lincoln. She scrabbled in her pocket for the remote key, unlocked the Lincoln's doors, and watched Sarah and Raf walk through the crowd of reporters like they weren't even there. Or more accurately, like they weren't important to the news media.

"If I gun it, will they get out of the way?" Aisling asked in a low, tense voice. She was a pretty girl, though her round face was pale with tension, except for the spots of high color on her cheeks.

"I wouldn't gun it," Megan said cautiously. "But put on a little speed, and they're likely to move, yeah."

The journalists did move, reluctantly, as Aisling did what Megan suggested. A minute later, she'd pulled out onto the road and cast a stressed glance over her shoulder. "Will they follow?"

"Probably, the jackals. And the car's a little hard to disguise. If you want to go around the long way, though, I've got a hotel room in Naas. I'm Megan Malone," Megan added. "Thanks for the rescue."

"No, thank you, you got between them and me, and I don't know what I'd have done if you hadn't." The poor girl's eyes filled with tears, and she dashed them away, obviously trying to concentrate on driving safely. "I only wanted to see where Da had died. I didn't know there'd be all those—those *vultures* there. I'm Aisling. Aisling Nolan."

"I gathered, yes," Megan said as gently as she could. "I'm very sorry for your loss."

"I heard them." Aisling's voice was choked. "I heard

them saying you were the murder driver? I've heard of you. Was Da killed, then?" A sob broke from her throat, and the car swerved a little as she tried wiping her eyes again.

Megan made an executive decision. "Pull over. I'll drive."

The girl gave her one despairing look and did what she was told. They switched seats, with Megan having to adjust the driver's seat to fit in it properly, and then, with a glance in the rearview mirror, she pulled back onto the road at a considerably higher speed than they'd been traveling. Aisling crumpled in the passenger seat, body-racking sobs filling the car for several minutes, until she lifted her head, coughing and shuddering with grief. "I'm sorry, it's just . . ."

"You have nothing to be sorry for. Have you water and a tissue?"

At the girl's wet nod, Megan said, "Well, get them. You'll need the hydration, and your poor nose is all red and runny. Give it a good blow, and drink as much water as you can, poor chicken."

She'd turned Irish all of a sudden, leaning into Niamh's pet names for people, but it seemed to help Aisling, who squirmed around to get an absurdly large, hot-pink water bottle from the back seat, then gulped down a great deal of its contents before saying, "I'm sorry," again.

"You're fine, love. Blow your nose, now." Megan flipped on the car's GPS and found a series of back roads that would eventually take them around to the hotel before a thought struck her. "Is there anywhere you need to be?"

"Uncle Adam is taking care of most of it," Aisling whispered. "All the—all the paperwork, all the—he's called me a few times to get my opinions, but I just keep crying. Da wanted to be buried on the estate, I know that. Not embalmed or cremated, although he'd take cremation if he had to. But he wanted to be part of the land. He's spent his whole life being part of the land." A fresh wave of tears took the girl, and Megan's own eyes stung with sympathy.

"I don't know where your estate is," she said quietly. "Is it in Kildare?"

"Wicklow," Aisling said hoarsely. "Just over the Kildare border, really."

"Will we go there?"

Gratitude shone through Aisling's tears, although it was replaced by uncertainty. "You were with somebody, weren't you? Someone you're supposed to be driving?"

Megan made a quick gesture at her jeans and jumper. "Off duty. On holiday, actually. Those were friends of mine." She was surprised the girl had even noticed, and flashed her a brief smile. "I'll text them and let them know I'm driving you home, and then I'll figure out how to get back to the car, which they don't have a key for."

"I'm sorry! Oh, god, I've made a mess of things . . . !"

"You've done nothing wrong," Megan said firmly. "They're adults who are not in the middle of a crisis.

They'll be fine at the visitors' centre for a while. What's the name of your estate?"

Aisling, miserably, said, "It's the Rathballard House. Thank you."

The Rathballard House, as if it needed no other address. And it didn't, of course: the GPS system recognized the house specifically, as well as the tremendous acreage around it. A part of Megan wanted to bounce with excitement at the idea of seeing the controversial rewilding project with her own eyes, although she couldn't give in to her inner child with a mourning young woman in the car beside her. "We'll have you home soon. It'll be all right, Aisling. Eventually."

"Really?" The girl sounded heartbroken. "Will it really?"

Megan sighed. "Yes. It'll never be the same, but you'll be all right. As all right as you can be. And it'll probably take a long time to even start to believe that, never mind to feel it, but . . . yes. Eventually. It will be. I really am so sorry for your loss."

Aisling gave a watery little nod, and after a long time, asked, "*Was* he killed, then? Do—do you know something no one else does? Were you . . . were you there?"

Megan, knowing she was hedging, said, "I don't know what you've been told," and braced herself for the storm of tears that she figured would follow.

Instead, Aisling took a harsh breath and said, "Not much. That Da was found dead in the well, he loved going to the well, and that he'd slipped and knocked his head and drowned of it. They didn't say anything about you. *Were* you there, Ms. Malone?"

"You can call me Megan. And I'm sorry, but yes, I found him in the well."

"So, he was murthured." Aisling's accent hadn't been particularly noticeable to Megan until that final word, which she hit so hard it barely sounded like "murdered" at all. She gave the girl a startled glance, wondering where she'd picked up the pronunciation, but let it go in favor of saying, "I don't know, Aisling."

"Well, if you found him . . ."

Megan winced. "I've found not-murdered bodies before, too. And that sounded better in my head."

To her relief, Aisling gave a short laugh. "I didn't know old people said that."

At forty-three, Megan hardly considered herself "old," but since she had roughly twenty-five years on Aisling, she decided it wasn't worth arguing about, either. "Old dogs do occasionally learn new tricks, and a lot of things sound better in our heads than they do out loud, so it's a useful phrase."

"Do you think Da was killed?"

"Maybe. I don't know. Do you think there's a chance of it?"

Aisling shot her a brief, hard look. "I wouldn't be asking if I didn't think so, would I?"

"Arguably not, but the guards think it's an accident, and most people would take their word for it."

"Okay, Boomer."

"I'm Gen X!"

"If Gen X thinks you can trust cops, then you might as well be a Boomer."

"You know, I had this conversation the other way around with somebody your age—what do they call your generation, Z? Zoomers?—a couple of months ago, so why don't we dispense with the rude generational divides and go back to why you think your father's death might not have been an accident."

The way Aisling's breath caught suggested Megan might have been a little harsh. Aisling went quiet for a couple kilometers, staring out the window and composing herself as they crossed the county border. When she spoke, it was to say, "Did you really? Have this conversation the other way around?" rather than address the bigger topic.

"I did, yeah. With a young woman a little older than you, whose impulse was to trust and talk to the guards. It almost cost her her job until I interfered." That was a little dramatic, but not inaccurate, and it earned Megan a quick look of admiration.

"You're always interfering, aren't you?"

"The guards certainly think so."

"They're—turn left up there," Aisling said abruptly. "I know it's not what the GPS says, but that'll have you drive all the way around the estate. This'll take us straight into it. The road's a bit rough, but it keeps people from coming onto the land all the time."

"It's your car." Megan turned down a country road lined by hedgerows and stone walls on both sides, offering little more than glimpses of the fields beyond them. There were forested grounds up ahead, visible in flashes, and she wasn't surprised when Aisling directed her down another couple of turns to eventually end up at a very, very high stone wall, populated on the far side by trees and split, where the road reached it, by an iron gate twice Megan's height. She stopped the car and leaned over the steering wheel, looking up at it. "I assume that *also* keeps people from coming onto the land all the time."

She probably deserved the dirty look Aisling gave her as the girl got out of the car to open the gate, but didn't feel like she did. She eased the MINI through, waited for Aisling to close the gates behind them, and fought the urge to creep along the country lane like a trespasser awed by her surroundings.

They were awe-inspiring, though. Despite it being the back way to the house, the road was lined with vast cedar trees, making it a literal avenue. On the road's left, just beyond the trees, a track that looked suitable for riding, walking, or cycling ran beside it, and past that grew what looked, from what Megan knew about trees, like old-growth forest. It probably wasn't: most of Ireland's original forests had been cut down centuries earlier, and these trees were more likely to be re-planted, managed growth rather than natural ancient forest, but they were still likely to be a century or two old. It looked peaceful, good for walking through, all soft and green in the undergrowth even if the trees themselves were bare-branched with winter.

The right-hand side of the road looked completely different. A huge, crazed tangle of growth burst up there, spreading as far as she could see as they bumped along the lane's twists and turns. "That's Da's rewilding," Aisling said quietly. "We've old forest for acres there on the north side, but the rest of the estate was cleared and farmed for centuries. He's been giving the land back to itself. He wants to be buried in the heart of it, where he worships."

"Is that even allowed?"

"I hope so. There's the house up there." She nodded, and Megan craned her neck a little, like she could see around the next bend. All she caught was a glimpse of a square gray corner, and for an instant, thought she knew what kind of house she'd see: one of the grim, blocky, neoclassical throwbacks that had come after the more ornate Regency era. Huge but ugly, at least on the exterior.

Then they came around the curve, and a squeaking laugh popped from Megan's chest. Huge, yes. Ugly, not so much: even at the back of the house, there were tremendous Grecian columns in white marble; broad, sweeping stairs leading to low-walled plazas; and peaked façades over tall doorways. The corner she'd glimpsed was being refinished, modern concrete waiting for its marble face to be replaced. Wings swept away from where they parked, reaching toward the front of the house in great curving arcs, like the whole house was a swan coming to land on the water.

The grounds immediately surrounding the house were well-kept lawns marked with smooth stone pathways to walk along as they wound through gardens, and the forests, both new and old growth, snuggled up to the lawn's edges like they were meant to be together. There were several cars parked behind the ridiculous building, and a driveway that curved off toward the front.

Megan laughed again. "This is the *back*?"

"The front is even more impressive," Aisling said with a little smile. "But I like this entrance better, because it's the one I used growing up. The orchards are right over there, and I'd go out and play in them all day. There's Uncle Adam." She ran forward to hug a small man with white hair who exited one of the house's huge back doors.

He had to be her great-uncle, Megan thought. Either that or Seamus had been much, *much* younger than his brother. Adam was at least in his sixties, with an interestingly lined face that looked as though he'd seen a lot of sun in his youth and had taken to wearing hats outdoors in his later years. He tucked her close, kissing her hair, and examined Megan with a kindly disinterest. "And who's this?"

"This is Megan Malone, Uncle. She thinks Da was murdered."

CHAPTER 7

The kindly disinterest fled from Adam Nolan's otherwise-pleasant face, leaving him pinched and angry. "Jesus, Ais, we don't need that kind of rubbish coming into this house. Isn't it enough that he's dead? Go," he snapped at Megan. "You're not welcome here."

"I drove Aisling home," Megan replied mildly. "She was in bits and needed some help. Until I arrange for a lift, I'm afraid I'm stuck here. And I didn't say I thought Mr. Nolan was murdered—"

"But she's the murder driver," Aisling finished with a note of triumph.

Megan took a heartbeat to wish a pox on the social media troll who had landed her with that hashtag, then tried to pull a smile together. "Which isn't actually the same thing as thi—"

"What business is it of yours?" Adam demanded. "It's our own private family matter, and you've no right to go sticking your nose into—"

"She found Da's body."

Nolan went entirely white, then colored the same way Aisling had, with hot spots high on his cheeks. "What? The guards never said anything like that."

"What did they say?" Megan asked, suddenly curious.

"That his body had been found at—" Anger coursed through Nolan's face. "At the holy well. They didn't say who'd found it, now that I'm thinking about it. They implied . . ." He stared hard at Megan. "They didn't even really imply it was the staff. They didn't say a word about it at all. They let me infer it, didn't they?"

"I'm very sorry, Mr. Nolan. The detective on duty recognized me and preferred to keep me out of the story entirely. I'm sure that's why he allowed you to think the staff had found your brother's body."

"Nephew."

"Nephew. My apologies. And I assure you, I didn't mean to become involved in any way. I'm only here because Aisling needed some assistance this morning."

"The media were all over." Aisling's eyes went red and blurry. "I just wanted to see where he'd last been, Uncle, but it was a madhouse. Megan put herself between myself and themselves so I could get in the car and drive away."

Conflict between gratitude and irritation surged across Nolan's face. "And how did she end up driving you, then?"

"They were coming after her once I was safe in the car," Aisling said. "So I threw open the door and had her climb in."

"I can call a taxi to take me back to the heritage centre." Megan took her phone out to open a countrywide taxi app she rarely used. "I assume the address is just the 'Rathballard House'?"

"I can drive you back," Nolan said reluctantly. "You've gone out of your way to help Ais, here."

Sympathy washed through Megan. "I appreciate the offer, Mr. Nolan, but you must have an awful lot on your hands already. If you don't mind me waiting around front for the taxi, it's no problem for me to take one. It's not very far, and I realize I'm already intruding."

Aisling's cheeks flushed again. "You're not intruding. You've been very kind and helpful, and you can wait for a taxi as long as it takes, but you have to tell Uncle Adam what you know about Da's death. He'd never slip like that, Unka, you know it."

"Not on purpose." Nolan spoke like a man weary of the conversation already. "People fall, Ais. They trip. Sometimes dreadful things happen."

"But—"

"Do you *want* your father to have been murdered?" the older man burst out.

Aisling took a shocked step backward, then stiffened, eyes bright with grief. "I do, maybe I do! At least there'd be some sense to it then, and not just him gone because of a stupid accident!" She bolted into the house, choking on tears, and Nolan, effectively forgetting Megan was there, shouted, "Jesus, Aisling!" and went after her. The door swung closed ponderously behind them, leaving Megan at the top of a set of marble steps all on her own.

"This is the moment you do the right thing by walking around the house and calling a taxi. You don't sneak around and try to talk to people about Seamus Nolan," she informed herself aloud. It was better when the dogs were there, and she could pretend she was talking to them. Phone in hand, she did at least back off the steps, looking up at the grand sweep of the enormous house. It didn't look like a place people *lived*, not in any meaningful way. It was too palatial, and Megan imagined at least part of the house was open to visitors who wanted to see how the rich Anglo-Irish landlords had lived in centuries past.

She breathed, "Well, you're here anyway, might as well find out," and did start working her way around the exterior toward the front of the huge building. A couple of groundskeepers paused to watch her, and after the third one gave her a funny look, Megan detoured toward him to say, "I *will* get to the front of the building if I keep walking, right?"

The groundskeeper, a kid in his mid-twenties with the shoulders of a working man and a shock of dark-red hair, grinned. "When I started here, I kept having a laugh at the size of the gardens. I'd imagine my own self living in this ridiculous place. 'I'll just take a wee turn around the gardens,' I'd say to myself, 'I'll be back in an hour or two.' It takes twenty minutes to walk around the whole building, if you're not in any particular hurry about it."

Megan laughed. "Not ten minutes? I thought everything in Ireland was a ten-minute walk."

"Well, we'd rather lie to you than disappoint you, wouldn't we? Ten minutes seems like a walk most of us can do, so we'll say ten minutes even if it's forty. You're American, then? And you came up the back drive? You're not a tradesman." He gave her a critical up-and-down. "What're you doing here, then?"

"I drove Aisling home after she had a bad spell at the holy well."

"Ah." The kid leaned on his rake like he was a ninety-year-old gardener posing for a portrait. "She's beside herself, she is. Her da was a good sort. Odd. But a good sort. He's got half the village employed here, and none of us knows what'll happen now that the old man's going to inherit."

Megan cast a startled blink toward the enormous house, then back at the lad. "Adam Nolan's inheriting? What about Aisling?"

The boy curled his lip. "Law of . . . what do you call it, the thing that the feckin' Brits got their pants in a bunch over and then it didn't matter when Willy's first child was a boy?"

"Primo, aaaah." Megan squinted, trying to remember the word. "Primogeniture. Male primogeniture, when everything goes to the oldest son, or to the next living male relative. Seriously? That's still in effect here?"

"'Tis. Mr. Seamus had been in and out of the courts for the past ten years, challenging it, and they keep pushing it up the line and telling somebody else to make the decision. And the old man hasn't any time for this re-wilding work. He'd as soon sell off half the estate to developers and spend the rest of his days in the Canaries."

A lump of excitement lodged itself around Megan's heart, making every thump ache a little. She shouldn't be thrilled at the hint of a motivation for murder, but the thrilling *zing* that shot through her didn't seem to care. "I didn't see anything about the inheritance in the news this morning."

"I'd say somebody's running hard interference, then." The kid gave a meaningful eye roll toward the house, and Megan, unable to stop herself, looked that way again.

"Adam Nolan?"

The kid sniffed. "You didn't hear it from me."

"I did not," she agreed, and a grin split his face before fading just as quickly.

"I wouldn't say he's a bad man, you know. It's only that this house *does* keep half the village in work, either from working here ourselves or because tourists drive through to visit the house and stop for lunch at our cafés or do a spot of shopping in the village centre. Without it, Ballyballard dries up."

"Ballyballard," Megan echoed. "Ballard's town?"

"Next to Ballard's Fort," he said with a tilt of his head toward the house. "It was Baile Lough Ceilidh back before the British took the land and changed the names to suit themselves, but the lake was drowned by the reservoir and nobody remembers it anymore, so it's Ballyballard now."

"Bally Lock Keely," Megan repeated carefully, getting the sounds right. "That's what, 'town of the dancing lake'?"

The boy smiled. "There was a waterfall, yeh. Poetical, isn't it?"

"The Irish are known to have a way with words. Look, I hope it turns out all right. Would the village be safer if Aisling inherited?"

"Oh, yeh, she's a sound wan, is Aisling. Like her da, that one. Look, do you know what he'd been doing out here? Have you seen it?"

"Um." Megan cast a guilty glance toward the house, although no one appeared to remember or care about her. "No? Except what I drove through, and I know he's rewilding and it's controversial somehow, but that's it."

"Right so. I'm Ian, by the way." He offered a hand with dirt-crusted fingernails, and Megan shook it.

"Megan. Nice to meet you, Ian."

"You too. C'mere to me now, I'll show you just a bit of the work. Are your shoes all right in the muck?"

"They'll wash." Megan wasn't going to lose the opportunity just to avoid mud on her shoes, although when she stepped in a section that sank her down to her ankle, she almost reconsidered. Ian, grimacing, helped her get free, then fished her shoe out of the mud and gave her a surprisingly rakish grin.

"See, the earth likes you. It's a good sign."

Megan laughed. "Did you just make that up?"

"Would I tell you if I had?" They didn't have much farther to go, and the one section was the worst for muck, although the border between the garden proper and the new rewilding looked more than a little dodgy to Megan's eye. Fortunately, Ian stopped just before that part and spread his hands. "What do you see?"

"Um. Honestly, it looks like somebody went absolutely nuts shoving everything they possibly could into the tiniest space available."

Ian beamed. "That's right. There's two major ways to rewild, at least two that I know of. One is to just stop the sheep and the cattle and the farmers going on the land and let it grow back. It's slow, but it does the job. The other is to over-seed the land on purpose, stuff it full of loads of this and loads of that, and when it takes root, it comes up fast and dense and diverse because of how the light and soil get used, yeh?"

Megan considered the tangle of new growth with interest. "And that's what you've done here? If it's faster, why doesn't everybody do it? Why's it so controversial? Don't we need all the forests we can get at this point?"

"'Cause it's not *as* diverse as natural growth," Ian said frankly. "'Cause you're seeding it on purpose, so nature doesn't pick and choose what grows, and that can make it susceptible to blight and bugs. Used to be they'd plant all one kind of tree, and it's hard for people to learn we've got past that and are trying to do better, but there's no denying that if you dump a load of one kind of seedlings into one place, it'll limit the diversity."

"Still, if it's fast . . . ?"

Ian nodded. "That was how Seamus saw it, and how the lot of us who work here do. Aisling's been out here growing things her whole life with the rest of us, so we only want to keep the work going."

"How much of the land is rewilded?"

"About eight hundred hectares. Two-thirds or so," he said to Megan's baffled glance. "And another hundred or so that's old forest, at least older than most these days. So almost three-quarters of the land has trees now, even if a lot of them are young scrub yet, like this."

"Holy moly." Megan's eyebrows rose. "And selling the land would . . . ?"

"See a lot of it ripped up, and our hearts with it, I'd guess. Even if only the land that's not been rewilded yet is all that was developed, it wouldn't be Seamus's vision, but you know how it is once development starts."

Megan sighed. "Yeah. Well, that's a mess I didn't expect to hear about. Thanks for showing me the rewilding. I had no idea there were different approaches. I thought people just stopped using it for farming or livestock and let it go."

"Oh, there's loads more things being done all over, in all sorts of ways," Ian said eagerly as they turned back. "C'mon, let me tell you about greening the Sahara. First, did you know it goes from desert to savanna every twenty thousand years or so?" He chattered on enthusiastically as Megan followed him back to the gardens, this time without nearly losing her shoe, then beamed at her as they reached the spot where she'd first stopped to talk to him. "Listen to me going on, and you with places to go. It's only that I'm not important enough to talk to anyone about the project, so it's exciting when I get to."

Megan laughed. "I'm glad you did. It was fascinating, and I now know more about reversing desertification than I ever knew there *was* to know. Thanks for your time, Ian. I hope things go well for the estate."

"Me too," he said a bit more solemnly, and Megan left him to work as she headed toward the front of the house again, now with her phone in hand to look up Seamus Nolan's case against male primogeniture.

There was a message from Paul, too, saying, *I don't know what's worse, being underappreciated or overappreciated*, with a link to a tabloid story featuring a flattering photograph of himself with Niamh, followed by an article gushing about the actress's redheaded fox of a detective. *Don't read the comments.*

Megan immediately read the comments, which seemed to be a fight club between people either drooling over, raging about, or envying Paul. She wrote back with *Thank god Niamh is fabulous*, and he sent a swirly-eyed emoji and a thumbs-up in response.

The primogeniture case had been going on for about four years, not ten, which was something of a relief: most legal systems didn't move fast, but a decade seemed really slow to overturn an obviously antiquated law. That said, there was apparently a *huge* amount of resistance to changing the law. Reading between the lines, it seemed like no one wanted to be responsible for making the decision, although Megan couldn't imagine why.

It wasn't like there were enormous numbers of landed gentry with firstborn sons to hand things over to, anymore. Most Irish nobility seemed to be as antiquated as the law, with the last generation having been born fifty or seventy years ago and most of their estates going to a random nephew whom someone had gone to a lot of trouble to locate.

That had been the case the only other time she'd come into contact with a historic landowner, too, although then, the heirs themselves had been invested in proving the connection. Megan wondered if calling them into the courts would have any effect on the law.

What the news articles *didn't* suggest was that Adam Nolan had any interest in stymying his nephew's attempts to make sure Aisling inherited the estate. His name barely came up in the stories at all, except as Seamus's only other living relative. Megan walked slowly around to the front of the building, not really looking where she was going as she read the various stories about it all. The newest was several months old, and ended with an expectation that the case would be heard in the High Court sometime in the new year.

Early January was a convenient time for Seamus to die, then. Megan had no idea what happened if the plaintiff died before the court heard his case, but she bet there would be a delay, at the very least. Or maybe it would be dropped entirely, and the inheritance would move on as the law was currently written.

Which would be very good for Adam Nolan. Megan slid her phone into her pocket and finally glanced up at the front of the house.

Another laugh escaped her. It looked even more like a swan's wings bending inward from the front. The center of the building was comparatively blocky, but had a long, pale stone walk reaching toward the main road from its impressive front steps, so there was even an impression of the swan's neck stretching forward between the broad, gentle curve of the house's vast wings. They were three stories in height, although the windows at the top were squat and square rather than tall and airy. The rooms there had almost certainly been servants' quarters once upon a time, and might even still be. Megan took a moment, trying to imagine living a life that included servants at all, then cackled.

She *was* a servant, in terms of social structure. Her job was literally driving other people around. Three hundred years ago, when this house had been built, she might have driven a horse and carriage, and been hired by a single family, rather than work for a company that hired her expertise out to multiple clients, but the gist of it was the same. She'd even used it to her advantage any number of times: people frequently didn't think anything of what they talked about in front of the help, as if she wasn't a person, or as if her temporary position in their lives meant anything she heard couldn't, in the grand scheme, be relevant to them. Mostly they were right, but occasionally she overheard something that—for example—might help her solve a murder.

Maybe she could get Adam Nolan to hire her for a few days, and listen in to what he might have to say about his nephew's death.

Except she was on holiday, Megan reminded herself. Her friends were visiting, and she should get back to them sooner rather than later. With a reluctant glance at the big house, which she would have genuinely liked to explore, she pulled her phone back out to actually *use* the taxi app.

There was a new text message from Niamh, a panic emoji followed by *I need to talk.*

CHAPTER 8

Megan's belly twisted so hard she thought she might lose what remained of her breakfast, and even though Niamh was presumably on set, she called anyway. Within a few seconds, a video image of the actress popped up against a background that looked like the interior of a film set trailer. "Oh, thank Jaysus, Megan, bless you for ringing."

"What's going on? Are you okay? Is Paul?" Megan's hands were shaking so badly her own image wobbled in its little frame. "What's wrong?"

"I've just gotten the best news ever." Niamh nearly dropped her phone, the picture swooping to show that she was, indeed, in her trailer on set before she righted it again. Then the whole picture zoomed around as she took a seat and put the phone into a stand of some kind that let her hide her face in both hands.

Megan's mind leaped places she was fairly sure it

shouldn't, and bit her tongue hard on asking, *Are you pregnant?* "What's going on? You look rattled for somebody who's gotten good news. Nee?"

Niamh looked up, expression torn between excitement and dismay. "D'ye remember that TV pilot I filmed a couple years ago? One of those prestige TV things, it's a massive project . . . ?"

"Sort of. Before you blew up a couple years ago with the Irish film, right? You had fun with it. There were some really big names attached, I mean, bigger than you were at the time . . ." Megan's stomach was still churning so strongly she went to sit down herself, clutching the phone in both hands so it would stop shaking.

"They've just green-lit it," Niamh said hoarsely. "Huge budget. Promotion like you wouldn't believe."

Relief crashed through Megan hard enough to make her dizzy. "Oh my God. Niamh! That's fantastic! Congratulations!" She thought her heart might start beating again normally in a year or two, if she didn't get any more shocks.

The actress met Megan's eyes through the phone. "It's filming in San Francisco, starting next month, for at least eighteen months and probably longer."

"Whoa. *Wow*. My God, that's incredible. So you're mov—" Megan drew a deep breath, suddenly understanding. "Oh. Oh, no. You're moving. And Paul . . . ?"

"I haven't even told him yet," Niamh whispered. "I just got off the phone with my manager. Ten minutes ago, no more. I texted you first. I don't know what to say. I can't turn it down, Megan. The script is incredible, the money is great, the cast is unbelievable, and it's a marquee spot. I'm second call. I can't turn it down."

"No." Megan sat back, pushing her hand over her hair and staring helplessly at her friend. "No, I get that. But eighteen months? Eighteen months *straight*?"

"There'll probably be a wee little bit of time off between series, so they can do postproduction at least far enough for us to see what we've done, where we are with the story. But two of the costars are kids, and they want them to be the same age through the whole production, which is part of why they're doing this crazy schedule. That, and . . ." Niamh gave Megan a sick smile. "Well, you know how much TV gets cancelled after a couple of series?"

"Yeah, of course, it's maddening."

"They, the producers, they've negotiated a three-series budget that they think they can get five seasons out of. But they only have the soundstage for a certain amount of time, so to keep inside the budget, they can't afford to risk anything being torn down. We're basically—you can't tell anyone this, Megan—"

"No, obviously not, but what am I not telling anybody?"

"We're basically going to try to film five series in three years," Niamh said in a low voice. "They've got the soundstage that long, and they want to get the whole story in the can before the streaming service pulls the plug. They're going to treat each series like a feature film, four months of filming, a month or two off except for pickups, then back to the main filming again."

"Pickups . . ." Megan racked her brain for a moment. "That's when you go back to shoot new scenes for things that didn't work, right? So . . . so you have to be there the whole time. You can't really fly back to Ireland for a couple of months between seasons."

"Not really, no." Niamh's eyes filled with tears. "I don't know what to do. I can't turn it down. It's such a great opportunity, Megan."

"Paul wouldn't expect you to turn it down," Megan said gently. "You know that, Nee."

"I *know*, but . . ." She buried her face in her hands again. Her hair was in cornrows today, beaded at the ends in gold and crimson, and her costume was a work of art, all oranges and brilliant greens with bangles on her wrists. She looked, Megan thought, *exactly* like a film star, so beautiful she was slightly unreal, particularly in the gorgeous, vibrant colors. Even when she lifted her head again, tears tracking down her cheeks, she managed to be glorious. Megan wished her unhappiness was a performance, too. "Do you think he'll come with me?" Niamh asked, sounding lost.

"I don't know, honey. You're going to have to ask him."

"I'm afraid he'll say no."

"I know." Megan was, too, although she didn't want to say so aloud to her friend. Worse, there was a knotty little part of her that selfishly didn't want *both* of them to go off to America, although she bet the comments section on that article she'd read would be united in thinking Paul was an idiot if he *didn't* go to the States with his movie-star girlfriend. "I know he loves you."

"I know, too. It's just . . . is it enough?"

"I don't know," Megan said again. "I hope so, sweetie. But, Niamh . . ."

Hope and curiosity spilled across Niamh's face, then burst into a complex laugh of joy and grief as Megan said, "*Congratulations,* babe. This is *huge.* This is *great* for you, and I'm so, *so* happy for you."

Niamh lost her movie-star beauty for a second as she gave a great snorting blurt of laughter and picked up her phone to hug it. "Thank you. I'm thrilled, I am, I'm excited, it's just . . ."

"Complicated," Megan said gently, once she was no longer pressed to Niamh's bosom. "I wish it could be not-complicated, but I'm still really happy for you, and you should be too."

"I am." Niamh gave her another messy smile. "I am so."

"And oh my God! San Francisco! Raf and Sarah live there! Niamh, you'll have friends!"

"Oh." Niamh's expression melted into gratitude. "Oh, do you think they'd really like to be friends? I mean, instead of just some rando they met on your phone once?"

"They'll be great," Megan promised. "And if you need somewhere to hide from the media for whatever reason, they'll totally sneak you in the back door and feed you jollof rice. It's Sarah's specialty."

"That sounds wonderful," Niamh said wistfully. Then her gaze rose to beyond the phone, and she made a face. "They're calling for me. I have to go pretend like everything's normal, because I'm not actually sup-

posed to tell anybody about this at *all* until it's been officially announced."

"Fortunately you're an actor," Megan said with a
wry smile. "Pretending is your stock in trade. And I
won't tell anybody, I promise."

"I know you won't. I'll tell you what Paul says," she
added quietly, then pulled together a startling smile,
proving her acting chops were still intact. "All right,
my pet! I'll talk to you soon! On my way!" she called,
and the call ended with a flurry of her colorful dress.

Megan put her phone down, then doubled to put her
head between her knees and breathe deeply for a minute. People should not *ever* reach out with "we need to
talk" without some kind of explanation, although in
this case, Megan didn't see what Niamh could have said
without potentially getting herself in trouble. Phone-
hacking scandals weren't, unfortunately, a thing of the
past.

Neither was her lurching heartbeat. Although it had
settled down, she still felt a little sick from the adrenaline rush of wondering what terrible thing had happened. At least it hadn't actually been terrible, in the
end, but Megan kept her head down for a minute or two
anyway, breathing until she felt steadier.

"Are you all right, ma'am?" A woman spoke from
behind her, making Megan realize she'd been sitting on
the Rathballard House's front steps for a while now.
She twisted around with an apologetic smile and nodded.

"Yeah, sorry. I just got some startling news and had
to sit for a minute."

"Oh!" The woman, who wasn't much older than Ian in the garden, got a determined look. "Then you'll need to come in for a cup of tea. Are you with one of the tour groups?" She flickered a glance down the driveway, where Megan, following her gaze, saw the dull gleam of a tour bus beneath the gray sky. The young woman went on, "They're all the rest of them upstairs in the drawing rooms by now, but you'll catch them up by skipping the Red Room entirely, it's dull as dishwater," she added confidently. "Come on, now, let me get you that tea."

Megan put up a token protest, but the truth was, a cup of tea sounded wonderful just then, and explaining who she was and what she was really doing there seemed unnecessary. "Thank you. There's a tearoom, isn't there?" She had no actual idea, but given the grandeur of the place, it struck her as likely.

The girl gave a pleasant nod as she ushered Megan through the house's tall doors into a massive hall, then veered off to one side, guiding Megan. "The groups usually take high tea at around four, when the tour ends, but I'll get you a bit of everything early, poor pet. Is it all right, the news you got? Are ye well?"

"It's fine," Megan promised. "Thank you. Oh, wow." The last was as the girl led her through an interior arch into a sitting room that would make strong men weep with admiration. Or at least, Megan thought as she sat gingerly in a sleekly padded Queen Anne–style chair, it would make limo drivers with a fondness for local architecture gasp with awe. "This is *beautiful.*"

The young woman smiled in a proprietary way, as if

she were personally responsible for three hundred years of selective architecture and furniture choices, then scooted off to fetch Megan some tea. Megan, for the third time, took her phone out to call for a taxi, but ended up deciding to wait so she wouldn't have to rush her tea. The girl came back within a minute or two with the tea itself, promised, "Just you wait for the rest," and bustled off again.

"Thank you." Megan poured herself a weak cup and wrapped her hands around it. Its heat stung her palms, but not quite enough to put it back down. Between chatting with Ian and sitting on the steps to talk to Niamh, she'd been outside longer than she'd realized, and the damp gray cold had sunk into her bones. She hadn't even taken a sip of the tea, grateful just to hold it, before the girl came back with a ridiculously wonderful three-tier silver platter of tea tidbits.

"Now," she said with satisfaction, "a bit of this is yesterday's, I won't lie, but the cucumber sandwiches and the salmon dip are fresh, and the cakes won't be any worse for being yesterday's. Eat as much as you like, love, it's a treat."

"Oh, I couldn't," Megan replied, startled. "I'll pay for it, of course."

"You won't," the girl began, and Aisling, coming into the tearoom, repeated it as she waved the girl away with a smile. The girl actually bobbed a curtsy as she scurried away, and Megan had the disconcerting thought about living a life with servants again.

Aisling looked better than she had half an hour ago, although she was still pale with grief as she gestured to ask Megan if she could join her. Megan nodded at the table's other chair, and Aisling dropped into it with no concern for its antiquity. Maybe, Megan thought, it was only a replica. A very good replica. "Sorry about my uncle," Aisling said. "He . . ."

Whatever explanation she'd meant to offer apparently wasn't good enough, because after a silence she only shook her head. Megan said, "It's all right. It's never easy when someone dies."

Aisling shot her a startled look. "You know almost no one ever says that. *Dies*. They say passed away, or gone on, or a dozen other things, but almost nobody's said to me that Da *died*."

"I won't, if you'd rather I didn't."

"No, it's good." Aisling picked up a cucumber sandwich and looked at it without interest. "I know people don't like the bluntness, but it's a blunt thing, isn't it? Death is, I mean. I don't know whose feelings they're trying to save, mine or their own. Nobody I loved ever died before. My mam is coming up from Cork. You'd think she'd be here already, wouldn't you?" Each sentence was delivered with a short pause between them, as if her thoughts were entirely disjointed. "Cork's not so far away."

"It's not far away, no." A couple of hours' drive, which meant, yes, Megan *would* have expected Aisling's mother to be there already, as Seamus had been found almost a full day ago now, and the family would have been notified first. "Your parents were . . . divorced?" she asked, trying to remember what the news articles had said.

Aisling gave a hard little breath that might have been meant as a laugh. "Separated. Not divorced, because Da was terrible at paperwork. I guess they both are. And it takes so long, anyway. But I don't even remember them being together, it was that long ago they split up."

Megan kept her eyebrows down with an effort. Divorce *did* take a long time in Ireland—the divorcing parties had to live separately for at least two of the previous three years for it to even be considered—and it could take anywhere from several months to years for it to be granted after the application had been made. Still, Aisling was in her late teens, and if her parents had split long enough ago that she didn't remember them being together, they apparently were *exceptionally* bad at paperwork. "I don't suppose they thought they might get back together?"

She would have clawed the question back if she could have. As it was, the last couple of words were strangled as she realized how inappropriate it was. "Sorry, that's really none of my business at all. I don't know why I asked."

The girl across from her gave another one of the hard breaths, a little closer to a cackle this time. "Because everybody does. Even me. But as far as I know, they haven't even seen each other since I was old enough to get on a bus myself to go down and spend a weekend with Mam, so no."

Since she was asking questions that were none of her business anyway, Megan, a little more cautiously this time, said, "Your father ended up with custody . . . ?"

Aisling barked a proper laugh this time. "Look at

this place. Wouldn't you say the parent who owned *it* would be the 'primary caregiver'? Mam's an artist," she added after a brief silence. "The kind who decided kids 'disrupted her creative flow,' even though she has three. My half sisters live with their fathers, like I do. All of them men with a lot of land like Da's got, like . . . I don't know. Like she was looking for Mr. Darcy. She grew up poor enough, down the country. My littlest sister is only four." She went quiet again, then, more stiffly, said, "Maybe it's not such a surprise she isn't here yet."

"Wow. That could complicate the inheritance, couldn't it?"

"Could it? Why?" Aisling blinked at her, and Megan wished she hadn't said anything.

"Because I think in Ireland the man you're married to is automatically assumed to be the father of your children unless you put something else down on the birth certificate, so if they never divorced . . ."

Aisling stared, then laughed again, sharp and disbelieving. "Holy Mary. I didn't know that. Well, Jaysus, they deserve something for being my mother's daughters, so if that's how it is, I won't contest it."

"But your uncle might, though, right?"

At Aisling's bewildered expression, Megan once again considered the wisdom of keeping her mouth shut, too late. "What's Uncle Adam got to do with it?"

"The law of male primogeniture?" Megan asked weakly. "Or, uh, I guess it's . . ." She'd seen it when she looked it up, but had forgotten already, so she got her phone to check again. "'Heirs male.' Men inherit in a noble line, even one that's been sort of discontinued like they have been in Ireland. Your father was challenging it in court, so you could inherit instead of your uncle?"

The color drained from Aisling's face, leaving even her lips chalky pink. "What?"

"You didn't know? He's had a court case going on for years!"

"Da was in and out of the courts all the time," Aisling whispered. "He was always causing trouble and fighting it in court, and usually winning on some technicality. It's part of how he got that silly nickname, there was some reporter who said he must have the luck of the old gods with him to keep winning, and he said that was right, he was a druid blessed by Brigid herself, and after that, he started with the robes just for the look of the thing, and after *that*, he turned into kind of a hippie, like, or a druid, I guess, but . . . *what*?"

She was a teenager, Megan reminded herself. A teenager who'd had no reason to expect her father's untimely death. Inheritance laws, even for an old, titled estate, would not be high in her list of important things to worry about. Still, Megan said, "I'm sorry, I assumed you knew," with a note of embarrassment. This wasn't information Aisling should get from a stranger.

Aisling's color had worsened until she was nearly green. "Do you mean it? The estate isn't mine automatically?" When Megan shook her head, Aisling put her face in her hands, then looked up with haunted eyes. "Uncle Adam had a phone call, that's why I came out front. When I left he was talking to someone about selling the land."

CHAPTER 9

"I listened for a minute outside the door," Aisling went on in a thin voice. "I thought he'd be giving out to them for being mental. He sounded angry, at least, and I heard him say something about the inheritance before I left. Promising to pay, or buy, or—I don't know. Megan, he wouldn't—this was my da's life," she cried. "His passion! Uncle Adam would never just let it go, would he? He couldn't! How could I stop him, if he tried?"

"Take it to court. I'm not a lawyer, Aisling, I don't know anything about this, but I think you'd better ring your father's lawyer right now and see if you can get an injunction to stop your uncle from selling anything before the High Court rules on the primogeniture case."

"I don't even know what that means!" the girl wailed. "I've never talked to Da's solicitor!"

She was a teenager, Megan reminded herself again, and swallowed her cooling tea in one gulp. "Okay.

Come on, sweetheart. Does your dad have an office in the house?"

"Yeah, of course, it's upstairs in the private wing . . ."

"Let's go up there," Megan said firmly. "We'll see if we can find your dad's solicitor's number and you can call and figure out what needs to be done. I'm sorry," she added, meaning it from the bottom of her soul. "You shouldn't have to be dealing with any of this, but if you think there's actually a chance your uncle would sell the land—and I hate to tell you, Aisling, but at least some of your staff thinks there is—you need to move now."

"He thinks it's a waste." Aisling rose shakily, and Megan, watching her wobble toward the door, looped her finger through the top of the silver serving tower and brought the snacks with them as they returned to the main hall and climbed the truly stupendous curving stairs there. "Uncle Adam does, I mean. I know that. He thinks it's mad to have thousands of acres gone to forest instead of being turned into housing developments. He and Da used to argue about it all the time, and it would always end with Da saying, 'Well, it's my land, Adam, and it'll be Aisling's after I'm gone.' Uncle Adam would grumble, but that'd be the end of it."

They turned deeper into the house after they climbed the stairs, going down hallways Megan could have spent hours in, gazing at the art, the view, the cornice and the cracks in the walls, trying to imagine all the history that had happened there. Instead, they moved at the pace of someone accustomed to living in historical splendor, until Aisling pushed on an old oak door that opened onto a strikingly modern office at the heart of the old house.

It had all the hallmarks of its heritage, of course: the ornate cornicing Megan had glanced at on their way into the room, and a ceiling rose that a massive glittering crystal chandelier hung from, not far above a solid wood desk that had probably been in the room for two centuries. But two computer screens and a laptop stand were on the desk, along with piles of paperwork and ballpoint pens, and the chair behind it was ergonomic, not ancestral. The built-in bookcases were filled with modern paperbacks and stacked haphazardly with books about gardening, growing, and wilding, along with innumerable others. A stereo system, including a turntable, had been fitted into part of the shelving, and the room's plank-wood floor was mostly hidden beneath rugs that looked, incongruously, like they might have come from IKEA. Then again, Megan realized, she wouldn't have any idea what a *real* Persian rug looked like.

Aisling froze just a few feet inside the door, then took a few jerky steps to a fluffy modern couch and collapsed into it, heaving for breath. Megan hesitated before closing the door behind them, then went to put her arm around the grieving girl, who turned her face against Megan's shoulder and sobbed helplessly for several minutes before finally managing to whisper, "I haven't been in here since . . . It still smells like him."

Since her father had been dead barely a day, Megan wasn't surprised Aisling hadn't been in the room, or that it still smelled like him. Not that she would say either of those things to a heartbroken teenager. She only nodded, and when Aisling could, helped her get up and tidy herself a bit before they went to his desk. The girl pushed a few pieces of paper around listlessly, until Megan, gently, said, "Do you happen to know his computer password?"

"Oh. No, but . . ." Aisling brightened a little and sat in the computer chair, moving it back so she could open a drawer and shuffle papers aside. To Megan's utter glee, she pressed a knot in the drawer's base and the whole bottom popped up with an immensely satisfying *click*. Under the false bottom lay a notebook and a scattering of photographs, all of Aisling at different ages. She took those out, running her fingers over a recent one of her and her father and tearing up again.

Megan, not wanting to be insensitive but also a little impatient, cautiously reached for the notebook, and when Aisling didn't stop her, took it out to open it. It was, as she'd rather hoped, filled with passwords, and also with notes that were so obscure to her that they might as well have been in shorthand, or ancient Greek. She flipped through it, hoping to find an actual address book, or at least specific information about the Nolan solicitor's name. Then, with an under-her-breath mutter, she put the notebook on the desk and took out her phone to ask it for "Seamus Nolan solicitor."

The first entire page of responses, annoyingly, were ads for solicitors *named* Seamus Nolan. Megan, muttering again, put in "Seamus Nolan Irish druid solicitor" and that time came up with a law firm in Dublin that matched information in some of the articles about his lawsuits. "Okay, Aisling? I'm actually a little surprised they haven't called you yet, but it looks like you want Gerry McHale at McHale and Sons. Does that sound familiar?"

Aisling wiped her eyes. "Oh, yeah. No, it wouldn't be Gerry, now that you're saying it. He died when I was only little. It's his son Patrick who took over the business. I suppose he'll have rung Uncle Adam. He wouldn't think of me at all. I'm only a wee lassie."

Megan made an incredulous sound in her throat, and Aisling gave her a bitter-edged smile. "He's like that, is Patrick. Da didn't like him much, I don't think, except he was in it to win, and because Da was always on some wild goose chase or another, he needed a solicitor who would back him."

"So he must have expected to win the primogeniture case," Megan said, mostly to herself. "Look, I think you should call him and find out what the situation is with the case, and if you don't want to do it yourself, hire a solicitor of your own to be your intermediary."

"How do I do that? How do I know who to trust?"

Telling this girl she didn't know wouldn't be of any help to anybody. Megan swallowed the impulse, said, "I'll ask some friends," and nodded at the notebook, where she'd written down the solicitor's number. "Ring. Ask about your father's will, and what this means for the court case. You can do this, Aisling." She stepped back to give the girl room to make the calls, and texted first her own uncle Rabbie, who knew everybody, and then a group chat made just for the purposes of saying, *I've got a teenage girl here whose father just died, and she might need a lawyer for the inheritance stuff. Any recommendations?*

To her eternal gratitude, the first several texts were actually useful responses, before the buzz of gossip lit up her phone. Between answering the more-obvious questions—yes, it was the Irish Druid's daughter, yes, Megan had found herself in another suspicious death case; yes, she would tell everybody everything later over drinks—she texted Sarah and Raf with an apology for the delay.

Never mind that, Raf wrote back almost immediately. *Have you solved it yet?*

No, but the plot thickens. I'll catch you up as soon as I'm able to get out of here. Megan put her phone away just as the office door swung open and a surly-looking Adam Nolan strode through. He saw Aisling at the desk first, and Megan watched him jerk with surprise, then visibly rearrange his expression to something relatively pleasant and sympathetic. "Ais, pet, what are you doing in here? I thought you went to lie down."

Aisling pressed the phone she held against her chest for a moment and nodded at Megan. "Megan offered to stay with me a bit while you were dealing with all those important phone calls, and I just wanted to spend a little time in here. You know how Da loved the view."

The view, overlooking gardens that turned into the thick, newly growing reforestation, *was* spectacular, but from Nolan's momentary blank look, Megan suspected Seamus hadn't liked spending a minute more in the study than he absolutely had to. But now Nolan's attention, however briefly, was on Megan herself, and as he tried to keep a scowl off his face, she saw Aisling gently close the open drawer and tuck her father's notebook into the back of her jeans.

"I'm so glad you're free again, Mr. Nolan," Megan said with the brightest, most sincere smile she could come up with. "I can't imagine how much paperwork you must be dealing with, while also supporting poor Aisling through this awful time. I know I'm really a complete stranger, but honestly, if there's anything I can do to help . . ."

"No, I'm sure we couldn't keep you. We do appreciate your time, Ms. Malone." Nolan's smile looked like it hurt. "I'll call a taxi for you now."

"Oh, I can do that," Megan promised, and Nolan's smile got tighter.

"I'm sure you can, and yet you've been here over an hour without doing so."

"*Uncle.*" Aisling gasped so credibly Megan thought she was probably actually offended on Megan's behalf. "Strangers are at the house for *hours* all the time, and you're never like this! It's Da's dying," she said to Megan in a quavering voice that Megan thought was as legitimate as the offense had been. "We're all in bits, and none of us are thinking clearly. Uncle Adam didn't mean anything by it. Megan's been a star," she said to her uncle, wetly.

Nolan looked as if he'd lost control of the conversation and didn't know how. "I'm not saying she hasn't been, pet, but this isn't her problem to deal with, and you've plenty of friends and family about."

"I've you," Aisling said, still wetly. "Mam isn't even here yet. Do you think she's really going to come?"

"I'm sure she will," Nolan began, and then to Megan's secret, terrible delight, a hurricane of a woman burst into the room to Aisling's cry of recognition.

Aisling was the spit of her; that was Megan's first thought, once she could see through the wild, loose hair and the remarkable number of brightly colored fabrics that Aisling's mother wore. She had beads and bangles everywhere, and a lovely openness to her pretty face. Aisling burst into tears upon seeing her, and although part of Megan realized she should sneak out while the drama was high, the drama *was* high, and she wanted to see what happened next.

Adam Nolan's jaw clenched before he wrenched his features into a tight smile that left cords in his throat. Megan wondered if he remembered Seamus had never divorced the woman, or what Seamus's will might say in regard to her. She almost wished she could take notes so she wouldn't forget anything her friends would want to hear about this meeting.

"My poor duck," Aisling's mother was saying. "I'm so sorry I couldn't get here until now, you know how the roads are in West Cork, and with all the rain, but oh, my darling, I'm here, and I won't leave you until you're ready to stand all on your own. Adam," she said a bit more coolly as she extracted herself from embracing Aisling. Her gaze slid off him to Megan, bounced back to Adam, and returned to Megan, tone cooling even more as she said, "And who have we here?"

"My name's Megan. I'm a friend of Aisling's." Megan felt that was stretching the definition of "friend" by a considerable margin, but Aisling gave her a grateful smile that was worth it. "It's nice to meet you . . . Mrs. Nolan?"

The ice vanished from Aisling's mother's expression, and she laughed, a bright, sweet sound completely in keeping with her artsy look. "God, no. I mean, yes, I suppose so, technically speaking, but I was a trendsetter even when we got married, and didn't change my name in the first place. It's Flynn, Jenny Flynn, lovely to meet you, Megan, although, God, the circumstances." The last several words were as if she'd abruptly remembered where she was, and why, and had put on a more solemn face like it was a mask.

"Ms. Flynn," Megan echoed politely. Jenny Flynn wasn't older than Megan herself, which meant she might have been as old as twenty-five when Aisling was born. Even if she and Seamus had been married for years before Aisling arrived on the scene, she just wasn't old enough to have been a *trendsetter* by not taking Seamus's surname. Not even by Irish standards: by twenty years ago, enough couples weren't getting married that adults in a relationship who didn't share a surname was borderline common.

"Oh, please, call me Jenny. 'Ms. Flynn' makes me sound so old, and an artist needs the freedom of youth, don't you think? Us women under forty have to stick together." She winked, and if she'd been any closer,

Megan was fairly certain Jenny would have elbowed her.

Adam looked pained. So, for that matter, did Aisling, which cemented Megan's certainty that Jenny was fairly close to her own age. It wasn't that she *couldn't* be under forty: Aisling was in her late teens, but even if she'd been in her mid-twenties, it was certainly possible for her mother to be just that side of forty. Not, however, from the Nolans' expressions.

No wonder Seamus and Jenny hadn't stayed together. Megan had only been in her presence a few minutes, and she was already tired of her. "I'll take 'we women have to stick together,'" she offered with the sharp certainty she was making an enemy. "I'm afraid I can't lay claim to the 'under forty' part, though."

The laughter drained from Jenny's face and returned again so quickly it was hard to say if it had really gone. "Well, you hide it well, then! Now, my duckling." She turned away from Megan to open her arms to Aisling again. "Tell me what Mama can do to help you through this terrible time. I'm here for you, my darling. Anything you need, as long as you need, my little chicken. Although I do have a show opening this weekend in Cork, so I really must be away by then."

She put the accent on the second "ma" in "Mama," in a way that Megan thought of as French and had never, to her recollection, heard in Ireland before. Megan glanced sideways, trying to hide her expression, and accidentally caught Adam's eye. For all that he clearly didn't want her there, the somewhat-grim glance he shot toward Jenny before meeting Megan's gaze again made them both suddenly have to look elsewhere to avoid bursting into a fit of inappropriate giggles.

Aisling, thank goodness, wasn't paying any attention. Her face was buried in Jenny's shoulder as her mother patted her hair and looked over her head at the computer and paperwork with an acquisitive eye. "When's the funeral to be, my darling? Did Seamus leave a will, or was that too ordinary and mundane for the Irish Druid?"

"There's a will," Adam grated. "I'm the executor."

"Shocking," Jenny murmured. "I'd have thought it would be Aisling. But then, you've only *just* turned eighteen, haven't you, darling. Perhaps he didn't update it yet."

"I'm twenty in three weeks, Mam," Aisling whispered.

"Twenty? Never. Where *does* the time go? But still, with a man out dashing about the countryside in his robes on his bicycle, what can you expect? And what does it say, Adam?"

Adam's smile tightened again. "You know I can't tell you that, Jenny, but if you're here just for the inheritance, I'd say Aisling and I can do well enough on our own."

"I'm his wife," Jenny replied with an airiness that had knives in it. "He'd have to exclude me specifically for me not to get anything, and the fact that you're hiding about it makes me think he hasn't. I'm sure I'll be staying. Maybe even for the funeral, after all. It'll be Saturday, will it?"

Adam, through his teeth, said, "It will," but Megan, watching Aisling, felt her heart break for the girl as she all too clearly understood that her mother was willing to stay for the public performance of a funeral on the weekend, but not for Aisling herself.

"No, that's all right, Mam." Aisling sounded very clear and sharp for the first time all day. Her gaze bounced off Megan's a little apologetically, but she focused on her mother. "Megan was just leaving, so if you could drop her back in Naas on your way south, that would be grand altogether."

"Naas isn't south of here," Jenny objected automatically, before thin lines appeared around her mouth as she realized she'd been outplayed. "I wouldn't want to leave you at a time like this, darling."

"I'll ring you at the weekend," Aisling said without quite meeting her eyes.

Jenny shot Adam a look, obviously not expecting help but still hoping for an opening. Instead, Megan stepped forward to tuck her elbow through Jenny's with a smile. "I really appreciate the lift. The Irish are *so* friendly and helpful. Now, Ais and I haven't really known each other that long, so I'm dying to hear all the embarrassing childhood stories that you've got to share. And you're an artist, right? She's so proud of you. You'll want to tell me all about that, too."

She steered Jenny out of the room, casting one last glance back at Aisling, and caught the girl's grateful "*thank you*" mouthed at her as the door closed behind them.

CHAPTER 10

"She's a beautiful girl. So kind and intelligent. Obviously she shares your own spirit. What a lucky woman you are." Megan kept up the stream of compliments until they were actually out of the Rathballard House and into Jenny's car, which was a little Ford Fiesta, about twenty years old, but, in the way of Irish vehicles, in startlingly good condition, with neither rust nor any danger of the engine banging or the exhaust system spitting fumes and smoke. "I really appreciate you giving me a lift."

The rules of polite society had Jenny in their teeth, which was clear from the way her smile briefly bared hers. "Of course, it's no bother. She's gotten so independent, my wee Aisling." That, too, was spoken with teeth.

"They do, don't they," Megan said ruefully. "Not that I have any of my own, but my friends with kids . . . what a handful! I don't know how you parents do it."

She didn't actually have many friends with children, but that wasn't the point, and Jenny would certainly never know the truth. "What a shock this whole business is, hm? Are *you* all right?" she asked solicitously. "I know it's so easy for partners to be overlooked when the relationship is strained."

It was as if she'd pushed the right button. Jenny's eyes filled with tears and she whispered, "Thank you," hoarsely. "No one has even thought to ask. It's so hard. Seamus and I had our differences, of course, but I never thought I'd lose him like this. He was such a kind man," she said rather sanctimoniously. "It was me that taught him about the woods, you know. The spirits of the forest call out to me, even now."

She trilled a little laugh and cut a glance toward Megan. "That must sound mad, to you."

It sounded like a load of hooey, but saying as much wouldn't earn Megan a drip of gossip, and she was after as much as she could get. "Oh, I don't know. I'm the farthest thing in the world from an artist, but even I get that feeling of connection in the woods. It must be a powerful force for someone like you, whose whole life is connected to the artistic and spiritual."

Jenny gave her a gratified smile through shimmering tears. "It's so kind of you to try to understand. So many people don't. But yes, of course, I introduced Seamus to the old ways, and it changed the course of our lives."

Megan turned her gaze out the window, partly to watch the stately drive go by, and mostly to hide her expression so it wasn't *completely* obvious she was choking on Jenny's sanctimony. The front road was lined with even more impressive trees than the back one had been, with lawn pressing up against them and snugging tidily to the sides of the road, with the rewilded forest beginning to make its mark on the soft, rolling land beyond. The sun brightened the mist lying over the treetops without quite cutting through the clouds for full light, or even rainbows. The whole drive had an air of ancient calm, as if it would have been the same three hundred years ago, and would be the same three hundred years hence.

When Megan was quite certain she had control of her voice, she said, "The old ways?"

Jenny trilled laughter again. "Oh, it sounds silly, doesn't it? But the ways of our ancestors, the druidic paths and the old gods. Seamus really embraced it." Her voice went flat at the last part. "And it got him noticed, too, didn't it. It wasn't enough he was born rich and an actual *lord*, oh, no. He had to make a mark of his own. Be the 'Irish Druid,' raising the old forests and bringing life back to the land. What a—" She caught herself at the last moment, and whatever she'd intended to say, she changed it to, ". . . noble soul."

Megan sucked in her lower lip, trying not to laugh at the woman's transparency. "Do you think his conversion to the old ways was political, then? Nothing really spiritual behind it? That must be heartbreaking to someone like you," she added, fully aware she was laying it on thick and astonished how well Aisling's mother responded to it.

A little to her surprise, Jenny sighed. "It was at first,

I'd say, but no, he bought in to it. Took it as seriously as any modern religion. If the old calendar said it was a high holy day, or even a low one, he would take himself into the woods to thank Brigid—she was his own patron goddess, even if she hadn't a thing to do with forests herself—and bring gifts, trinkets . . . offerings, you'd call them. There's a whole rag tree of them somewhere on the estate, and his worship circle. It's all quite the thing." Her voice flattened into disapproval with the last few words.

"A rag tree?"

"Where you tie ribbon or cloth to a tree to make a wish, or ask for healing, and as it decomposes, your wish comes true? Do you not have that, in America?"

Megan smiled briefly. "Probably in places, but not that I'm familiar with. What a lovely idea. I imagine you taught him that too?"

Jenny glanced at Megan like she'd just dropped considerably in her estimation. "It's an old Irish custom. There's one at St. Brigid's Well, where I'm taking you."

"Oh." Megan dropped a little in her *own* estimation. "Right, of course, I've seen it. Really, thank you again for going out of your way. I appreciate it so much."

"It's nothing," Jenny said in a tone that made it clear it was something. "I'm sure I'll drive back up to the house after. It's only a little ways."

Megan had to admire the audacity it took for Jenny to even consider that, after she'd been sent packing. "I'm sure Aisling will be . . ." She couldn't come up with a way to end that sentence that wasn't a flat-out lie. "She's being so strong, after all. And it seems like her uncle is there to help her with as much as he can."

"Adam Nolan's interested in what benefits Adam Nolan and Adam Nolan alone," Jenny said with heat. "He opposed me and Seamus marrying, wore black the day Aisling was born, and has had developers on the long finger waiting for a chance to sell. I'd say he hasn't any money of his own, nothing but what Seamus provided for him, and he lived beyond those means too. I'd have stayed married to Seamus until the end of time to stand in his way."

"Does it work that way?" Megan asked, trying to sound as lightly incurious as possible. "I know the inheritance laws are more complicated than usual because it's an actual landed gentry estate. Someone mentioned a lawsuit to allow Aisling to inherit, but of course under regular Irish law, a spouse would usually inherit half unless there's a will that says otherwise, right? I don't know much about Irish inheritance law." That much, at least, was true. Most of the rest of it was fishing, and Jenny, jaw snapping, took the bait.

"It's a great fecking mess, is what it is. I *deserve* my half of it for putting up with that bloody fool as long as I did, but you're not wrong about the gentry rubbish making a wreck of it. Adam's in line to inherit as it stands, even though Aisling is Seamus's only child. The *bloody* patriarchy preferring to bounce back generations to find a man instead of passing to a woman! And with the last hearing coming up, Seamus might have won, so it's bloody convenient he's dead, isn't it!"

Megan flickered another quick look out the window in an attempt to hide her expression. They were on the motorway now, with nothing interesting to see, and would be at the holy well within a minute or two. She couldn't decide if she wished the drive was longer to see how much further Jenny's mask could fall apart, or if she was relieved she'd be getting out of the car and away from the other woman's reach soon. Cautiously, she said, "You don't think . . ." just to see where Jenny would go with it.

Jenny snatched it right up. "I do think. I think if he'd waited another minute, Adam might have lost his whole claim to the estate, and he couldn't risk that. I think he pushed Seamus into that well and probably held him down to make sure he stayed dead, and now he's going to take everything from me! And Aisling." Chest heaving, she fell silent a few seconds. From the corner of her eye, Megan saw her realize that she'd completely lost the charming, flaky artist persona she'd put on. Her face darkened, and for an alarmed heartbeat, Megan wondered if Jenny Flynn was actually dangerous.

"I'd feel so strongly too," she heard herself say in the soppiest voice she'd ever used. "You try so hard to provide safety for your children, and to build a gentle world of art and music, and when it's snatched away, what else can a mother do but be passionate about it?"

Appreciative tears flooded Jenny's eyes again. She dashed them away theatrically and smiled tragically at Megan. "You're so understanding. No wonder my darling Aisling is so fond of you. It does my heart good knowing she's got caring, intelligent women like your-self around her. You *will* give me your number, won't you, Megan? I'd like to keep in touch."

"If you give me your phone, I'll put it in," Megan of-fered. Jenny nodded at a purse between the seats, invit-ing Megan to open it, and shrugged carelessly when Megan said, "Is there a passcode?"

"Who can be bothered? It's only a phone, after all."

Megan bit her tongue on responding to that, too, and put a wrong number in, off by one digit, with a silent apology to her number neighbor, if such a person ex-isted. She also checked for Aisling's number in the phone, found it, did her best to memorize it, and put it into her own phone as soon as she'd put Jenny's away. They were just pulling up to the holy well's visitor site as she did, and she climbed out of the car to offer Jenny another smile. "Thanks again."

"I'm so glad we had this time together," Jenny re-plied soppily, and drove away.

Rafael and Sarah, who had apparently been hanging out with the car and the dogs all afternoon, came up to Megan, who stood waiting until Jenny was safely out of the parking lot and well out of earshot before saying, "*That* woman is a piece of *work*. Holy *moly*."

"Tell us everything. And also bring us back to town because I'm starving." Rafael looked hopeful, and Megan laughed.

"Yeah, I'm sorry. I didn't mean to be gone so long. Let me just try to text Aisling . . ." She sent a text to the number she'd copied, and at least didn't get a bounce back, so either it had gone to Aisling or to some poor

random stranger who would wonder why she'd said *Hi,
it's Megan, I got your number from your mom. Are you
doing okay?* Phone back in her pocket, she said, "Are
we going back to Naas, or Dublin, or . . . ?"

"Naas is closer, and I need foooooood. We can figure out what we're doing after that, after that," Rafael
said decisively. "If we're staying, we'll have to check
back into the hotel. Are they going to have room?"

"It's a weeknight in January. I'm pretty confident
we'll be okay on that front." The drive back to Naas
only took a few minutes, but it was long enough to
summarize the events that took place at the Rathballard House. "We have to go out there," Sarah said,
as wide-eyed and eager as her husband. "For one thing,
it's a legitimate tourist site, right? But also you've gotten so much dirt already, there must be more if we all
go talk to people!"

"So you're on board with the whole investigating
the murder—*not that we know it's a murder*—thing
now, huh?" A pang ran through Megan's chest, and she
rubbed below her breastbone, trying not to think of
Jelena.

Sarah's gaze went sympathetic in the rearview mirror before sliding toward embarrassment. "Well, we
are here and all, and you *are* the murder driver . . ."

Megan chuckled. "And it *does* make for a particularly
great vacation story, doesn't it? 'Oh, no, we didn't go to
the tropics, but we did solve a murder mystery . . .'"

"Can you imagine the views you'd get on *that* vacation reel?"

Megan shot Rafael a look. "Please tell me you're not taking pictures to put up on social media."

With some effort, he arranged a credibly injured expression across his face. "Would I do that?"

"You probably would," Sarah said placidly. "I, however, would not let you."

"Thank goodness you've got a sensible wife. Okay, right, so I guess we're maybe staying overnight in Naas again. *Oh!* I forgot to tell you about Niamh! You can't tell anybody this!" Megan pulled into the hotel parking lot and twisted around to tell her friends about Niamh's job offer. "She'll be lonely. I mean, she won't be, because she charms people at the drop of a hat, but it'd be nice for her to have some real friends there. I told her you'd make jollof rice, Sarah."

"Oh!" Sarah's dark eyes lit up. "I could do that! Speaking of which." Her stomach growled audibly as they got out of the car. "Bring me to food, please."

They went to the hotel restaurant while Megan went and checked back in so she had somewhere to put the dogs while they ate. Neither of them had even wanted to wake up to walk from the car into the hotel, and both collapsed on the room's floor dramatically as soon as she let them off their leads. Dip went so far as to flick one reproachful ear, as if informing Megan she had simply expected *too much* by asking two small, energetic dogs to walk five hundred meters, and then went straight back to sleep. Thong spent a little time artistically arranging herself until Dip made an ideal pillow, and let out a huffing sigh of contentment as Megan left them in the room.

Her phone buzzed on the way back downstairs with a text saying, *sorry, I think you got the wrong number* in response to the text she hoped she'd sent to Aisling. She shot a *whoops, sorry* text back at them, glanced at the group text she'd sent lawyer questions to—there were more answers, but she didn't read them—and went into the restaurant muttering at herself for getting the number wrong. Sarah and Raf had already ordered, including food for her, and the appetizers arrived just as she sat. Her own stomach growled audibly, and the other two laughed, not quite covering their own tummy rumbles. "I thought I'd eaten a big breakfast," Sarah protested.

"You did, but that was seven and a half hours ago!" Raf bumped his shoulder against Sarah's, and for a moment they shared a sweet, dippy smile that made Megan smile too.

"I love you two together," she said a little soppily. "I'm so glad you're here. Thank you for coming."

"Well, we wanted to anyway." Rafael reached across the table to grab her hand for a moment. "But under the circumstances . . . how are you doing, anyway? You know, with everything?" The emphasis he put on *everything* made it clear he wasn't asking about the investigation they were helping her with.

Megan drew a deep breath, held it, then let it out in a huge raspberry. "Okay, I guess. I miss her horribly, like, all the time, but I guess it's getting better. And . . ." She withdrew her hand from Rafael's to bury her face in it, then looked up over her fingertips. "I know the guards want this to just be an accident, and I don't know, maybe it is, which would be fine, actually. But is it . . . weird, or wrong, or stupid, to be sort of relieved I found another body?"

"I mean, it might be weird," Raf said without hesitation. Sarah elbowed him, and Megan laughed as he looked injured. "A little weird," he insisted, "but no, it makes sense, Megs. Like if you'd never come across another body in your life, then it would feel like that whole relationship ended for nothing, but if this really is just how you're gonna be, then it's really better for both of you that it ended."

"That's what I told myself—in fact, I think I told Paul and Niamh that too, but . . ."

"But you wanted to hear somebody agree with you in a deeper voice," Sarah said.

Megan gave a startled laugh, considered that, and laughed again. "I don't know that it had to be a *deeper* voice, but yeah, hearing somebody *else* say it out loud, that actually helps. And I'm *really* glad you're here. I still feel like . . ." She trailed off again, eyes dropping to the plate of mozzarella sticks, and ate a couple before trying to put her thoughts into words. "First, *none* of my friends have been telling me this, it's all in my own head, but I'm still going, you're forty-three years old, Megan, it's just a breakup, why are you so broken up over it?" She smirked, hearing the answer in the echoed words, but shrugged. "And so I'm also going, it was two months ago, you should be over it by now. And I'm not, like, crying in my pillow every night anymore, but it still *sucks*, and, I don't know. I feel stupid because of that."

Sarah, in a remarkably sarcastic voice, said, "Yeah, Megan, you were only together three years, it should definitely take you less than three months to work your way through the feelings there, what's wrong with you?" and when Megan snorted, added, "You would never say anything like that to a friend of yours, would you?"

"No! Obviously not! And like I said, my friends aren't saying it to me, either!"

"Well, then, treat yourself like you're one of your friends," Rafael said gently. "C'mon, Megs. Sarah's right. You even know it. You just said so. It's okay to take a while to get over having your heart broken. Especially when the circumstances are, frankly, weird."

Megan, feeling sort of injured, met his eyes with surprise, and he gestured with the last mozzarella stick. "Megs. I love you. You know I do. But normal people don't just go tripping over dead bodies all over the place, and I swear to God, if you say that technically speaking, you hardly ever *trip* over them, I will push this mozza stick up your nose."

Surprise burst out of her in a laugh loud enough to draw attention from the handful of other diners, but Megan ended up grinning at Rafael through a sheen of tears. "I love you, too, man. *Mi amigo mejor.*"

"*Mi amiga,*" he said fondly. "Now, c'mon, tell me, how are we gonna finagle our way into the rest of this investigation?"

"There isn't a 'rest of it,'" Sarah pointed out. "Megan's the only one doing any investigating!"

"Yeah, but I don't know how to invite myself into it, whether there's an investigation or not. I tried to get Aisling's number from her mom's phone, but I got it wrong. Oh, but wait, let me check . . ." She pulled her phone out and checked the group text for the lawyer stuff, then looked up with a delighted grin. "We're in. Rabbie sent a recommendation for a personal solicitor for Aisling, so I've got an excuse to go back and see her."

Rafael glanced at the waitress, arriving with their dinner, and eyed Megan. "Are we going as soon as we've eaten?"

"You know what, I think it'll be easier if we wait until tomorrow, during the hours the house is open to the public. If we pay our fee, they can't kick us out."

"That's not how trespassing laws work," he pointed out. "At least, not in the States."

"No, not here, either, but give this to me, Raf. I'm doing my best."

"Yeah, okay. Dinner now, a leisurely evening tonight, and a murder to solve tomorrow. A perfectly normal Irish vacation. Tell me how this works. Do we go over the clues during dinner? Discuss who we've interviewed and who we still need to talk to? Do we—" He broke off as Megan blinked at him. "What?"

"Know who we *haven't* talked to?"

He rolled his eyes and grimaced theatrically. "Most of the Irish population?"

"I swear to God, Raf. No, I mean, yes, but we haven't talked to the *priest*. Father Columbkille or whatever he was. Colman."

Sarah's eyebrows rose slowly. "Who's Columbkille?"

"An Irish saint, but don't ask me anything else about him. I know how to pronounce his name and that he's kind of big here. Okay, first things first," she ended triumphantly. "Dinner, a leisurely evening, and in the morning, we find out if the priest did it."

CHAPTER 11

Sarah and Rafael had an air of palpable excitement about them in the morning, which, Megan had to admit, was a nice change from the usual attitude of people around her when she got tangled up in an inexplicable death. Even Paul, who was fond of her, spent a lot of time exasperated that she was involved at all, and Jelena obviously hadn't liked any of it.

To be fair, Niamh basically always thought it was a riot, but her presence was more hit-and-miss because she was so often off being famous.

Rafael, though, looked like he desperately wanted a trench coat and one of those Sherlock Holmes hats. When Megan said as much, he positively lit up. "A deerstalker? Can we find one?"

Megan said, "Probably," at the same time Sarah said, "No," and Raf's expression went to war with itself, trying to be thrilled at Megan and pout at his wife. Both women laughed, and Megan added, "But also, probably not now. I have no idea if there are any hat shops in Naas."

Raf, brightly, said, "I have the internet in my pocket. I bet it can tell me," and made a show of sulking off toward the car when Sarah, not very sternly, shook her head. He muttered, "Fine. I guess we want to get to the scene of the crime nice and early anyway . . ."

"We're not *going* to the scene of the crime," Megan pointed out, but facts had no hold on him as he skulked around, pretending to hold up a magnifying class and saying, "Egad!" to the dogs.

"I'd ask if he's always like this, but—" Megan said to Sarah, and they both laughed again.

"He's much sillier with you, though," Sarah murmured. "Part of it is that he really needed the holiday, but it's you too."

"I know his true ridiculous self, and have since we were six," Megan agreed. "Did he ever tell you about the time he broke his leg falling out of the tree?"

Sarah squinted as they trailed after her husband and the dogs. "He mentioned breaking his leg and said it was your fault."

Megan's jaw dropped with indignation, even though that was, in fact, Rafael's version of the story, and always had been. "He fell the wrong direction!"

Rafael yelled, "I did *not*!"

"Me!" Megan said, still indignantly, but to Sarah, gesturing wildly to animate the story as she told it. "Me on the ground here on this side of the tree branch! Him up on the branch, terrified because he couldn't get down! He's facing me! I said, 'Let go and I'll catch you!'

He lets go and *falls backward*! Away from me! Onto another log! *Of course* he broke something! He's lucky it wasn't his wretched head!"

"You said you'd catch me!" Rafael called with the remembered injured pride of an eight-year-old.

"I would have if you'd *fallen toward me*! He spent the whole summer in traction," Megan told Sarah gloomily. "It was the most boring summer of my life."

"Like that was my fault!" Rafael, at the car, scooped the dogs up and waited for the women to catch up with him, then, more sentimentally, added, "She was great. She did spend practically the whole summer hanging out with me. Mom bought me a brand-new Game Boy, and we played Super Mario Land and Tetris until we were having nightmares about being crushed by blocks."

"Sometimes I can still see the tetrinos falling when I close my eyes," Megan reported dolefully, and beneath that, Rafael mumbled, "Tetrominoes."

"Oh my God. Whatever. Get in the car, you pedantic dork."

Sarah, getting in the front seat herself, breathed, "I had no idea they even had a name. Those are the blocks, right? They're actually called something?"

"Welcome to the terrible knowledge earned by bored children over a video game summer," Megan replied solemnly. "Also, now that I'm thinking about it, I bet I should have hired a dog sitter for the day. Today, not that summer. Just to clarify."

"There's that one woman, Gwinny somebody, the actress?" Raf said. "She's a dog sitter. I was reading an article about her the other day. She's gotten pulled into a couple of things like you keep doing, Megan. Minding her own business, walking the dogs, finding dead bodies. Maybe you could hire her."

"Gwinny Tuffel, right, I know her from EastEnders or something. No, that was somebody else." Megan paused, trying to remember where she knew the actress from, then shook her head. "Anyway, yes, I know who you mean, but she's British and probably not available in County Kildare, Ireland, on five minutes' notice, so, no, I'm more thinking about asking the hotel."

"Why do either of you know about a British dog-sitting, murder-solving actress?" Sarah asked, mystified, then considered her own question. "I feel like that answers itself. Never mind. Let's take the dogs, Megan. At least over to the church. I assume we're going to a church?"

Megan waved her phone. "Yeah, I got directions to where Father Colman works. Is stationed? Is registered? What do Catholics call it?"

"Assigned, they're *assigned* to a parish," Rafael said, "and I can't believe you don't know that after growing up with me."

"If you'll recall, I was stunned and horrified to discover that church was something you had to go to during the summer, too," Megan pointed out, and said to Sarah, "In so far as I'd ever thought about it, I assumed it was something you had to do in winter, like school."

She laughed. "Are you suggesting Raf broke his leg to get out of going to church all summer?"

"It was a *bad* trade," Rafael assured them both. "How'd you find out where Father Colman works?"

"Secret murder-driver-investigation stuff," Megan said in as dramatic and arrogant a tone as she could manage. Her friends looked sort of offended, and she laughed. "I asked at the front desk. Nobody knew, but one girl was sure her ma would, and when her ma didn't, she rang her da's grandma, who did."

"Her ma rang her da's grandma, or the girl who works at the desk did?" Sarah asked curiously as they got in the car.

"Believe it or not, her ma did, and then rang her back at work. All aboard the Irish gossip train, I guess."

"I love it. Aunties the world over never miss a beat when it comes to gossip. How far are we going?" Sarah held up a finger. "What I'm asking is if there's time for a nap between here and there. All this murder-mystery stuff is hard on my sleep."

Rafael coughed, and Sarah gave him a warning look that made Megan laugh. "It's only a few minutes, sorry. We could probably walk, but the weather . . ." The skies above were leaden, not quite raining, but certainly threatening it, and a few thick, spattering raindrops did fall as she pulled out of the hotel parking lot. They seemed to just be a warning, though, and the car was still dry when they arrived at the parish house on the church grounds.

Despite the relatively early hour, Father Colman was out on the grounds, clearing brush, and it looked like he'd been at work for some time already. His pale face was flushed pink from effort, and he was dressed much more traditionally than he had been the other morning, in an actual cassock with a white shirt beneath it, and the dangling accoutrements of the clergy: a cross, a long belt, a rosary. It struck Megan that save for the colors, it really looked very similar to the outfit Seamus Nolan had been wearing when he died.

Colman paused when the car pulled up, took a bottle of alcohol spritz out of his pocket, and cleaned his hands as he came down a small hill to greet them. Sturdy, practical black work boots were visible beneath the cassock's hem, and Megan wondered if that was *de rigueur* for priests in old-fashioned clothing, or if he wore nicer shoes inside the church.

He paused as they got out of the car, examining them as the spritz bottle went back in his pocket. "Megan Malone. The murder driver. Patrick Doyle told me to watch out for you. I'm Father Colman."

"Father," Megan said as politely as she could with dismay sluicing through her. "I'm not used to this whole 'my reputation precedes me' thing. Did he tell you not to talk to me?"

"Yes, but I'm rarely a man to do what I'm told, and besides that, I'm desperate curious to hear what it is you want of me." He smiled rather beatifically, first at Megan, then at her companions. "And you are?"

"Rafael and Sarah Williams," Raf offered. "Murder-driver hangers-on."

"Oh my God." Megan put a hand over her face, and Colman laughed.

"Will you have a cup of tea? Come in, at least. The weather's threatening." He turned in a swish of robes, inviting them along as he angled for steps placed into the low hill rather than walking them up over the grassy knoll itself. "I expect you'd like to ask me about Seamus Nolan's death, and whether I saw anything."

"Well, yes. And also why you're wearing a cassock," Megan admitted. "I thought those went out of fashion decades ago, and you weren't wearing one on Monday."

"They're warm and easy to move in," Colman admitted. "Western men have been sold a bill of goods on the emasculating effects of dresses. They're *grand*."

"Right?" Sarah asked, audibly delighted. "Agbada are still the traditional dress for Nigerian men, and it's one of the things I miss from being a child there. American men dress so stodgily."

"It's Beau Brummell's fault," Colman informed her as he ushered them into the rectory. It was a small, beautiful old building, the exterior of cobbled stone and the general structure being what the Irish called "two up, two down": a public room and a private room downstairs, and two bedrooms upstairs, although Megan bet the second room upstairs had almost always functioned as an office for the priests assigned there. The downstairs was mostly open now, the wall between the two main rooms knocked out for internal French doors. Colman took them through a living room filled with oversized leather seating. The usual kind of crosses adorned with rosary beads hung on the walls, interspersed with smaller variants of known as Brigid's crosses. It was homey and comforting, but Megan ended up bringing her attention back to Colman as he led them into the kitchen.

"I'm sorry, what? Beau Brummell? Wasn't he, like, *the* fashion maven of the Regency era? How can boring men's clothes be his fault?"

"My understanding is that he wasn't wealthy, so he couldn't afford the brilliant colors and fabrics that the rich men around him wore, so through sheer force of personality and an eye for well-fitted clothing, he convinced the rich that their colors and flashiness was crass, and that dark, subdued, tailored trousers and coats were more suitable for men of class. Two hundred years later, and the Anglophile world is still wearing what one poor but persuasive British dandy convinced the elite was appropriate menswear." By the time Colman had finished his explanation, he'd poured tea for all of them and gotten them settled around his small dining room table, which sat in a square of light from the window.

All three of the Americans were gazing at him in astonishment as he wrapped up. Megan eventually said, "I had no idea," and Colman beamed with pleasure.

"Most people don't. There, that's your history lesson for the day. Now I suppose you'll want to interrogate me." He sat with his own cup of tea and made an inviting gesture with it. "Have at."

"Em." Megan was surprised into using the Irish version of "um," although she didn't usually hear herself doing that. "Well. You were at the holy well very early. Why? And did you see anything?"

"I'm very fond of Saint Brigid, and I like to think she's fond of me," Colman said earnestly. "I go there often for a morning devotional, and I've encountered

Seamus any number of times. I didn't see him Monday morning, though."

"Tell me about your devotional," Megan said, partly out of real curiosity and partly, she admitted privately, to see if she could get the priest to slip up.

He smiled briefly over his cup of tea. "I like to pray at the stone arch over the closer well. I suppose in the vanity of my heart I hope that someday I'll look down to see my knees have worn grooves in the stone and cement, to say that I was there, and that I worshiped. I fear the granite is harder than my knees, though, and I haven't enough years left to make my mark. I feel that I can speak directly to Brigid there at her well, and through her, to God."

"What do you talk about?"

Colman chuckled and ducked his head. "Some days it's a desperate prayer to set the world to rights, isn't it? Begging for people to find enlightenment, in whatever form that may take, so they might follow God to a brighter future. Other days it's smaller. A sick child, or an ailing mother, or a father out of work and a family growing desperate. And some days I've nothing to ask at all, save to be quiet in God's embrace, and find some peace within myself." He sucked his teeth, then sighed. "Monday was one of the latter. I don't often go to the upper well at all anyway, but I felt too old and tired to even think about it then. So I didn't see anything, or hear anything. I suppose he must have already been in the water when I arrived, God rest his soul."

"Did you get along with him?" Megan wondered. She could almost feel Sarah and Rafael exchanging glances as they sipped their tea, being quiet so they didn't interrupt.

"Someone will tell you this if I don't myself, so I'll say to you that I'm mostly sorry to see him dead because I think dying now curses his immortal soul to hell," Colman replied steadily. "There's no good in worshiping pagan gods in these times, Ms. Malone. Brigid found her way to Christ, and it's as a saint she should be revered, not as a heathen goddess adulated by an unenlightened people."

Megan kept her eyebrows down with an effort. "Weren't the goddess and the saint different people? I mean, I know there's a lot of crossover, but wasn't there supposed to have been a Christian Brigid too? A nun? I know she was supposed to represent an awful lot of what the goddess did, but I'd have thought you'd see them as separate?"

"Who knows," Colman said as if it pained him. "But if we're to accept that God could take a mortal form in Jesus, we could also presume that the ancient heathen goddess might have taken form as Brigid of Kildare, and in doing so, cast off her pagan origins and dedicated herself to Christ."

"I never even considered that as a possibility." Megan took a swift sip of hot tea, using it to avoid saying the wrong thing, then shrugged a little. "But then, I'd never heard that Beau Brummell was responsible for boring clothes, either, so maybe there's a lot for me to learn today. So you thought Nolan might convert back to Christianity, or Catholicism, given time? That he might have given up on Brigid-the-goddess in favor of Brigid-the-saint?"

"No," Colman admitted, "not really. But where there's life, there's hope. I wish he hadn't brought so much attention to the well as a site of the goddess, though. Do you know there are people who actually believe the goddess will bless them with children if they come to there to pray and ask it of her?"

Sarah spoke in a neutral voice, through thinned lips. "But if the saint and the goddess represent the same things, how do you know which one they're asking for help from?"

The faintest curl of disdain pulled at Colman's mouth. "I know. You can tell. Especially the ones *he* encouraged to come there, with their fiery columns and their three circles and their sun signs. They're searching for the old, dark paths, not the way into the light."

"The triskelion?" Megan asked, surprised. At Rafael's breath of a question, she took her phone out and used a fingertip to draw three spirals on a sketchbook page, each leg of the spiral feeding back toward the others so they made a single unit. "I didn't know that was a symbol of Brigid. I just thought it was an old Irish thing."

"True believers would carry her cross, woven of straw or—" Colman lost a bit of his high-handedness. "Or of toothpicks and yarn, to be honest, these days. But it's that cross that belongs to the saint, not the old circles. They were the goddess's. So you know," he said, more darkly, "you know which of them they're coming to ask favors from."

"And Nolan brought more of those pagan worshipers around than you felt comfortable with?" Megan asked. "I wasn't clear on how serious his whole druid thing was. He really believed, huh?"

"He played it up for the news and made light of it, but he did. He wouldn't have come to the well all the time, in times when no one would notice him, if it didn't mean something to him. I only wish it had meant the right things."

"I don't suppose you killed him," Megan said lightly.

Colman blanched, hands suddenly shaking so hard with emotion he had to put his teacup on the table. "And risk my own immortal soul? I did not."

"No, I didn't suppose you had." Megan put her own cup down and conjured up a smile for the priest. "Thank you for your time, your patience, and your interesting history lesson about Beau Brummell. I appreciate it. And . . ."

She hesitated, and he chuckled. "And you'd also appreciate it if I didn't mention you came sniffing around to Detective Sergeant Doyle?"

"I wouldn't ask you to lie about it, but if you didn't feel like bringing it up, I wouldn't *hate* that."

"I'm sure I'd have no reason to be talking to the man again," Colman assured her as he led them back out. The Brigid's crosses in the living room caught Megan's eye again as she followed him. Straw and rushes, she thought, none of them the cheap yarn ones he'd disdained. There was even a three-legged one she'd never seen before, closer to the triskelion she'd drawn than to the shape she thought of as Brigid's cross. Maybe the old priest wasn't quite as anti-pagan as he made himself out to be, although she couldn't see any profit in saying so aloud.

Instead, at the door, she smiled and offered a hand to shake. "Thanks for your time, Father. We'll get out of your hair now."

"The tea was excellent," Rafael said to the older man as they left, and when Megan glanced back, the priest was in the doorway looking satisfied.

None of them spoke until they were in the car, and even then there was a brief, loud silence before Sarah blurted, "Well, *I* feel a real urge to go back and sit on one of those stones and draw, what did you call them? Triskelions? All over my body now. What a bigot."

"I offer myself as tribute," Rafael said immediately. "I'll be glad to help with that. Megan, you in?"

Megan laughed. "No, no, sorry, but I think that would be weird."

"Yeah, okay, fair. Still, I'm all in, baby." That was directed at Sarah, who beamed at him.

Megan laughed again. "So does that mean you want me to drop you two off at the holy well while I go on to Rathballard House?"

They chorused, "No!" as one, and Sarah shook her head for emphasis. "No, we're in it this far, I want to see how it all works out. And besides, I've always wanted to look around one of those old grand house's gardens. Let's go ahead and do that, and maybe you can drop Raf, me, and some body paint at the holy well *later*."

"Mmm-hmm. And then you two can call a taxi and

make out like teenagers in the back seat while they drive you back to the hotel."

"Somehow that sounds both disgusting and perfect," Rafael said. "C'mon, let's go to the big house so Sarah and I can get on with being gross later."

"He does not pitch things well, does he?" Megan said to Sarah. "I'm suddenly afraid to ask exactly how he proposed."

"Oh, *believe* me, you don't want to know." Sarah waited a dramatic beat. "I'll tell you on the drive over."

Megan hastily turned the engine on, then perked her ears for the gossip as she drove.

CHAPTER 12

Much as Megan enjoyed the idea of driving up the Rathballard House's back road and really throwing Adam Nolan for a loop, she didn't have the passcode for the back gate, so they went the long way around. Rafael and Sarah's jaw-dropped silence and then brief gasps of laughter as they made the approach to the big house's massive edifice was worth it, though. "All of a sudden I get why Keira Knightley giggled when she saw Pemberley," Sarah said. "That . . . you sort of don't . . . *wow*."

"You really sort of don't, do you?" Megan agreed. It was hard to appreciate the sheer ridiculous size and grandeur of an old manor house without seeing it in person, even if she was fairly certain the Rathballard House didn't actually have anything on Pemberley itself. Or, at least, not on the houses that had played Pemberley on film. "You two should definitely do the real tour while I try to barge in and talk to Aisling."

"But that wouldn't be any fun! For you, I mean. Don't you want to see it?" Sarah wrinkled her nose. "Or maybe pursuing murder cases is more fun. I'm not sure how that works on a scale of fun to not fun."

Megan, without thinking, said, "Honestly, if Seamus was actually murdered, I think I need to solve it to be okay with the breakup," and then parked the car to stare out the windshield, dismayed at the truth in that. Rafael and Sarah were both very quiet, exchanging glances in the rearview mirror, probably imagining Megan couldn't, or didn't, see them. "Yeah," she said after a moment. "Yeah, I guess that's it. It's not just finding another body, that's not enough to make it seem okay. But if there's really been a murder and I can figure out who did it . . ." She sighed. "I'm a mess, aren't I?"

Rafael, stoutly and with the confidence of a best friend, said, "Of course not, Megs," and shot a look at his wife that Megan probably wasn't supposed to see. It made her laugh, even if it was sort of a watery, uncertain laugh.

"Of course not, but also definitely."

Raf scooted over in the back seat so he was behind Megan, and looped his arms over the driver's seat to give her an awkward, but heartfelt hug. "Well, yeah. I mean, welcome to being human, babe."

"Why is being human so awful?" Megan half-wailed the question, because she meant it a little more than she wanted to, at least in the moment. "Or complicated, or something, and why aren't I better at it after this long?"

"You're not really asking why you're bad at it. You're asking why things still hurt," Sarah replied softly. "And that's because you're not bad at it. We're supposed to feel a lot and be messy and complicated, and when things don't go the way we hope, we mourn. Now," she said, still gently, "snap out of it, because you've still got a murder to solve."

Megan, startled, snickered, then made a face at Rafael as he said, "Or a suspicious death to investigate, at least."

"Or a perfectly normal accident that I should leave alone so the family can try to get on with their lives," Megan concluded, then shook herself and straightened her shoulders like she was putting armor on. "But okay. I'm fine now. Let's give this a shot. The dogs are probably okay in the car for an hour—yes, I'll crack the window open, as if it was ninety degrees in Los Angeles, not forty-eight and cloudy in Ireland—and hopefully I'll really only be a few minutes, anyway. I just have to give Aisling this lawyer's number."

The other two paused, examining her, before Raf said, "Do you think she believes that?" in a low voice to Sarah.

"I actually think she does. Oh, wow, what's going on there?" As they were getting out of the car, a news van and two radio buses pulled into the Rathballard House's huge driveway, and a number of people piled out. Megan recognized one as the reporter who'd border-line-accosted her the day before, and another from the evening news, but the man they were circling like sharks was a stranger to her.

He towered over almost the entire media crew, a well-built, handsome white man who wore a perfectly ordinary, cream-colored button-down shirt and khakis and somehow made them look like it was a nod to Indiana Jones. Maybe it was that he had his sleeves rolled up to expose his forearms. He had a vibrant energy to him, a ready white smile, and dark sandy-gold curls that managed to be artfully tousled in a careless way, as if he'd never thought about his hair and just woke up that way.

Megan, suddenly remembering Jelena's love of fan fiction, said, "Oh my God, he's a Main Character," out loud, and clapped a hand over her mouth to keep herself from laughing audibly.

Raf breathed, "He's a *what*? Who is he?"

"No idea who he is." Megan giggled behind her palm, and kept her hand more or less over her mouth to answer the other question. "A Main Character. A, uh, a, oh, God, what did she call them? A Gary Sue or something like that. No, that's a perfect version of yourself that you put into the story. I think he's just a Main Character. I mean, look at him! He looks like the world is here just to let him tell his story!"

"On the one hand, I'm fairly sure you've lost your mind. On the other hand . . ." Rafael eyed the guy, who was shaking hands and chuckling with the evening news reporter. "I'd probably think I was a main character, too, if I looked like that."

"Right?!" Megan laughed again, then bit the inside of her cheek to silence herself and edged toward the media group. They positioned themselves so they were

filming the Main Character with the Rathballard House
as the background, and although she didn't get close
enough in time to hear his name, Megan could hear his
practiced, confident speech as he gazed into the camera.

"—loss to the rewilding community, of course, and
we extend our sympathies to the Nolan family. But despite Mr. Nolan's efforts, I can only see this beautiful,
ancient estate as under attack from the worst-possible
approach to rewilding. Let's have a look around." He
held an incredibly sincere-appearing expression for
several seconds after he finished speaking, then offered a brilliant smile to the cameraman. "Will that do,
or should I do it again?"

"You're grand," several people said at once, and the
cameraman said, "As always, Jack."

Megan took her phone out to search on 'jack ireland
rewilding' and came up with a hit immediately. "Jack
O'Malley," she murmured to her friends. "Natural
rewilding proponent. That means he believes in just
taking the animals and the crops off the land and letting nature creep back in. Really hates the approach
Nolan was taking. My *God*, he's good-looking." She
turned the phone to Raf and Sarah, scrolling through
photographs that looked as if they'd all been staged on
film sets. Even when he was literally knee-deep in
muck and filthy from digging, Jack O'Malley shone
the same way Niamh did, charisma pouring from the
page.

"We can creep after him," Raf offered, then gave his
wife a rueful glance when she visibly perked up at the

idea. "You could at least *pretend* I'm as hot as that guy, hon."

Sarah opened her mouth, glanced at Jack O'Malley, looked back at her husband apologetically, and closed her mouth again. After another moment, with a note of false sincerity, she said, "Of course you are, Rafael."

"Back me up here, Megs."

"Raf, you're a good-looking guy, but I'm sorry, he belongs in a movie-star lineup."

"Maaaaan, you think your family has your back . . ." Rafael grinned, then jerked his chin toward the group. "That reporter's the one who recognized you yesterday. He might notice you again. But it's perfectly reasonable for a couple of American tourists who were just over at the holy well yesterday to be at the, uh, what's it called? The Rathballad House? Today."

"Ballard," Megan said absently. *She* wanted to follow O'Malley. But Raf wasn't wrong, and the longer she stayed there, the more likely it was she'd be noticed. "Right, you're right, go for it, look, I booked tickets for the whole day, the house, the gardens, the maze, so you've got every reason to be anywhere they go. I'm gonna sneak up to the house."

Fortunately, the film crew and their gleaming subject had veered toward the gardens, giving Megan a chance to scurry past while their attention was diverted. Once on the house steps, she glanced back and got a thumbs-up from Raf, who, with Sarah, was approaching the gardens at a slightly different angle. Megan murmured, "Move along, move along, nothing to see here," and hurried inside.

The staggering size and imposing beauty of the foyer stopped her for a moment, awakening a ridiculous sense of being too small and ordinary to even step into a place like this. It was extraordinarily effective propaganda. Not a word had to be said: she simply *felt* she didn't belong.

On the other hand, if a nineteen-year-old could breeze through the place like it was nothing, then surely Megan's own forty-something self could manage to overcome a sudden bout of insecurity. She went into the tearoom, delighted to see the same young woman there who had helped her yesterday. "Hi, I don't know if you remember me?"

"Oh, yes. Are ye well? You weren't feeling well yesterday." The girl—Nora, according to her name tag, which had been missing yesterday—dimpled as if genuinely pleased to see Megan.

"Much better, thank you. Look, do you remember that I left with Aisling Nolan? She's an acquaintance, a new friend, and I've got some information she asked for yesterday, but we forgot to exchange numbers. I'm sure this puts you in an awkward spot because you probably don't interact with the family all that much, but is there any way someone could let her know I'm here?"

"Ah, Aisling, she's a dote, she's always in and out to chat with us, actually. Not her uncle, he's not that sort at all, but Aisling and her da always treat us like people." Nora's eyes suddenly went wet. "Treated, I guess. Poor Seamus. He was a decent man, trying to do best for the estate and the world." She dashed the tears away, composing herself, and added, "I wouldn't be able to reach Aisling myself, but go around to the gardens and see if you can find a lad called Ian. He'll have her number."

"Oh! Ian, about this tall, nice-looking young man? Red hair?"

"That'll be him," Nora said with delight and satisfaction. "You know him, do you?"

"We spoke yesterday. He was very knowledgeable about the rewilding project."

"Oh, yes, I'd say he'd have been tapped to run the project in a few years. Lord Nolan wanted to step back and spend more time trying to expand, now that the estate's been such a success." Worry creased Nora's forehead. "Who'll run it now, do you think? Ian's only young still, but he'd be well able. Aisling would let him, but Mr. Nolan would never. Ah, Jaysus, is *he* Lord Nolan now? I hadn't thought of it. It ought to be Aisling," she said fiercely. "She'd do right by us. But I'm keeping you. Have a scone," she finished, and pressed two of them, still warm from the oven, into Megan's hands.

"I just ate . . ." They smelled so good, though, that Megan cast a covetous look toward the butter, jams, and whipped cream. Nora shooed her that way, and Megan wasn't woman enough to refuse the opportunity. A minute or two later, she was outside, balancing four scone slices on a plate the girl had insisted she take, too, and making the long trek around the house's wing toward the back gardens.

The scones were absurdly good, and the thick blackberry jam had probably been made in-house. Megan sank her teeth into the second half of one, trying to avoid getting a dot of cream on her nose, and closed her eyes for a few steps, savoring the rich buttery flavor merging with the tart jam and mellowing cream. She could get used to this, if it was how the rich lived.

If she was a good person, she'd save the second scone for Ian, when she found him. Megan was still considering the idea as she rounded the house's corner and met someone coming the other way at considerable speed. She yelped and bounced back, prepared to offer an apology until she looked up to see whom she'd nearly— literally—creamed.

Detector Inspective Doyle stood at a dead stop just in front of her, his jaw clenching with anger. "What the hell are you doing here?"

"Having a scone?" Megan offered the plate, both as an explanation for what she was doing there, and to see if she could head off Doyle's ire with food. Neither worked: he curled his lip at the plate, and scowled even more deeply at her attempted humor. Before he could give out to her for making a joke, she added, "Looking for Aisling. She asked me for something yesterday, and I'm delivering it."

"How the—" Doyle clenched his teeth on what was obviously going to be a curse, perhaps because he'd remembered he was a representative of An Garda Síochána and *probably* shouldn't be swearing volubly at passersby. Even ones who were nicknamed "the Murder Driver." Megan watched with interest while he searched for a word that would both satisfy his need to snarl *and* not get him in trouble for haranguing a member of the public. "—*devil* do you know Aisling Nolan?"

"We met recently," Megan replied breezily, then tilted her head to the side, curious. "What are *you* doing here, Detective Sergeant? I thought there wasn't a case to investigate."

The detective's face went florid by inches, starting beneath his collar and creeping up until his hairline stood out bright and white against the hot blush. "That's none of your business."

"Well, no, it's not. I was just curious." Megan took a moment to try to figure out logistics, then handed Doyle the plate. He took it more out of surprise than intention, then glared helplessly as she got her phone and lowered it just far enough for him to see she was opening one of her social media apps. "Don't worry, I'm just updating my followers on the morning so far. I mean, who would have guessed I'd run into the investigating detective at the dead man's house when there's nothing to investigate?"

She had no intention at all of doing any such thing, but Doyle made a satisfactory noise of strangled outrage and tried to snatch her phone out of her hand while simultaneously handing the plate back. Neither worked, but the remaining scones made a brief, tragic arc through the misty air before landing face-down on the grass with a *splat*. Megan raised a betrayed look from the lost scones to Doyle, and nearly choked on laughter. Actual, profound distress was writ large over his face. He said, "I'm sorry," with genuine agony.

"You should be," Megan said, humor dissolving into anger. "What do you think you were doing, trying to grab *my property* out of my own hand? I'll have you written up for this, Detective Sergeant!" Her ears flamed with heat, and she found herself taking an actual threatening step toward the guard.

To her astonishment, he stepped back, his own face ruddy again. "Now, there's no need for that, Ms. Malone. It was only a bad moment on my own part, and I'm sorry for it. You're after asking what I'm about here, well, I'm here to tell you Adam Nolan asked for me himself, he did. The household got word that himself, Jack O'Malley, was coming to the grounds today, and there's enough bad blood between the Nolans and himself that they wanted a police presence here, they did."

The spill of words came at such a pace Megan could hardly keep up, although it wasn't *what* he said that was hard to follow; it was that he said it at all. She said, "What do you mean, 'bad blood'?" while still trying to figure out what had prompted the sharing of information at all.

Doyle's gaze flicked to her phone, and he rolled his jaw before answering in the same rapid, conciliatory way. "Do you not pay attention to the news? They've been fighting each other in court for years. O'Malley claims Nolan's caretaking approach to his estate is antithetical to the good of the land. He's been suing to have the whole estate turned over to the State for proper maintenance and rewilding for at least a decade. The courts keep finding in Nolan's favor, but there's always another angle O'Malley's ready to try. Or there was. The last round, the courts told O'Malley to stop wasting their time and that he wouldn't be heard again."

"And you think Seamus *accidentally* fell into that well?" Megan asked incredulously. Doyle's jaw tightened again, and his glance dropped to her phone a second time. A penny dropped with it: he was afraid she *would* report him. That was why he'd suddenly started sharing all of this. Megan moved her thumb over to bring up the keypad, and color scalded Doyle's face again.

"I think he was a madman who made an arse of himself pretending to be a druid," Doyle snapped. "And I think stone is slippy when the dew is upon it, and that the poor bastard slid, cracked his skull, and drowned in the name of acting like an old story was a real goddess who would hear him. So, yes, Ms. Malone, I *do* think he accidentally fell in that well, and that's the end of it. Now, if you'll excuse me, I've another bloody lunatic to get off this land." He took an abrupt step forward, enough to make Megan fall back this time, and his departure would have been dramatically impressive if he hadn't stepped in the fallen scone.

He cursed sharply, hopping on his opposite foot and trying to scrape the scone off, while Megan choked down laughter, then hurried the other way.

CHAPTER 13

Ian, the young gardener, was deeper in the metaphorical weeds today than he'd been yesterday, and Megan badly wished she had a change of shoes to tromp into the mud with. Instead, not wanting to shout and draw everyone's attention, she minced her way through mist-laden muck that got wetter with each step. She'd made it about halfway across the workspace when a laugh met her and Ian called, "Stop, I'll come to you."

Megan, grateful, found a patch of earth that looked more or less solid and did stop. Ian, pink-faced from work and smiling, eyed the plate she still carried as he approached, and lifted an eyebrow at her.

"I was bringing you a scone, but it met a sad end under Detective Sergeant Doyle's boot," Megan explained.

Ian, straight-faced, said, "I knew I didn't like that man," then spit a grin. "What can I do for you today, Megan?"

"Nora in the house said you might have Aisling

Nolan's number? I've got some information she asked for, but we forgot to exchange numbers, and I don't think I'd be welcome walking through the house yelling her name."

"Oh, but I'd like to see that, I would," Ian said with a sparkle in his eyes. "She'd love it. The old man would have palpitations. It'd be grand so. Yeah, I've her number."

He took his phone out of a deep pocket, and Megan, hastily, said, "If you want to text her and give her *my* number, that might be less weird than handing hers out to relative strangers."

Ian paused, then crooked a smile. "You're a good egg, aren't you? I'll do that so. What's your number?" He put it into the message, sent it, then contemplated the phone for a moment. "It strikes me that this might be one of those situations where it might have been better to use the phone for its intended purpose, and rang her."

Megan put on her best bewildered look. "'Rang her'? I'm sorry, I don't understand. Are phones supposed to be used for something other than texting, taking pictures, and internet browsing?"

"They tell me there was a time when all you could do with one was ring somebody," Ian informed her solemnly, then gave a performative shudder. "Can ye imagine such a backwards and dreadful time?"

Megan laughed. "Actually, yeah. I lived it. It wasn't all bad."

"Never," Ian said with obliging sincerity. "You're never old enough to remember a time before smartphones. Ah, there she is," he added as his phone chimed.

"She says go on up, the same way you took yesterday if you can manage it without getting lost, and that I'm to give you her number in case you do."

He did so, and Megan said, "So, you're actually friends, then, not just acquaintances," as she put the number into her phone.

A little to her surprise, Ian went rosy, which clashed terribly with his red hair. "We are so. She's a lovely girl."

Megan sucked her cheeks in, trying not to grin. "Oh, is *that* how it is."

"It's never any how!"

"Uh-huh." The grin got away from her, and Megan lifted the phone in thanks. "I appreciate your help, and I'll put in a good word for you with the lady of the house."

Ian's cheeks turned positively scarlet, freckles standing out in pale tan blotches against the heat of his skin, and Megan, grinning, minced her way back toward the house. The poor squished scone had acquired a number of crows and pigeons disagreeing over which of them got the better part of the feast, and were so intent on their argument that she passed within a few feet of them without scaring them away. One of the pigeons, a particularly pretty bird with mostly white feathers lined with tan, did eyeball her warily, but jam and scone were of far more interest, and it went back to pecking and wing-buffeting after she'd walked by.

She hadn't thought she'd been gone from the front of the house all that long, but a visibly increased number of visitors were now climbing its steps, or stopping to take pictures of each other with the huge house as an awesome backdrop. Megan avoided being in the background of those pictures as much as possible, not wanting to end up as a splash on somebody's social media if they recognized the murder driver. Fortunately for her, there were other, more interesting-looking people also gathering: a small group in clothes ranging from the perfectly ordinary to the theatrically pagan were hugging each other and speaking quietly at the foot of the steps. Megan didn't know any of them, but she guessed they'd known Seamus Nolan in his religious practice. She slipped into the house on her own and detoured to the tearoom again in order to return the scone plate.

Nora waved another greeting that turned into a beckoning gesture. Megan, uncertain, approached her, and Nora nodded toward the table of scones and other pastries. "That detective garda came in here and paid for a scone he said was to be given to you."

Megan's eyebrows shot up. "Seriously?"

"Not a word of a lie," Nora promised. "Are you that hungry, then?"

"No." Megan laughed. "No, he knocked the scone I had out of my hand and apparently felt guilty for it." Or, she thought, he was worried enough about the possibility she would report him that he'd decided he'd better cover his tracks as thoroughly as he could. "Thanks. I'm not hungry, but I'll take one anyway, just in case."

"Just in case." Nora gave a satisfied nod and flitted off to do her job, leaving a bemused Megan to depart the tearoom on her own.

It was earlier in the day than she'd been there yesterday, which might account for the greater number of people visiting the house. Megan bore left when most of the visitors were going right, and a staff member moved to block the stairs, producing an artificially apologetic smile. "Sorry, ma'am, this part of the house is private. The tours go through the other wing."

"I'm here to visit Aisling," Megan said with a somewhat more sincerely apologetic smile of her own. "I can ring her, if you like, so she can verify it's okay?" She held up the phone with Aisling's name visible, and the staff person blanched, then stepped out of the way. Megan nodded her thanks and went up the stairs, but thought they should have made her call, just to be sure she was legitimate. Otherwise, sneaking into the Nolans' personal quarters was far too easy.

Which would make it easy to commit a murder. She went up the stairs considering that, and only remembered as she got to Seamus Nolan's office that he hadn't actually died in the house. "Too bad," she breathed to herself, since she didn't have the dogs to talk to. "I bet there are security cameras that could see who went places they weren't supposed to, here."

She raised her hand to knock, heard voices, and paused, ear not *quite* pressed against the door to listen in. A man and a woman were arguing, using the low, tense pitch of people trying not to be overheard. Megan felt her ears actually perking, like she was one of her Jack Russells, and she actually did press up against the door, listening hard. She couldn't make out a word, and she fought the temptation to crack the door open so she could hear.

Heavy footsteps sounded, and she failed to stand back fast enough. The door yanked open, and Megan more or less fell into the room, narrowly missing Adam Nolan as he skipped an angry step backward and barely rescued a second scone from an undignified end. "What the *hell*!"

"I am so sorry," Megan said as she straightened, face hot. "I heard voices and was trying to decide if I should knock."

"By listening in?" Nolan demanded.

"By trying to listen to tone," Megan replied, starting to recover her equilibrium. Nolan's antagonism made it easier: she could hide in offended dignity, even if she had, in fact, been trying to listen *in*. "I didn't want to interrupt something important."

"You didn't." Aisling, in her father's desk chair, spoke in a thin, quiet voice that belied both the tense talk from a moment earlier and her uncle's irritation. "It's nice to see you again. Come on in, please."

Adam Nolan made a sound in his throat that sounded remarkably like a growl, then stalked past Megan into the hall. She stepped aside, getting out of the way, and pushed the door mostly closed behind her. "I'm sorry for interrupting."

"Well, you didn't, really." For all her youth, Aisling looked worn and exhausted, with shadows under her eyes and her skin dry and pale. "He was leaving because he thought he'd won the—discussion—and he didn't want to give me a chance to find my feet again."

"Oh, well, that sounds lovely. You look wrecked, Aisling. Have you eaten anything? I brought you a scone."

Megan lifted the plate, and pure gratitude washed over Aisling's face.

"Thank you so much. No, I forgot to eat this morning. I don't think I even ate anything yesterday, except that tray you brought up with you. You're a lifesaver, you are." She took the scone and slathered it with the jam Megan had brought along, eating big bites as Megan sat across from her and lifted her phone.

"I got a number for a solicitor my uncle recommended. Someone who'll represent you alone, although they might want to coordinate with your father's lawyer once you've got someone on your side. I just wanted to bring it by for you, because I didn't have your number." Megan smiled suddenly. "At least, not until young Ian out there got it for me. He seems like a nice young man."

Aisling turned a becoming shade of pink that helped her color considerably. "He is, yeah. He's a great help—he *was* a great help to Da. I'm hoping I can promote him." The momentary pleasure drained from her expression. "But Uncle Adam wants to sell it all. He was trying to talk me into the idea of it, telling me how desperate the estate is for money and how mad it is to hold on to all this land for some dream of my da's. That's what we were arguing about before you came in. I'm glad you did. I was starting to be afraid I'd agree just because I'm too tired to fight about it."

"I'll get you some more food, but then I'm going to stay right here with you while you ring that lawyer," Megan said a bit fiercely. "You need somebody on your side."

The young woman's eyes welled, and she dropped

her gaze, dashing tears away with buttery fingertips. "It ought to be my mam, but God, she's awful," she whispered before glancing up again with a mix of misery and rue. "Look, I didn't say thank you, did I? For getting her out of here yesterday. That was incredible. You could do that for a living."

Megan smiled. "You didn't say it out loud, but I got the idea. And sometimes I *do* do it for a living. Sometimes I get a famous client or somebody who's just trapped in a conversation, and it's useful to be good at maneuvering them out of it. He can't sell it right away, anyway, can he? Never mind the question of who's the heir, but isn't there a waiting period? A year or something before the will is executed?" She held up her hands. "Not that I expect you to know, and I sure don't know for certain, which is why—"

"I need to call the solicitor," Aisling said with a nod. "You don't have to get me food. I'll ring up for it." She reached for a house phone on the desk, making Megan remember something, although she held her tongue until the girl had finished asking for a meal.

"I noticed you moved your father's book of passwords out of your uncle's sight yesterday," she said cautiously once Aisling had hung up. "Is everything all right there?"

"Oh, we were arguing about that too." Aisling slumped. "I told him I didn't know where it was. I don't want him going through Da's stuff. He wants to look at Da's computer, but I'm afraid he might—I mean, he wouldn't, would he? He wouldn't . . . change anything?"

"His solicitor should have a copy of anything so important that changing it would have an effect on the estate," Megan guessed, "so even if he would, and I'm not saying he *would*, you should be safe. Which isn't to say I think you should share that information with him. Not just him. Anyone. Look, I'll stay in the room, but I'll go over there where I'm not in the way so you can call the lawyer. How's that sound? I'll be moral support, just out of earshot."

"Perfect." Aisling managed a wan smile, then took the number Megan offered, stared at it, and said, "I don't want to do this. I don't want any of this to be happening."

Megan sighed. "I know. I'm sorry you have to, and I'm sorry it is. But if you put it off, things could get even worse, so I'm going to encourage you to do it."

"It hardly seems like it could be worse." Aisling nodded, though, and picked up her phone with clear reluctance. Megan offered a supportive nod, then moved to the other end of the room, as promised, and took her own phone out so she at least *appeared* not to be paying attention.

She'd missed two texts, one from Paul and the other from Rafael in their group chat. With a glance at Aisling and the assumption the girl would need support and the chance that Paul might too, she decided not to read that one yet, and checked Raf's instead.

Megan, Raf's text read, and she knew something was wrong immediately because who bothered to use somebody's name in a text, *there's a toxic waste dump on this estate.*

CHAPTER 14

Megan squawked, "What?" out loud, although she tried to keep it quiet, as Aisling, chewing on a knuckle, sat with her phone pressed against her ear at the other end of the room. Then the girl straightened, taking a deep breath and pulling herself together in a professional manner. "Hello, I'm Aisling Nolan. I've been given your number through—"

She cast a panicked look at Megan, who said, "Rabbie Lynch from Sligo Town," just loudly enough to be heard. Aisling echoed it, and relief slid across her face as the person on the other end apparently recognized the name, or the strength of the reference. "Oh, he did? That was lovely of him. Yes, I'm calling—" She went into an explanation, holding herself together through the need for a professional demeanor, and Megan let herself look back at her own phone.

A second text had come through from Raf: *O'Malley knew where he was going. He took the camera crew straight to it. It looks like farming waste, not that I know much about it, but that's what they're saying. There's at least a dozen barrels, and it's been here awhile, the ground is bleached and dead and stinks.* Another text, this one with a couple of photos, followed that, and Megan blanched. Rafael had undersold it, if anything.

The barrels weren't barrels, for one thing. They were tanks, splitting along their seams and stained with foam and acid streaks. There *were* at least a dozen of them, spilling over a small, bereft-looking hollow of land that had somehow been overlooked in the rewilding scheme. No one had made any effort to improve the regrowth there, even aside from the threads of discoloration spread across the earth from where each tank lay, reaching toward each other like a lethal spiderweb. Megan, horrified, typed, *where are you?*

Raf sent a flat-expressioned emoji and *on the estate?!?* back, then, after a moment, a map screenshot with the GPS coordinates on it. Megan pulled it up in relation to the rest of the estate, startled to find it closer to the house than she'd expected. She zoomed out, realizing the house itself wasn't planted squarely in the middle of the estate as she'd supposed, but rather sat almost in a corner of it, the land fanning out around it.

He knew exactly where to go, Raf wrote on the tail of that thought. *He's had this planned.*

Think he planted it? Megan asked, then, *how'd **you** get there, you're not media!*

Sarah told them we were with the Murder Driver's investigation team.

Megan groaned loudly enough to make Aisling look toward her, although she shook her head hastily, indicating the girl should go back to her conversation. *Oh, no, tell me she didn't.*

She definitely did, Sarah wrote in the group chat. *And he lit right up and welcomed us along.*

Megan whispered, "Oh my *God*, you two," at the phone, and scrolled back up to the pictures. Raf was right: the tanks hadn't been put there recently. There was too much death around them, encroaching on land that looked like it *had* been rewilded. That might be a good place to hide waste, she thought: right in the middle of a reserve, where, in theory, nobody would even be looking. And the environmental damage could be incredible—not just the groundwater seepage, but also the effect on the rewilding attempts. It could make the whole effort look poisoned, if an outside party was responsible.

Megan groaned quietly and scrolled back down to see that Sarah had sent a voice message through the app. She put it to her ear and played it, listening to the quiet, "The media is eating it up. O'Malley's line is that forced regrowth—that's what he's calling Nolan's method—is as toxic to the natural development of the land as this waste site is. He's very carefully *not* saying Seamus Nolan was responsible for it—"

Megan breathed, "Because libel laws are way stronger here than they are in the States," and briefly tried to remember whether it was libel or slander that referred to written works. It didn't really matter: O'Malley was being careful in what he said, and if the papers weren't careful in what they printed, they themselves would be in trouble, not O'Malley.

Sarah's voice message went on like she really was an investigator, focused on echoing O'Malley's words truthfully. "—and he's actually really upset about the dump in the first place, I think that's real emotion, but he's obviously not above trying to use it to bring Nolan down." She paused like she'd heard herself say that, and ended with a sigh. "As if being dead wasn't brought low enough."

"But how did he know about it?" Megan asked as if Sarah could hear her. The better question, though, was how *long* O'Malley had known about it. Long enough to plan a path for a media team.

Long enough that he could have killed Seamus Nolan in order to cause a stir that would draw attention to the estate in the first place. Megan shivered, surprised at how dismaying she found the thought. She'd encountered premeditated murders before, though, so she wasn't sure why this one bothered her, except for the fact that Jack O'Malley was so incredibly good-looking. Someone that handsome shouldn't have to resort to murder to get what he wanted.

Of course, from what she understood about beauty, somebody that handsome would also be considerably more likely to get away with murder, too. Whether it was a cultural or an innate thing, people equated attractiveness with goodness. She remembered reading an interview with some movie star who'd talked about realizing, when he was a kid, that he could get away with things his classmates couldn't, just because he was ridiculously good-looking. Even at the time, he'd thought it was unfair.

He'd also admitted to having taken advantage of it on occasion, even if it *wasn't* fair. Megan doubted anybody born with more than their fair share of good looks hadn't taken advantage of it from time to time, and if Jack O'Malley had in this case . . .

Aisling was still on the phone, her feet pulled up onto the desk chair so that her whole body was tucked into as small a space as she could possibly take up. She looked fragile and in need of defense, but the occasional words Megan heard were relatively steady, as if she had at least some degree of emotional control. A tap sounded on the door, and she lifted her head, but Megan waved and went to get it, smiling to find a timid-looking staff person with a plate of soup and sandwiches. "I'll take it," Megan whispered. "Thank you."

They nodded and hurried away as Megan pushed the door closed and brought the tray to Aisling's desk. She gave Megan a quick, grateful smile and tested the soup's heat with a fingertip before retreating into her phone call to let it cool down. Megan went back to the other end of the room, scanning through a few more messages from Raf and Sarah about the severity of the waste site, then holding her breath to look at Paul's text.

If you've talked to Niamh, ring me when you can.

Megan winced and nodded as if he could see her response, then sent, *I have and I will. Probably tonight, if that's okay?*

After a moment, a thumbs-up appeared on the message, followed by *still solving a murder?*

Megan grimaced like he could see that, too. *Still trying to figure out if there was one, but it's looking more likely, I think. I'll update you when I ring.*

He sent a wobbly smile back, along with, *well, get on with solving it so I've your undivided attention.*

"Oh, God, that bad?" Megan breathed, typed, *Will do*, and turned her phone off as Adam Nolan threw the door open and stormed back into the room.

Aisling shot a sharp glance at him, then rose to leave, phone still pressed to her ear. He said, "You don't need to go," without any motion toward stepping out again himself, and Aisling, looking weary, left anyway. He stalked to Seamus's desk, taking the seat Aisling had been in without seeming to notice Megan's presence. She cleared her throat, and he surged to his feet again, jaw tense. "What are you still doing here?"

"Keeping Aisling company," Megan replied. "I gather you know Jack O'Malley's on the estate?"

"That bastard. Yes, of course I knew. If anyone did murder Seamus, it was him."

"You think so? Why?"

"Because they're after the same grants from the European Union, aren't they?" Adam snapped. "There's not much money in this rewilding nonsense, and even Seamus tried not to beggar the estate by applying for grants. Ireland's got one of the worst forest coverages in the entire EU—"

Megan, genuinely startled, interrupted with, "Really?

But it's legendarily green. I mean, like, that's Ireland's whole *thing*."

Nolan bared his teeth as if annoyed that he even knew this. "Oh, believe me, it's true, I heard it often enough from Seamus. 'Only eleven or twelve percent, compared to an average of over thirty percent continent-wide.' Even I'd say that's a travesty, when this whole country was covered in trees once upon a time. Not in anybody's living memory, but still, it's an embarrassment."

"I guess so! Look, I'm sorry, you were saying about the grants?"

The older man half-growled again, impatient with the whole thing. "Most of them are for people who want to grow trees to harvest. I could understand Seamus wanting to do that. It's a profit-making venture. But no, he wants to regrow old forest, broad-leaf forest, slow-growing . . ." He gestured as if Megan should know and understand all of this already. "And there aren't many grants for that. For long-term projects. So himself and *himself*," he said, obviously referring to O'Malley, "were in constant competition for those few grants available. I've no interest in continuing this rewilding, so I'd say it's to his benefit that Seamus is dead, all right."

"Right," Megan said. "Did you know he's just exposed a toxic waste site on the estate?"

Adam paled so dramatically Megan thought he might actually fall. "He's what? How big? How bad? Where?" He swayed, then reached for the desk chair and sat heavily. "Are you sure?"

If he was responsible for the mess, then he was also an extraordinary actor. Megan almost felt sorry for him. "I'm sure. Someone sent me pictures."

He put his hand out, demanding to see. Megan rose and walked the phone to him, holding it up so he could see. She didn't really expect him to snatch the phone from her hand, but given Doyle's behavior earlier, she also didn't want to take any chances. A thread of hope tightened his features, and, guessing what he was going to ask, Megan turned the phone around, flipped to the map and its GPS coordinates inside the estate boundaries, and showed him that too. Adam slumped, nearly green with horror. "This will scupper the sale."

"*What sale?*" Aisling's voice rose sharply as she came back into the room. "Uncle Adam, what have you done? You've got something already *set up*? Jesus, what are you doing? You can't do anything." The last few words were almost snarled, color rushing her face. "I've spoken to my solicitor. They're filing an injunction to make sure you *can't* do anything until the courts have decided on the legality of gender-based discriminatory inheritance laws. And it's a year before the estate is even out of—" Her breath caught slightly as she reached for the word, although Megan thought she'd already done brilliantly in defending herself. With a note of triumph as she remembered the word, Aisling finished, "*Probate.* Even if you're the executor of the will, and I don't even know if you are because I've only your word for it, you can't sell or change anything until the executor's year is over!*"

"What solicitor?" Adam demanded. "You haven't a solicitor. Your *father* had a solicitor!"

"And now I have one." Aisling thrust her jaw out as color rushed into it. "I'll be ringing Da's lawyer, too, but I've someone representing *me* now."

"You don't need any such thing—"

"Apparently I do! *What sale?*"

"It's a big old estate, Ais," Adam said cajolingly. "A few hundred acres toward development won't even be missed, and the money for it is more than this bloody rewilding project has made in a decade. I've the buyers all lined up. We're desperate for the cash, Ais."

"Jesus, were you *waiting* for Da to die? He wasn't even fifty, Adam, he had decades left in him! Far more than you've got." Aisling's color reversed, blotchy pale patches standing out in the red. "Jesus, you killed him, didn't you? Megan's right. It was a murder, and my own uncle did it!"

"I—"

"*Detective!*" Aisling full-on bellowed the word, voice so deep with rage there was no danger of it cracking. "Detective Sergeant Doyle, where the hell are you?"

Megan, once more fully aware she was witness to something she had no business seeing, texted Raf and Sarah with, *is that detective with you*?

They both responded with variations on *no, why?* almost immediately, and Megan, knowing she probably shouldn't draw attention to herself, said, "He's not with the media group that went with Jack O'Malley. Which is strange, isn't it, Mr. Nolan, if you called him here to run O'Malley off the land? Which, now that I think about it, is also strange. Why didn't you just use your own security? A house like this, open to the public, must have security. And it's private property. You'd have the right of it."

Adam flushed, but his stuttered protest was overridden by Aisling's snapped, "Not if he's not the master of the house." She folded her arms defensively as Megan and Adam both looked toward her. "Well, wouldn't it be my decision? I *ought* to be the heir to Da's plans and dreams, not some ancient son of a bitch wh—"

"Aisling!" Adam Nolan actually sounded shocked, but his grandniece rounded on him.

"Oh, I'm sorry, what did you think I should say? Me beloved auld uncle who's been there for me through thick and thin? You're trying to sell the estate, Adam! Da's not yet in the grave and the land isn't yours to sell and you're trying to sell it! Cozying up to me and trying to talk me into it when you've got buyers lined up already! Wouldn't you say a man who did that was a son of a bitch?"

"You have no idea what you're talking about," Nolan growled. "I've spent the past twenty years watching your idiot father turn good arable land into a forested mess, spending every cent we couldn't spare on his dream project, and not gotten him to budge an inch on finances. You've no idea what a disaster this estate is, Aisling. You don't want to inherit it. It'll destroy your life. I'm trying to protect you from your father's mistakes."

"I'm not yours to protect, and the land's not yours to decide what to do with!" Aisling's eyes were bright with fury, her whole young self crackling with angry energy. "And it's not mine, either, not until the courts decide who inherits, anyway, so you can't do anything, and if you try, I'll have you up on legal charges before you can turn around!"

A heavy thudding on the door made them all jump. Detective Sergeant Doyle let himself in without an invitation, his face flushed like he'd run through the house. "The staff said I was being called for. What's going on? Ah, Jaysus, what's *she* doing here?"

Every gaze jumped to Megan, who managed not to flinch under the attention. "I brought Aisling some information she asked for, and she invited me to stay awhile. Detective Sergeant, are you aware of the toxic waste dump on the land?"

"The what?" Doyle and Aisling spoke at the same time, the girl blanching again, then whirling toward her uncle in a fury. "What have you done?!"

"Why in God's name would I dump toxic waste on land I wanted to sell?" Adam yelled. "Do you know what I'd say it was, I'd say it was your own father, desperate for cash and willing to wreck a corner of his precious project to hide somebody's waste. You've no idea the desperate straits the property's in, Aisling—"

Aisling, savagely, said, "Da would *never*," and to Megan's acute horror, the door bounced open again and Jenny Flynn trilled, "Oh, you're right, my darling, your dear father would never!"

CHAPTER 15

For a single heartbeat, everyone in the room was temporarily united in surprise at Jenny Flynn's reappearance. Adam Nolan accidentally caught Megan's eye, and she jerked her gaze away to keep from laughing at the abject exasperation in his expression. Worse than exasperation, really: borderline horror. Jenny was clearly the last person he wanted mixed up in the conversation, and Megan, catching a glimpse of Aisling's face, saw just as much unhappiness in her pinched mouth. Even Doyle looked pained, although his irritation was probably just that yet another party had been added to the mix. Megan knew her own distaste wasn't much better hidden.

Jenny somehow seemed not to notice any of it, descending on Aisling with a happy trill. "I'm sorry, my darling, I realized I never should have left you in these dreadful times. I drove back to Cork last night, but only long enough to arrange for someone to stand in for me at my gallery opening, and then came back up this morning immediately. I can't believe how insensitive I was being, leaving you alone with all of this to deal with." She draped her arm around Aisling's shoulders in a protective manner, but also leaned on the girl hard enough that Megan had the sudden thought of vampires draining the strength of those around them.

Aisling made a visible effort to keep from curling her lip and swallowed before turning a thin smile toward her mother. "You really shouldn't have, Mam. I'm all right. I've got the solicitors in hand and all."

"I'm sure you do, my pet," Jenny cooed. "But Mama is here to help now anyway. What would your dear father never?"

Another extremely brief silence swept the room as the others took in, and adjusted to, the idea that she'd roundly defended Seamus Nolan's reputation without having a clue what had been said. In that time, she noticed Doyle for the first time, and her eyebrows drew inward.

"Detective Sergeant Doyle," he said before she could come up with any questions. "Here at Mr. Nolan's request, ma'am. There are unwanted parties on the property."

Adam flushed heavily around the collar, and Megan took a glorious moment to revel in the suspicious squint tightening Jenny's eyes, as if she had to briefly consider the possibility that *she* was one of the unwanted parties. But her expression cleared, because the police officer had obviously been there before she ar-

rived, which let her off the hook. Megan bit the inside
of her cheek to keep from grinning, although the impulse faded fast as Jenny trilled another laugh. "Oh my
goodness, Detective Sergeant, not *ma'am*. I'm never
old enough to be a ma'am!"

She shot Megan a warning look as she spoke, as if
afraid Megan would bring up the whole over-forty
thing again, like she'd done the day before. Megan tried
for a politely reassuring smile and got one corner of
her mouth to lift briefly, which was evidently enough.
Doyle, however, said, "I'll remember that, ma'am,"
evenly, and after a pause said, "or should it be 'Mrs.
Nolan'?"

To Megan's astonishment, Jenny simpered and gave
a little wiggle of her shoulders that almost devolved
into a childish curtsy. "I suppose, if you must."

Adam Nolan shot Megan another look, this time
clearly intending to get her attention, and Megan popped
her eyes at him in return. Given the rejection *she'd* gotten for using "Mrs. Nolan" the day before, Jenny's
change of heart was enough to make even Aisling stare
at her mother. Then, almost as one, Aisling and Adam's
expressions cleared, and Megan felt her own doing the
same. Jenny, she thought, was trying to stake her claim
to the Nolan fortune by suddenly being willing to be
"Mrs. Nolan." And she was doing so in front of the law,
specifically, which would arguably be considered more
strongly in a court case. Megan refrained from giving a
low whistle, but only just.

"Mrs. Nolan," Doyle said obligingly. "Mr. Nolan,
you called for me?"

"I did—" Nolan strangled the words. "Get O'Malley off my property!"

"*My* property!" Both women spoke, and Aisling, cheeks bright with furious color, shook her mother off.

Adam ignored both of them. "And get someone in here to investigate an environmental disaster cleanup."

Doyle's eyebrows rose. "That'd be beyond An Garda Síochána's remit, sir. You'd have to ring the government."

"Then ring them! Jesus, I'll have to talk to the press, it's already too late to get ahead of it if O'Malley's out there showing it to them, but I've got to do something—" Nolan strode out of the room while Aisling, still pink with anger and hands shaking with emotion, turned her focus to her phone. Jenny slipped over to Seamus's computer and sat, trying a password and then opening the drawer that had contained his password book and effortlessly checking its secret compartment.

A flicker of irritation darted across her eyebrows, although her voice was syrupy sweet. "Aisling, my love, where's your father's password book?"

Aisling shrugged and put her phone to her ear. Doyle looked around the room, attention landing on Megan, and for a moment she felt a surge of sympathy for the detective. Even without her presence, this was a family drama writ large, and she couldn't blame him for not wanting to be in the midst of it. She tilted her head toward the door cautiously, an invitation, and after a tight-jawed moment, he followed her into the hallway. Neither of them made any effort to close the door behind them, and both paused to watch Jenny opening and closing desk drawers and growing increasingly agitated as she didn't find the password book. "I wonder what she thinks is on the computer," Megan said quietly.

"Probably Nolan's last will and testament," Doyle said in the irritable tone of a man who wanted to discuss things with *somebody*, but definitely not *her*. "What's the story with that one? The three of you looked like you'd bit lemons when she swanned into the room. She's Nolan's estranged wife, I know that, but what's the rest of it?"

"She's manipulative and cloying. I only met her yesterday, and she set my teeth on edge. Detective Sergeant . . ." Megan sighed. "Look, for what it's worth, assuming Seamus Nolan *was* killed, at the moment, Aisling thinks Adam did it so he could inherit and sell off the land before the courts decided Aisling could inherit. Adam thinks Jack O'Malley did it because O'Malley believes Seamus's tactics were destructive to the environment *and* he's up for the same grants Seamus was. Jenny showed up to get her piece of the pie, and somebody dumped toxic waste in the middle of Seamus's rewilding efforts. At the very least, there's been a mess brewing here for a long, long time."

To her surprise, Doyle gave her a thin smile. "Isn't that always the way at the big house. What do you think?"

Megan was surprised enough to be asked that she hesitated, and Doyle's mouth went thinner and flatter. "Don't mistake me, Ms. Malone. I'm not looking for your help. But you're in the thick of it, and somebody might have let something slip to you that they wouldn't say to me."

"I'll answer, but does this mean you're considering the possibility there was a murder after all?"

Doyle exhaled heavily. "I think the man slipped, cracked his head, and drowned, but where you are, there's fire."

Megan started a protest, then let it go with a short nod. "All right. Adam Nolan or Jack O'Malley look like the most likely suspects, but it's not to either of their benefit to set a toxic waste dump on the land, so I don't see how that's connected to them. Jenny's awful and as far as I can tell must have a head for the long game, or she'd have divorced Seamus years ago, but with the way the inheritance laws stand for landed gentry, I think she'd have been better off waiting until the court cases cleared and declared Aisling the legal heir. Even if it meant she didn't get anything officially, she could probably leech off her daughter for the rest of her life, but if Adam inherits, I don't think he'll give Jenny a red cent. So if she was going to kill him, I wouldn't do it now." She paused, aware her pronouns had gotten mixed up there, but Doyle nodded, apparently understanding.

"Anyone else?"

"There's a young man called Ian who works in the gardens. Aisling fancies him and thinks her father had plans to promote him into a position of overseeing the whole wilding project, but he fancies her, too, and killing somebody's da isn't a great way to cozy up to them. Father Colman didn't like Nolan much, and says he didn't see him at the holy well that morning, but he would be the closest we have to being the last person to see him alive. And there's still the matter of the bicycle."

"The bicycle," Doyle echoed grimly. "Nolan's bicycle, in the hedge where some gombeen threw it."

"It was missing the next morning. Which, Detective Sergeant, points at you. You're the only person I told about it, anyway."

Doyle's eyebrows shot toward his hairline. "Are you seriously considering me a suspect?"

"You didn't want to investigate, I told you about the bike and you dismissed it, and now it's missing. So, yeah. You're on my list."

The detective stared at her for a few seconds. In the silence, Megan heard Jenny swearing, and glanced into the office to see her glaring, red-faced, at Seamus's computer. Then, her tone wheedling, she said something quiet to Aisling, who turned to emphasize that she was still on the phone. Doyle, after a long pause, followed Megan's gaze, and in a relatively neutral tone, said, "How about that one?"

"Aisling? She's nineteen and been thrown in over her head with estate law while grieving. I could be wrong, but I don't think she'll have killed her own da."

"And what about you?" Doyle asked sourly. "Miss Marple, always at the heart of the scene, why isn't it you?"

"Because I was at the Dublin airport picking my friends up at half eight in the morning on the day Seamus Nolan died."

"It's an hour between the airport and the holy well," Doyle challenged. "You could have done it and gotten back to collect them."

Megan stared at him. "With weekday traffic on the M50? Seriously? But okay, let's say I had. Why would I have brought them to the murder site, when I could have just *not*, and kept myself completely out of the picture?"

"Killers always return to the scene of the crime." For the first time, Doyle looked like he might be enjoying himself.

Megan snorted. "First, no they don't and you know it, and second, I'd have to have either taken public transport, which wouldn't have gotten me back in time, or a vehicle that went on the toll roads, in which case you can check the CCTV to see if there's any hint of me driving either north or south before about ten a.m. on Monday morning."

"You'd be a good killer, wouldn't you, Ms. Malone?"

"I'd like to imagine I wouldn't make any really obvious mistakes if I found it necessary to secretly murder someone, but people like to imagine they could fight off a lion with their bare hands, too, so I'm not sure what I imagine is a great baseline."

Doyle's eyebrows rose again, and Megan ducked her head to chuckle. "Sorry, it's something I read online. The percentage of American men who think they could fight off a lion with their bare hands. It's something like six or eight percent."

"Have they ever seen a lion?" Doyle asked cautiously.

Megan laughed out loud that time. "Maybe not in real life. I don't know. I think the list of animals went from, like, house cats to grizzly bears or something, but man, I've seen cats fight. I don't think I could beat a nine-pound one, never mind a lion. To be fair, I'm pretty sure I'd stand a better chance against humans, generally. They don't usually bite as a first line of defense." She fell silent, suddenly aware she wasn't necessarily making the best argument against being a killer.

Doyle shook his head. "I'd say I walked into that, but I'm not sure how I could have. I've known Adam Nolan thirty years," he added with a sigh. "I wouldn't have said he was a killer. That, and he's an old man. A fight against Seamus could as likely go badly for him."

"There's a back road," Megan said suddenly, aware it hardly tracked. As Doyle's expression turned questioning, she went on. "The front driveway's got security, right? So they can keep track of the visitors coming and going. But the back way might, too. If it does, we might be able to see whether Adam or anybody else went out the morning Seamus died."

"*We*," Doyle said icily, "will do nothing of the sort."

A pang of irritated disappointment sliced through Megan, although she only shrugged in response. Partly because it was Doyle's job to look at that kind of thing, and partly because if she didn't make a fuss now, he might not think to tell the on-site security not to let her look at any potential footage later.

As if following her thoughts, Doyle added, "I'll look into it," in a grudging tone. Megan nodded, wondering if he would, or—now that she was thinking of security cameras—whether the heritage centre had any pointed at the road outside their parking lot. She tried not to let her head snap up at the thought; Doyle pretty clearly had no intention of looking into the matter of Seamus's bicycle, and if she made it clear *she* wanted to, he'd forbid her.

Of course, Paul forbade her to do things like that all the time, and she did them anyway. Paul, though, was a friend and an ally, willing to use what she learned toward a common goal of solving a mystery. Doyle was neither friend nor ally, and would be just as likely to have her arrested on the grounds of interfering with an investigation as not.

Even now he eyed her suspiciously. "You've gone awfully quiet. What are you thinking?"

It wouldn't go over well if she said she was thinking it was hypocritical of him to listen to her analysis of who might have done it, without being willing to let her help look into it all a little more. Instead, Megan said, "I was trying to think if anybody had said anything else that might be useful to you," which wasn't far off the truth. "Where's your young man? The young guard, I mean," she corrected as Doyle's eyes widened. "The one who was with you Monday. Garda Farrell, I think. Shouldn't he be here, if you're here on official business?"

Doyle's jaw snapped shut, and color flushed his jowls, which Megan bet meant he wasn't there on official business at all. That was interesting. She grabbed for the next thought she had, trying to go on casually as if she hadn't really meant anything by the question at all. "I thought Aisling might fancy him. Although what am I doing matchmaking when the poor girl has just lost her father . . . listen to me go on. Look at her mother," she added with a little more sincerity, and Doyle, the tension in his jaw loosening a little, glanced into the office toward mother and daughter.

Jenny Flynn had borderline ransacked Seamus's desk—all the previously tidy stacks of papers, books, and notes were scattered everywhere—but had evidently failed to find what she was looking for, because she'd left the desk and was cooing at Aisling's side. The angle of her head said she was trying hard to hear both ends of the phone conversation her daughter was having, although every time Aisling spoke, she walked away from her mother. It led to an odd-looking little chase around the room, Jenny scooting along in Aisling's wake like a particularly needy puppy. "I wonder if I can distract her again. Although it didn't do enough good yesterday, if she's back again today."

"I'll talk to her," Doyle said with a grim note. "If she's after Nolan's fortune, then maybe she'll let slip how she took herself down to the holy well and pushed him in." He went into the office, and Megan, not prepared to find herself thrown out, followed so she was back in Aisling's eyesight and memory. The girl gave a quick exhalation of relief at seeing her.

Doyle, deft as a sheepdog, separated Jenny from Aisling and escorted the older woman out of the room with a brief show of charm that Megan hadn't previously seen displayed at all. Aisling finished her phone conversation and threw herself into one of the office sofas, face swelling with tears and emotion. "I thought she was gone. I wish she was. Isn't that awful of me?"

"It's not." Megan came to sit beside her and offered a hug. "I've only known her for ninety minutes and I'm already exhausted by her, so, no, I don't think it's awful at all. Ais, I don't mean to be pushy, but both your uncle and your mother really want access to your father's computer. Do you know why?"

Aisling, sniffling, said, "No, but I think we should find out. There's a key in the office door, go on and lock it so, and I've got his password book." She darted a glance at Megan. "You won't tell Uncle Adam and Mam, will you?"

"Definitely not."

Aisling sniffled again. "Then let's see what Da was hiding."

CHAPTER 16

Megan went to lock the office door while Aisling booted the computer up, then dragged another chair over to the computer desk. Aside from the computer chair itself, the furniture in Nolan's office was not intended to be dragged: the lightest piece was an upholstered armchair, although after Megan had wrested it into place, she realized there were also at least two footstools that would have been much easier to move. At least she'd earned sitting down, after all that effort.

Aisling had the computer unlocked by then, although they both stared at Seamus's desktop in dismay for a moment. There were dozens of folders, files, pictures, and notes piled on top of each other, as if the computer desktop was as physical as the wooden one in front of them. Aisling, faintly, said, "This always drove me mental when I'd watch Da looking for things, but he knew where everything was. I kept after him to tidy it up, but he said, why bother when he knew where things were? This is why, Da." Her voice shook with frustration and grief. "This is exactly why. So somebody else can find their way through your mess."

She pushed the keyboard out of the way and put her head down, sobbing with sudden, overwhelming grief. Megan rubbed between the girl's shoulder blades, making no effort to calm or direct her attention elsewhere. After long minutes, Aisling lifted her head again, face swollen and red, a wet spot of tears and mucus dribbling off the edge of the desk and onto her shirt and lap. She wiped futilely at her face, and Megan rose to find a mostly empty box of tissues next to one of the couches. Aisling blew her nose and did her best to dry her tears while saying, "Sorry," hoarsely.

"Not at all," Megan said gently. "You're going through a lot, sweetheart. It's okay to fall apart as often as you need."

"You're kinder than Uncle Adam," Aisling whispered. "He's telling me to pull myself together, put on a brave front, when I can barely breathe from one minute to the next."

Megan sighed. "People react to grief differently, and he's an older man, a different generation, with different social expectations of how he shows emotion. Generally, men are allowed to be angry and women aren't, but men are almost *only* allowed to be angry. Everything else has to get crammed down. So it might be that he's doing his best to help you in the only way he knows how."

"Or he could be an arsehole," Aisling whispered harshly.

"Also possible," Megan agreed with a brief smile.

"Look, that tea is probably cool enough to drink, so why don't you have some of it, and eat the soup while we try to go through these files? It'll help."

"Will it really?" Aisling pulled the tray of food to her obediently anyway, then scooted to the side so Megan could take over the mouse and keyboard.

"It actually will," Megan promised. "Not with the big-picture stuff, but it'll help in the moment, and we get through the big picture one moment at a time, so, yeah. It'll help."

Aisling nodded and, between spoonsful of soup, mumbled her way through suggestions as to where and what Megan should open on the computer desktop. Megan followed her instructions at first, then opened the file explorer window and searched on "Aisling."

Floods of files came up. One, helpfully, was actually titled "Last Will and Testament," and Megan clicked that open in the background while scrolling through hundreds of other files. Most of them were pictures, and after a minute of trying to remember how, she convinced the computer to disregard photo files in favor of documents and pdfs. That reduced the number from thousands to dozens, and both women exhaled in relief, then shared a half-smiling glance as they heard each other do so.

"Can you look at the will?" Aisling asked in a small voice. "I'm not sure I'm brave enough to."

"If you're sure." At Aisling's nod, Megan opened the will, and Aisling turned away, concentrating on her soup while Megan skimmed the legal document. "Your father has you listed as his sole heir, Ais."

194   *Catie Murphy*

A shudder of relief went through the girl, although she looked back at Megan with huge, uncertain eyes. "Is that right, though? What about Mam?"

"She's not in the will." Megan started to open a web browser on Seamus's computer, then, feeling peculiar about doing so, used her phone instead. "Um. Okay, the internet says . . . oh, man. Your father should have divorced Jenny, Ais. She's apparently entitled to a third of the estate even if the will provides otherwise."

"A *third*? Jesus wept!"

"It's better than it could be," Megan said with a wince. "If he hadn't left a will, she'd have been entitled to two-thirds. I don't suppose they did get divorced and you don't know about it?"

"It'd be a weird thing not to tell me," Aisling said under her breath, but shrugged. "I don't . . . well, look for divorce papers, maybe? My name wouldn't be on them, I wouldn't think."

"Mmph, yeah." Megan searched the computer first for "divorce," then "separation," and exhaled sharply as the second came up with a hit. The file spilled open, date stamped almost five years earlier, with a scan of a petition for legal separation signed by both Seamus Nolan and Jenny Flynn. "Oh, holy . . . that could change everything. This"—she waved her phone—"says a deed of separation will frequently mean the married couple have renounced their entitlements to inheritance in the case of the death of the spouse. And it's been long enough now that they could have been divorced, if they wanted to be. Or maybe not wanted to be, but you know what I mean."

"I do. I know it was a big step forward when they made divorce legal at all back in the dark ages, but I don't know why they had to make it so hard. Years of legal separation before you can file for divorce and every bloody divorce has to go to court to be heard. I'm never getting married," Aisling snarled.

Megan, torn between sympathy and a touch of laughter, said, "It was the *nineties*, not the dark ages, Ais."

The girl sniffed. "It was *ages* ago. Way before I was born. Christ, I wish he'd divorced her, though. Does it say?" She finally looked at the screen, reading the separation document. "Does it *say* she gave up her inheritance rights?"

"It doesn't look like it," Megan said as she skimmed the document. The language in it was remarkably informal, making Megan wince. "It looks like they might have hammered it out on their own without solicitors. Which seems stupid, honestly. Why would your father not use his lawyer?"

"Because Mam couldn't afford one of her own," Aisling said through her teeth. "I'd bet that's why. She'll have wheedled and cajoled and promised him it would all be grand and they didn't have to do things the hard way. He'd have offered to pay for hers, and she'd have said how could she trust a solicitor he was paying for, and he'd have said how could she trust an agreement they came to without a solicitor then, and she'd have said that was different, she *knew* him, and she'd give him that huge soppy-eyed look he was so weak for, and he'd have agreed."

Megan's eyebrows rose through that whole speech,

until she felt like they'd melded with her hairline. "That sounds like you knew your parents pretty well."

"I loved Da with all my heart, but he was stupid when it came to Mam, and you've met her. She's a weasel. I used to wonder why she'd left me and I hated her and I loved her and I was desperate for her approval, but when I was twelve or thirteen . . ." She trailed off, eyes losing their focus as she looked at something out of memory. "She needed money, and came by with Aoife, my wee little sister, who was only three. She left her in the kitchen with the staff, because she couldn't have the reminder of her other lovers right there when she was asking Da for money, now, could she? And I listened to her cozy up to Da, and I could hear him . . . *melting*. It was like he was made of sugar, and she was the rain, falling down all around him and washing his will away. She didn't ask about me once. After a while I went to play with Aoife, and I heard her drive away."

Aisling fell silent, still looking at nothing, before eventually saying, "It was four hours before she came back to get Aoife. She must have been most of the way to Cork when she realized she hadn't brought her home. We were still together, Aoife and myself, and she said to me, she said, 'thank you, darling, what a lovely child you are, watching my baby for so long. Does your mother work at the house? Let me give you a tip, for your troubles.'"

Megan inadvertently said, "Oh, Ais," in horror, and the girl blinked at her, slowly refocusing.

"I took the tip," she said in a thin voice. "Forty quid

it was, and I watched her walk away with my half sister without her ever knowing it was me, until Aoife looked back and cried 'Aisling?' She went white, she did, my mother. She came back laughing, trilling like she does, saying how funny she was and did I think she was funny, but I knew then, didn't I? She literally didn't know who I was. And from then on I could see her. It's not fun, being twelve and seeing your parents for who they are. So, yes, I knew them well enough. Da would do anything for her, and she'd do nothing for anyone but her own self. If the inheritance rights weren't written out of the deed of separation, it's because she'll have simpered at him and said an artist's life is so precarious, didn't he want to provide her with some kind of support if something happened to him, and he would have bent right over. The weak bastard," she said without heat. "The poor, stupid, weak bastard, and now he's left me fucked, hasn't he."

"Your solicitor is going to have to answer that," Megan said, all too aware it ended with an unspoken "but."

One corner of Aisling's mouth turned up in a thin smile. "'But.' Yeah. Great. Grand. Brilliant. Let's see what other shite we've got in store." She turned back to the computer, randomly opening files and waiting for them to load before finding the newest ones according to their date stamps. "Useless, garbage, rubbish," she announced to most of them, clicking them closed almost faster than Megan could glance through their text.

One flashed by, and Megan blurted, "Wait," as

Aisling clicked it shut, then pulled it up again from the recent documents list. "What the heck is a '*banchomarbae*'? Oh, Brehon law, I know . . . absolutely nothing about that except I've heard the words."

"It's the old law of Ireland, the law of the kings and poets," Aisling said vaguely. "I don't know what *banchomarbae* means, except something to do with women, obviously. Oh, because 'ban'—"

"Is the Irish for 'woman,' I know. Scroll down."

Aisling did, both of them reading fragmented notes that Seamus Nolan had clearly left for himself: - *banchomarbae: female landholder in absence of male kin, - Brehon law overturned/illegalized by James I, - argument to now overthrown British law in favour of ancient Irish tradition, - full of shite, I know, but it'll play well and maybe gain support/time to get the law properly changed, - also ah the irony, Anglo-Saxon landholder reverting to Brehon law for daughter's inheritance of the damn title, - approach British crown??? as Irish courts obviously reluctant to make a decision on this*

Megan, typing into her phone, said, "*Banch* . . . I can't say that one, but this says he's right, it was an old law that said women could inherit if a father didn't have a living son. It was a, huh, they call it a 'life-interest,' basically inheriting for the woman's lifetime, after which it would revert to her father's kin."

"I don't have any," Aisling said. "Except Uncle Adam, obviously, but if he doesn't die before me, I'll make sure he does." She paused briefly, trying to make that make sense, then muttered, "You know what I mean. What if I had kids, though? A son, if we're being patriarchal about it. Wouldn't he inherit? Because he'd be my father's line, too, right?"

"Apparently not, according to Brehon law," Megan said in mild astonishment as she read on. "Not unless, ha! Not unless the landholding is 'insubstantial.' I think your three thousand acres would be considered substantial. But if you don't have any other relatives, I don't see how it *couldn't* go to your theoretical kids, yeah."

Aisling curled her lip again. "Some bastard would probably run a DNA test and find some eighth cousin nine times removed living in Australia under an assumed name and claim they were the male heir. No wonder Da was trying to get the law changed."

"See," Megan said almost absently, "see, that's like defining new species of whales based on minute genetic differences. I mean, I *guess*, but as a non-scientific layperson, if you can't tell the difference from the outside, it seems it's like cutting it very narrowly. So if you have to rely on a DNA test to locate an heir, especially one who isn't trying to locate *you*, that seems sort of like it's cheating, to me. It wouldn't have worked, a hundred years ago."

"Aristocracy would one hundred percent have used genetic testing a hundred years ago if they could've," Aisling pointed out dryly. "But yeah. It'd be a load of crap."

Megan, glance bouncing between Seamus's notes and the Brehon law information on her phone, said, "You're sort of aristocracy in name only anyway, right? Because Ireland's a republic and the government doesn't recognize any of the titles. How come your dad didn't just renounce his peerage?"

Aisling sighed explosively. "Believe it or not, he couldn't. There's a way to renounce it in Britain, but because Ireland isn't under British law anymore, there's actually no way to renounce a British title under Irish law. You can not use it, and Da didn't, really, except to be theatrical in the papers, to gain attention for his re-wilding project and whatnot, but you can't actually renounce it. It can only die out."

"That's a little morbid."

"Yeah, but if it didn't come along with Uncle Adam wanting to sell off the estate, I'd just let it die with him anyway. I don't need to be a peer."

"Arguably nobody needs to be a peer."

Aisling's sighs turned to a soft laugh. "Legit. I'm sure there are loads of posh bastards in Britain who would disagree, but it's bad enough being rich. Having a title to pretend you're superior with is taking the piss."

"Well, if your uncle is right, you're not that rich anyway, because your father put all the money into rewilding." Never mind that the estate was thousands of acres of salable land, which amounted to being rich on paper if not in practice, and never mind, Megan thought, the likelihood that there was rather more cash on hand than Adam wanted to admit to. The goal was to make Aisling laugh again, even if only briefly, and she did. Megan, reading about Brehon law and the *banchomarbae* one more time, added, "Did you actually talk to your father's solicitor yet? I wonder if they know about his plan to try using ancient Irish law in his favor. Or in your favor, I guess."

"I haven't. I don't know. Will it even matter, if Mum's going to get a third of the estate anyway? If I can't protect it *all* . . ." Sadness crept over Aisling's face again. "Well, I guess protecting part of it is better than nothing, but—and then there's the waste site? Who could have dumped farming waste on the estate, Megan? Like, there's loads of land that used to belong to the estate that was returned to tenant farmers a hundred years ago, and I don't know what kind of relationship my great-grandfather and grandfather had with them, but Da, at least, he's worked with all the farmers around here. I think—I thought—we were friends, but if they've done this, if anybody's done it . . ." She slumped in her chair, visible exhaustion crashing through her. In a tiny voice, she said, "I don't want any of this to be happening."

"I know." Megan sighed and leaned over to offer an awkward hug. "I know, sweetheart. I'm sorry. Who—" She broke off as the doorknob rattled, and an angry, questioning sound echoed in the hall outside. Aisling shot her a wide-eyed look, shut off the computer, and Megan dragged the armchair back into place as Aisling got up to wobble toward the door.

Seamus's password book was still on the computer desk. Megan lunged for it and shoved it under her jumper as Aisling unlocked and opened the door to admit her uncle, whose face was a mask of tension.

"Why was the door locked? Those bloody pagans are out front wailing like banshees and surrounding

O'Malley's media team. If Patrick doesn't get them out of here—where is he?" Adam glowered around the office. "What'd you do with Detective Sergeant Doyle?"

"You mean the detective who's apparently running personal security for you out here on your private property?" Megan asked coolly. "He left with Ms. Flynn a while ago. I must have accidentally locked the door when I closed it after the staff brought food for Aisling, sorry about that. What happens if Doyle doesn't get them out of here soon?"

Nolan went red and white and back again in stages as Megan threw answers and questions alike at him. "They're obstructing media access—"

"On private property," Megan said. "Aren't you allowed to throw them out? Either the pagans or the media," she added thoughtfully. "Although I guess neither would play well. I suppose that's why you want Doyle doing it. He's an official presence, even if you called him up on his own time for your own reasons. Why *do* you want him here, Mr. Nolan?"

Aisling's gaze ping-ponged between them, the question of how Megan knew Doyle wasn't there officially writ so large on her face it could probably be read from the moon, but she didn't ask. "Is it," Megan wondered, "that if he's here, he can't be somewhere else actually investigating? I'm beginning to think that would be to your benefit, honestly. This all looks pretty bad for you, doesn't it? Wh—"

"Get out!" Nolan advanced on her, and to Megan's astonishment, Aisling grabbed her hand and ran.

CHAPTER 17

Megan whispered, "What?" as Aisling pulled her through the door and along the hall, and she only managed to drag the girl to a stop halfway down a set of narrow back stairs Megan hadn't seen before. "Aisling, why did you run? Has your uncle been violent to you in the past?"

To Adam Nolan's credit, Aisling looked so completely shocked that Megan believed her startled, "What? No, never. But you're my only friend here," she added more quietly. "I don't want him to get the staff to throw you out, especially because I'm really not sure if they'd listen to me over himself. I need somebody on my side."

Megan, thinking of Nora in the tearoom and Ian out in the gardens, said, "I think you might have more friends here than you know, but I *am* here to help you if I can, and you're right, getting into a power struggle isn't going to help you at all." She bit her lip, suddenly feeling sly, and said, "Should we go see if I'm right about more friends than you know?"

"Yes? How?" Aisling's expression wobbled between hopeful, curious, and grief-stricken. Megan opened her arms impulsively, offering a hug, and the girl sniffled gratefully as she accepted the embrace, standing there until another set of footsteps on the stairs was followed by an apologetic throat-clearing.

Aisling sniffled again, wiping her eyes and patting uselessly at the teary spot she'd left on Megan's shoulder as she stepped away. "Oh, I'm sorry, I'm a mess."

"It's okay," Megan promised.

The woman who'd cleared her throat, standing several steps below them with an armload of household materials, looked mortified to have interrupted Aisling's mourning. "I'm so sorry. And I'm so sorry, Miss Nolan." The first was clearly an apology, and the second, condolences, both of which wrung weepy smiles from Aisling.

"It's okay. And thank you. Here, please." She squished back against one wall, and Megan stepped back, across from her, so the woman could pass between them. She ducked her head apologetically and scurried between them, shoulders hunched like she could make herself small and invisible through body language. A moment later she disappeared through a different door than the one they'd come through.

"Actual servants' stairs," Megan said with a brief smile. "I knew that's what they were, but I didn't expect to meet staff on them."

Aisling tried for a wobbly smile of her own. "Most

of the staff who don't work in the public part of the house do use them. I used to, too, all the time when I was little. They're faster, a lot of the time. And good for hiding if your da is looking for you to do a chore." She fought off tears again, trying to distract herself by asking, "You were planning something?"

"Oh! Does the back road have security cameras? Also, here." The hug had reminded Megan she'd put Seamus's password book under her jumper, and now she offered it to the young woman, who blinked, then smiled unhappily.

"Thanks. And yeah, of course. All of the estate's access points do."

Megan's eyebrows rose, thoughts leaping ahead. "How long do you keep the footage for?"

Aisling looked blank. "I've no idea. Why?"

"Well, let's start with the back road. I was talking to Doyle about suspects, and it struck me that if there was footage, we could see if anyone left the house early Monday morning."

Brief confusion fell to dark comprehension in Aisling's eyes. "You mean, we can look to see if Uncle Adam snuck out after Da to knock him in the well."

"I wouldn't have put it that way, but . . ." Megan spread her hands in agreement. Aisling nodded and, equilibrium temporarily restored by having a goal in mind, tottered down the steps ahead of Megan. The stairs were steep and covered with heavy-wearing, plain carpet that, like the handrails, came from a more recent era than the steps themselves. Unlike the main halls of the magnificent old house, there were no beautifully worked cornices or ornate baseboards: these were plain, intended to render servants invisible, and not made with their comfort or appreciation for beauty in mind.

This set also opened straight into the kitchen, although the door swung inward, not outward, so that someone coming out of the stairs wouldn't risk slamming the door into someone on its other side. That was another sign of it being merely practical: Irish houses tended to have doors that opened inward, with the bulk of the room hidden by the door as it opened. Megan, accustomed to American doors that generally opened into a room against the wall, had yet to adapt to the custom of "hiding" the room behind its open door, and found it irritating.

"Aisling!" A few voices chorused the young woman's name, along with another one or two who called her *Miss Nolan*. For a moment, people—mostly young women—swarmed around Aisling, offering hugs and comfort while either completely ignoring Megan, or eyeing her with a little suspicion. She waved a small, unobtrusive greeting, and stayed out of the way while the staff and friends checked in on the young lady of the house. Ais *did* have more friends here than she thought, but Megan suspected there was still a slight class barrier that could make things uncomfortable unless Aisling came into the staff's space, as she'd just done.

Within a few minutes, they were let loose to go to the security room, which actually turned out to be set in a modern outbuilding far enough away from the main house that Megan hadn't noticed it before. Ais-

ling led the way confidently, though, and knocked briskly
before letting herself and Megan into the building.

To Megan's relief, Doyle wasn't there. Maybe not
yet, or maybe he'd already been and gone, but either
way, they wouldn't be interfering with each other.
There were two young men, one of whom lurched to
his feet and swayed when they entered, trying very
hard to look like he hadn't been napping. Unfortunately for him, he'd had his head down, and there was a
large, round red mark on his forehead from its weight
pressing against his arms.

The other, more awake and therefore less guilty,
stood up more slowly, in obvious surprise. "Miss Nolan?
What can we do for you?"

"It's Johnny, right? And Mick," Aisling said with a
smile toward the red-marked youth. "I just wanted to
review the security footage for Monday morning, if
that's possible. For the back road first, please."

Both of them blinked at her, then slightly more cau-
tiously at Megan before casting questioning looks at
Aisling, who gave a rather fierce little smile. "This is
Megan Malone. You'll know her as the Murder Driver."

Megan bit back a groan as the lads' faces absolutely lit
up. The awake one—Johnny—blurted, "You're deadly!"
and Mick stepped up to elbow him with a cackle. "Deadly,
like! No pun intended!"

Johnny looked startled, then gleeful. "Yeah, like!
Deadly-deadly!"

"She doesn't kill people," Aisling told them both se-
verely. "She only solves mysteries."

Neither of them were in the least derailed by the inconvenient truth as they kept elbowing each other and giggling. Then Johnny got the run of himself and sat back down at the desk to start pulling up files from earlier in the week. "Monday morning shouldn't be hard. You'll want it early, yeah? From when your da went out, I'd say." His laughter fell away and much more solemnly, he said, "I'm dead sorry, I am, miss. Your da was a nice old duck."

Aisling, teary-eyed again, managed a smile anyway. "He was, wasn't he? Thanks."

Johnny nodded as Mick sat beside him, and for a minute or two they got the right files loaded and then jumped to the early-morning time stamps, which took a matter of seconds. Megan, thinking of how security tapes had been reviewed in the media of her childhood—and presumably in real life at that time, too— couldn't help chuckling quietly at the speed of it all.

"Oh, there's Da," Aisling whispered. Her father, robes girded, rode down the long back avenue on his bicycle, its headlight a bright spot in the dark morning. There were three cameras along the avenue, one near the house, one at the ridiculously tall iron gate, and one in between. The time stamps on the videos indicated how long it took Seamus Nolan, helmet balanced precariously atop his head, to get from the house to the back gate, but without the bike's headlight, Megan didn't think any of it could be seen. It was *dark* in the woods at six o'clock on a January morning. If someone had walked out, trusting their knowledge of the road, she wasn't sure the security cameras would have noticed them.

A light did come on when he opened the gate, though, so anybody, on foot or otherwise, would at least have triggered that. Once he was gone, Johnny fast-forwarded through the next several hours. Three tradesmen's vehicles came in, and two of them left again in that time. Megan noted down the names on the sides of the trucks, and very quietly said, "I don't suppose there's another angle to see into those trucks as they're leaving?"

"Mmmnnn, yeah, I dunno," Johnny said rather noncommittally, but Mick scrolled through another set of files and opened one that showed the back parking lot from the house's point of view. The trucks—one butcher, a milkman, and a delivery of veg—drove up one at a time, parking in view of the camera, and the two that left only had one person in them. Johnny said, "Well done, mate," and Mick looked satisfied, then turned inquisitively to Megan to see if she thought he'd done well too.

She nodded. "The last one didn't leave until—" She hesitated, hating to say it in front of Aisling, but ended up sighing and finishing, "Until after I'd found the body anyway, so no one slipped out that way. What about the front drive?"

"Those gates don't even unlock until nine without a house key," Johnny said, but he pulled the files up anyway.

To Megan's astonishment, just a few minutes after the time stamp said Seamus had left through the back avenue, Aisling's unmistakable MINI Cooper drove up to the estate's front gates, opened them, and disappeared down the driveway.

* * *

A long, shocked silence fell before Aisling protested, "That was never me," in bewilderment. "What would I be doing up that early?"

Megan, who distinctly remembered the only reason she'd ever been up that early at nineteen was because she'd joined the military and *had* to be, instinctively felt that was a perfectly reasonable question.

It wasn't, though, one that could provide any kind of meaningful alibi, or explanation for why Aisling's MINI was going for a drive at six in the morning, whether she was in it or not. She turned to the girl, genuinely baffled. "Does anybody else have your keys?" She paused, trying to remember from when she'd driven the vehicle. Aisling hadn't shut it off when they'd traded seats, so Megan hadn't entirely noticed. ". . . do new MINI Coopers even *have* keys?"

"There's a power switch that's kind of like a key," Aisling said faintly. "But no. I mean, yes? There's a fob to unlock it with and I've the only one, but the key doesn't even come out. If I left it unlocked, and I do at home—why wouldn't I?—someone could drive it away." The implications were beginning to set in, and her color went from white to red and back again. "I never killed my da!"

"I believe you." Megan spoke gently, but there wasn't a gentle way to ask, "But do you have an alibi for Monday morning, Aisling? Just in case?"

Aisling stared at her, eyes bugged. "Why *would* I kill him? The whole bloody inheritance mess, I didn't even know about that, why would I bring it down on my own head? My mother, my uncle, all of it, and I *love* the rewilding project, Megan, I'd never do it any harm, and nothing but harm can come from Da's death!"

"I know," Megan said, still as gently as she could. "I take it you don't have an alibi, then?"

The girl flushed scarlet from her collarbones to her hairline. "Ian was with me until he had to get up for work at half seven."

"Oh! That's brilliant!" Megan heard herself and barely stopped a laugh; the two young men completely failed to stop theirs, and the entire room very briefly dissolved into a kind of catcalling, hooting cheer of gleeful approval. Aisling put her face in her hands, blushing so hard her skin nearly glowed through her fingers, and Megan, embarrassed for her, said, "I mean—!"

"I know what you mean," Aisling said into her palms. "But c'mon, lads!"

"But it's grand so," Johnny said, still laughing. "A little bloody *Lady Chatterley's Lover*, yeah mate?"

"Oh my *God*! It's not—we're not—it's not—!" That, apparently, was the extent of Aisling's ability to defend what was certainly, at least on the surface, a cross-class romance.

"It is, and ye are," Johnny said happily. "Ian's a sound lad, that's brilliant so. Well done you, I say. Look, though, who's driving your car, then?"

"I don't know," Aisling said, drawn back to the topic at hand. "Most of the staff aren't here overnight, so it's . . ." She trailed off, then, unhappily, said, "It's most likely to be Uncle Adam, isn't it?"

"Is there a camera at the gate so we can see into the car?" Megan asked. "Or would it have been in the camera looking at the back parking lot's field of view?"

"I'd parked 'round the side," Aisling said with a shake of her head. "There were trucks in the way when I came home last."

"And the gate cameras look out, not in," Johnny said, but skimmed forward through the video. "They had to come back, though, right?"

They clearly had, because Aisling's car hadn't gone missing, but there was no footage of their return. Johnny stared at the screen a few seconds, then switched to the back-avenue cameras, which did show the MINI coming back up the drive later in the morning, after the delivery trucks had made their runs. Reflections from the trees against the windshield made it too hard to see into the car, and Megan made an impatient noise. "You can't really blow it up and fix the resolution like they do in movies, can you."

"Wouldn't that be grand," Johnny said dryly. "Maybe they park in the camera's view, though."

"They didn't," Aisling said. "I'd have noticed if the car had moved."

Megan wondered if she *would* have, given she'd have learned about her father's death in the meantime, but she didn't bring it up, because the car had, in fact, been returned to the out-of-camera location where Aisling had originally parked it. "Was anyone visiting? Anyone who didn't like your father?"

Aisling sat, weariness slumping her shoulders. "No.

Not that I know about, anyway. Maybe there's CCTV footage from the main road?"

"Oh!" Megan straightened. "That reminds me, I was going to ask the visitors' centre—but also, Johnny? How far back do you keep these archives? And do you review them before they're deleted or anything?"

"We've a server for them." Johnny gestured toward a second door in the office, one Megan hadn't taken any particular notice of. "That's the cool room for it. Video takes up a lot of storage space, even low-grade security video, and we've a lot of cameras around the estate. It's wiped quarterly, but not all at once. So today we'd be overwriting what we captured three months ago like."

"Oh." Megan exhaled noisily. "I don't suppose anyone here knows how to tell at a glance how long toxic waste has been sitting somewhere."

Even Aisling, who knew what she was talking about, gave Megan a dubious look, and she ended up chuckling quietly. "Yeah, no, I didn't think so. Well, okay, look, are there any cameras or access points near these coordinates?" She got out her phone and the map Rafael had provided with the GPS coordinates of the waste dump, and the two young men, now nonplussed, scanned through the estate's cameras' locations to see if any of them matched up.

"The closest is half a kilometer away," Mick finally said, volunteering almost the first words he'd spoken since Megan had been there. "On a corner of the estate where a footpath went through before the walls went up. The story has it that the tenant farmers couldn't fight the landlords over the land, but by God, they'd keep their footpath. They kept knocking the wall down, just wide enough to walk through."

"I'm surprised they weren't shot for it," Megan said flatly.

Mick shrugged one shoulder. "They said some men were, and that four watchmen were killed and two had their legs broken before the next viscount on the land gave up the fight and walled the pathway itself off. You can see it in the satellite imagery."

He pulled one up, and indeed, there was a section of narrow, walled pathway connecting one side of the estate's corner to the other. The path's walls had clearly seen better days, and the new-growth forest was obviously eating its way into it, but Megan made a humming sound and leaned in to look more closely. "Do you think there's enough broken wall there you might be able to drag tanks through? Can you overlay that with the GPS coordinates I gave you?"

"Yeh, a'course." Mick did, making it clear that the old pathway was by far the closest entrance point to the waste site, but also showing that whenever the satellite images had been taken, the waste hadn't yet been dumped. Before she asked, Mick said, "Most of this imagery is a couple years' old, see, here's the date." He zoomed in, hovering his cursor over the image, and a date popped up: nearly three years earlier.

Megan stepped back. "Rats. And your video surveillance only goes back a few months. That's a lot of time in between."

"We can look." Johnny shrugged helpfully as Megan glanced toward him. "It's no bother, is it? And if we find something, we'll be helping the murder driver solve a crime, yeah?"

Whether Seamus Nolan had been murdered or not, the waste dump was definitely a crime all by itself. Megan, a little startled at the thought, nodded, and Johnny looked delighted. "We'll get on it, boss."

She eyed him. "Was that an American accent?"

The kid blushed almost as brightly as Aisling had, and she laughed and patted his shoulder. "A good attempt, anyway. At least I could tell what you were going for. All right, look, I want to go check something else out—and oh, God, the dogs!—but I'll come back later this afternoon to see if you've found anything, okay?"

Johnny opened his mouth, obviously prepared to take another stab at the American accent, then blushed harder and only nodded. Mick, rather hopefully, said, "Dogs?"

Megan grinned. "I'll bring them back to meet you later, too, okay?"

"Brilliant." Both the young men turned back to their computers, and Megan offered Aisling a hand out of the chair she'd taken.

"I don't want to," Aisling said dismally as they left the security office. "Whatever it is, I don't want to."

"Tell you what," Megan suggested, "why don't you go spend a little time with Ian, and stay out of everybody else's line of sight for a while? If I can find anything useful out at the visitors' centre, I'll text, okay? And in the meantime, you just be gentle with yourself."

"Okay. I'll try." Aisling offered a weak smile, and they walked back to the gardens. Aisling peeled off to go find Ian, and Megan, feeling like a fire had been lit under her, marched around to the front of the house, then slowed to a startled halt.

There wasn't exactly a blockade of human beings spread over the greens that the great, swan-like façade reached across, but the gathering of people who stood out a little from the conventional norm had expanded. Nearly all of them were long-haired, men and women alike, and a considerable percentage were in robes not unlike the ones Seamus Nolan had died in. Some were of a more formal nature than Seamus's: exquisite embroidery splashed across hems and necklines, and made of heavier materials than the lightweight cotton Seamus had worn, with rosary beads that she still found incongruous for pagan practitioners. A lot of those people were also wearing sandals or going barefoot, which Megan thought must be pretty cold on a misty January afternoon.

Others were dressed a little more like Seamus himself had been, hiking boots and jeans and tunics or robes over those, but they were still unusual compared to most modern wear. As Megan watched, a few of the more formally garbed people gathered together, taking one another's hands and lifting them. They lifted their voices, too, in a song as unexpected as their look, because it was familiar to Megan: it was called "The

Parting Glass," a traditional song sung for funerals and final goodbyes. They had sung it at her grandfather's funeral, and his family had sung it when he had emigrated from Ireland nearly a century earlier.

Megan found herself standing alone on the grandiose steps, watching the gathering of Seamus's pagan friends, and weeping as they sang.

CHAPTER 18

Media had gathered as the druids sang, although Megan didn't realize it until the song was done and the vocalists had come down from the steps, forming little knots of embraces and quiet discussions. She could hear the sorrow in their voices, and, as various people from the media began to intrude on their mourning, exasperation. "No," someone said impatiently to a microphone, and then a woman with wild black hair and a mildly forbidding expression put herself between the speaker and the interviewer.

"No," she repeated more politely, "it wasn't a planned gathering. More of a—" Humor creased her face, making her look considerably less formidable. "More of a pagan flash mob. Seamus Nolan was a well-loved member of our community, and a number of us felt we should come here today to show our support for each other and his family."

She spoke very well, clearly and with good projection, like someone who was accustomed to not only talking in public, but also to handling people who made mockery of her faith. Megan moved closer, trying to hear the reporter's questions, too, as the woman shook her head. "Why would we not sing it? Surely you're not gatekeeping traditional music now. It's a song to say goodbye to someone you've lost, no matter what faith you come from, and as you well know, it's not the first loss in our community recently."

The reporter, who, Megan now saw, was the man who'd recognized her at the heritage centre, stumbled in his answer, and the druidic speaker took the opportunity to press her advantage. "Now, I'll be happy to answer more of your questions if you'd like to approach my personal assistant to set up an interview, but you are, at the moment, interrupting a gathering of mourners, and I'm quite certain you wouldn't want to intrude on our grief."

She turned away with a rush of dark hair, leaving the reporter looking as if he hadn't quite caught the number of the bus that had just hit him. Megan ducked her head, smiling, and tried to slip by without being noticed.

It almost worked, but then his voice followed her, sharp and enthusiastic, like he knew she was a story that wouldn't handle him the way he'd just been handled. "Megan Malone, the Murder Driver, here at the scene of the crime again! Does this mean Seamus Nolan met with foul play? How is your investigation going, Megan? This is Peader Haughey with FMRadio Now on One Oh One Point—"

"No comment," Megan said as charmingly as she could, and scurried away while he was still finishing his station's call information. The smooth radio voice kept rolling right along, but he glared at her as she ducked into the gathering of druids with a mumbled apology at interrupting. The woman who had been talking to the reporter shot a look past Megan at him, then, with an expression of recognition and joy mingled with grief, drew Megan straight into an embrace and said, "Thank you for coming, it's good to see you," as if they were old, old friends.

Megan almost laughed as she returned the hug. After a long heartbeat, the woman murmured, "He's fecked off now," and released her with an apologetic smile. "Sorry for grabbing you like that."

"Not at all. It works, doesn't it?"

"Best way I've ever found to protect other women," the dark-haired woman replied. She was considerably taller than Megan, with golden undertones to her pale skin, and had dark, snapping eyes. "Pretend you know them, ignore the arsehole, run away together. I had a two-year relationship start that way once."

Megan did laugh then. "Really?"

"Well, it was a bit on and off," the other woman admitted. "Are you all right?"

"I am. He's just looking for a story. Are you? You handled him beautifully."

The woman grinned and curtsied, which worked well with her robes, and made the rosary beads she wore swing nicely. "I'm grand so, and he's a leech. Did

I hear him say you're the Murder Driver, though? It's Megan, isn't it?"

"You know, I did not know I was going to end up, like, more famous than most people, if not exactly famous, because of all this. Yeah, I'm Megan. And you're . . . ?"

"Carla. Nice to meet you. You were a friend of Seamus's?"

"I found the body." Megan winced as she said it, wishing she'd chosen softer words, but Carla took it in good stride, sympathy flashing across her face.

"That must have been hard for you. Are you well?"

"It wasn't my favorite way to start a day," Megan admitted with a sigh. "But yeah, I'm okay. You're a druid?"

"A witch," Carla said with a smile. "But there's some solidarity between the pagan practitioners, and Seamus was a sound lad. A friend."

"Why do you all wear rosary beads?" Megan blurted curiously. "They're not exactly pagan, are they?"

Carla curled her hand around her beads—black and white stones, almost marbles—and smiled as she lifted them to dangle their pendant, which was a carved Crann Bethadh, a Tree of Life. "Prayer beads, not rosaries. Rosaries *are* prayer beads, but—"

"Right," Megan said sheepishly. "Right, of course. I was thinking like all prayer beads were rosaries, not that rosaries were a subset of prayer beads. Okay, that makes sense. Thank you. And look, before I let you go, can I say, you all sang 'The Parting Glass' beautifully? I love it, and I wasn't expecting it, and it made me cry."

"A job well done, then." Carla's smile turned regret-

ful. "We've had a lot of chances to sing it lately. Well."
Weariness swept over her, aging her before she drew a
deep breath. "Not *lately*, but over these past few years.
Partly the way the world's gone, you know, with everything that's happened. That's been bad enough, but then
this is the third or fourth stupid accident that took
someone from the community on top of that, and none
of us have the spirit for it."

Megan breathed a wince. "Oh, God, I'm sorry.
That's awful."

"It is. It feels like more than we can handle, sometimes. Like we're already beaten down, everybody is,
and then just these stupid random accidents. It's exhausting." Carla smiled wearily. " 'Brigid's Curse,' that's
what some of us are calling it. I even know a few people who have left her worship to find another goddess,
to stay safe."

"Really? Do you think it'll work? I mean. Also: is
Brigid cursing people?"

"I doubt it," Carla said to both questions. "And if
she was, I assume she wouldn't have picked Seamus,
unless he had some dark secrets only known to him
and herself. No, there was a death down in Clare a few
years ago, and another in Galway not too long ago.
One was in the middle of a pilgrimage with half a
dozen other people there, so I'd say there was nothing
suspicious about it, only wretched luck."

"Pilgrimage to . . . ?"

"Other holy wells." Carla sighed. "The truth is, a lot
of them are a bit manky and not well-kept, and people
get careless. It breaks my own heart, but there's not

much to be done except raise funds to make them safer, and that puts up barriers to worship in its own way. The world's a complicated place."

"That's true enough. So you think Seamus just slipped?"

"On a dark misty morning? I'd say so. It doesn't make it any easier, though. Or any harder, maybe." Carla's gaze went beyond Megan, then returned for a brief smile. "Sorry, love. I've someone to talk to there. It was nice to meet you."

"You too. Thanks." Megan glanced over her shoulder as she slipped out of the druidic gathering, and accidentally almost caught the radio reporter's eye again. She grimaced and ducked behind somebody, mumbling, "Sorry," as she tried to get out of his line of view.

"No worries," a perfectly delicious male voice said. Megan blinked upward, realized she'd hidden behind Jack O'Malley, and barely cut off a laugh. He was even more attractive up close than he'd been from a stone's throw away, and his smile was inviting and sympathetic. "Vultures, aren't they?" he asked in a low voice. "They can be useful, but once they've got your scent . . ."

"Do vultures hunt by scent?" Megan wondered, and O'Malley's eyebrows furrowed so flawlessly that there really should have been a Hollywood film crew on hand to capture it.

"You know, I don't know. I'm going to have to look that up, but not until I'm no longer in the presence of the most interesting person within three square miles. You're Megan Malone, right? Jack O'Malley." He offered a hand, and Megan took it with a faint sense of disbelief. He had big square palms, slightly rough with calluses, and a warm, solid grip that didn't try to overwhelm. "I met some of your team earlier. I assume you're up to speed on the environmental disaster unfolding on this estate."

"Do you mean the waste spill or the rapid regrowth approach?"

O'Malley's brown eyes actually sparkled. "Oh, you are quick, aren't you? I mean the waste dump," he said more seriously. "Look, between yourself and myself, I *don't* like the Miawaki Method, but I can't truly fault Seamus for his efforts. Look what he's done with the estate inside of what, fifteen years? Would I rather he'd chosen a natural regrowth approach? I would so, it's true enough, but there's two thousand acres here that was field and meadow when his daughter was born, and now it's new forest at all stages of growth. And these ones," he said with an unexpectedly fond note as he made a small but encompassing gesture at the robe-clad mourners around them, "I mean, do I think they're mental? I do, a little, but they do love the land and will show up to put their bodies between the trees and the axes, which is a fair bit more than most people can be arsed to do, so I won't let the likes of Peader Haughey run them over if I can stand in the way."

"Wait, then why—I thought you and he were rivals?"

"Well, we are, were, in the papers like, weren't we? There's not much love for rewilding in this country, Megan Malone. Maybe not in any country, but certainly not this one. So Seamus and I, it's true we were always desperate for the same grants, but look," he said with a gesture at himself, "look, if you've got this, you use it, don't you?"

Megan, ill-advisedly, said, "I certainly would," and Jack laughed out loud.

"When we're done here, I'll be asking if I can get your number, then. But I know what I've got, it's true, and it makes for good airplay, doesn't it? And Seamus, the truth is, the man really believed, or believed as much as anyone does in anything, in his connection to Brigid and the land. So it was a game, wasn't it? Himself with the long hair and the connection to the roots of Ireland and myself with the pretty face and the conservative clothes, and together we made a fair good team, I'd say. Where one of us couldn't draw attention, the other could."

"But court cases? Isn't that a lot of drama and expense if you were really basically on the same page?"

"Well." O'Malley sighed. "Look, even those raised the profile, didn't they? Brought attention to rewilding projects, not just in Ireland, but across the European Union. And it wasn't that we didn't each of us believe in *our* methods over the others', so some of the fights got pretty tense, I won't deny that. But look, that waste site down there, I did find it—"

"How?"

O'Malley jolted, then let out a slow exhalation as Megan gazed expectantly up at him. "I was tipped off," he admitted. "I've no idea who. An anonymous letter, weeks ago, postmarked from the GPO. They didn't give me the exact coordinates, but they told me where to go looking, and I did."

Megan wrinkled her face. The General Post Office in Dublin was the largest post office in the country, and if she'd wanted to send something anonymously, she'd have used it, too. "I'm sorry," O'Malley went on. "If I knew, I'd tell you, or the authorities, because whoever tipped me off is probably the person who planted it. And I'd be lying if I said I was a man above using the tip to get this next grant that's coming up, but there's no way Seamus was aware of it, or permitted that on his land. There's a bad actor here somewhere, and whether they killed the poor bastard or not, they've really made a mess of his legacy, and I don't like that for him at all."

"You're not really what I expected you to be," Megan said slowly. "I don't know what I expected, but not that much forthrightness."

"I like to surprise people. Now, look, no, I won't ask for your number, but I'll give you mine if you'll take it. I'm old-fashioned, so I've even a card to offer." Jack dipped a hand into a pocket and came out with an old-fashioned-indeed card-carrying case, stainless steel with Celtic knot work embossed on its surface.

"Oh, that's pretty."

"Isn't it? It caught my eye." O'Malley extracted a card and handed it to Megan. "I'd love to hear from you, but I won't take it amiss if I don't. Do you think he was killed, then?"

Megan shook her head. "I'm not even sure it matters

at this point. There are so many people who wanted things from the estate, his death leaves things in a complete hash. But if not, boy, he died at a really convenient time. For a lot of people, including you."

For a few seconds, O'Malley's immense charisma faded and he was simply an unusually handsome man at Megan's side, looking sad and tired. "I've spent the past three days wondering if I should withdraw my application for the grant we were both up for. I wanted it, of course. I want it still. But not because my rival is dead, for God's sake."

"But it won't do anyone, including the rewilding efforts for this whole country, any good if you *don't* get it," Megan said, and O'Malley's shoulders dropped wearily.

"That's it, though, isn't it? I don't even know if withdrawing would make me look any less guilty, because I know I'd be an obvious direction to look. I do have an alibi," he said, gazing down the driveway.

"Is it the six different people who were all vying to get into your bed?" Megan inquired with polite amusement, and he glanced back at her with another startled laugh.

"How flattering. No, I was up from half five planting trees down in Waterford in the pouring rain with thirty other volunteers. There's an experimental project going on to warm the land with tarp on a grand scale before planting, and they'd finally gotten the ground up to temperature. Dig a hole, plant a tree, cover it up again before it loses the heat, or before you do. Miserable to do in the rain."

"But it is an alibi."

"And you're the only person who's asked about it." O'Malley gave her a brief, curious smile.

Megan forbore to mention that she hadn't actually asked: he'd volunteered the information. But still, Doyle really *should* have asked, if he was doing any sort of investigating at all.

Which reminded her of where she wanted to be going, so she lifted O'Malley's card in two fingers, said, "Thanks for talking to me," and headed back to the car, texting Raf and Sarah as she went. *Where are you two? I've got an idea and want to go back to the holy well for a minute. Am I bringing you with me, or are you two on the scent of something here?*

Raf typed *Scones* back and sent a picture from the tearoom of a plate of them. *We're on the scent of scones. Why have I never had scones before? They're amazing. Are we going to paint tinnitus on Sarah if we go back to the well?*

Megan stopped and said, "Tinnitus?" out loud, staring at her phone.

Tetrahedrons, Rafael typed. *Trellises. Tr . . . what the hell did you call that thing, Megs?*

A triskellion?

YEAH! That! Rafael sent a whole series of laughing emojis while Sarah followed it with a bunch of facepalm emojis and *No one would believe me if I told them he was a doctor.*

Megan actually vone called them rather than texting anymore, saying, "I'm going to use this equipment for its originally intended use," as Raf picked up and scooted around the table so he and Sarah could share the screen.

"The debate over whether cell phones were intended for video calls or if you're dumping all phone calls of every kind into one lump aside, why are you going back to Kildare?"

"I want to see if they've got security cameras on the road leading to the holy well site. I think they might. I remember seeing reflections when I was out there the other night."

Sarah lit up. "You're looking to see who took the bicycle?"

"If I can, yeah. Do you want to come along, or hang out here and do the house tour?"

"House tour," Sarah said immediately. "Partly because I'm a tourist and want to do tourist things, but also that way if you need us to waylay anybody and keep them from leaving the premises, we'll be here."

Rafael beamed. "I knew you'd be all in on the murder investigation thing if I just gave you some time."

"It is," Sarah admitted, "weirdly appealing. *Once*. I don't want to make a habit of it."

Megan blew a kiss at both of them. "Okay. I'll run back out to the holy well and see if I can charm anybody into showing me footage, if they've even got it on-site, which they probably don't, but don't harsh my squee here, okay? I'll text you if I learn anything."

As she hung up, she heard Sarah saying, "'Harsh my squee'?" as if she hadn't quite heard Megan correctly. A minute later, she was at the car, where the dogs began leaping around as if they'd been cooped up miserably for days.

"You can't fool me," she told them as she opened the door enough to put a lead on both of them. "I could see you as I walked up. You've been sleeping like babies, not suffering from endless boredom as the mean humans have fun without you. Quick walk now, and then we'll have a better one at the holy well, c'mon, pups." She ran them a short distance up and down the manor house's driveway, then tucked them back into their carrier for the drive into Kildare. Dip complained the whole way, making Megan grateful she didn't have actual children.

She came in the wrong way to look for a security camera facing the direction she needed it to, but there was one facing the other way, and she gave a hiss of triumph that made even Thong whine inquisitively. "Oh, it's okay, sweetie," Megan said absently. "Everything's okay. I just need to see if . . . well, look, don't let me get my hopes up, okay? The odds of them having access to the security feeds are really low."

She still parked, got the dogs out, and took them for a decent walk through the park, letting them stretch their legs and sniff around, before going into the visitors' centre. Margaret, back at the desk, smiled brightly as Megan entered, but the smile fell away into a dead glare as she saw who it was. "You again."

Megan winced from the bottom of her soul. "Yes. Hi. I'm sorry. I just had one little question."

The flat look in the woman's eyes didn't change at all. "The detective told me not to talk to you."

"Yes. No. Fair. Reasonable. I just wondered if the security cameras out there on the road have a feed you can check?"

Margaret's jaw clenched. "If I tell you no, will you go away?"

"Do they have a feed someone *else* can check?" Megan offered her best, most-winning smile. "It probably wouldn't really be your job anyway, right?"

"They're for show."

Megan started to speak, paused, and blinked her confusion for a few long seconds. "The security cameras are for show? You mean, they don't work at all?"

"That's right," Margaret replied tightly. "They're meant to scare people off, but the centre can't afford to pay for actual security. Now will you go?"

"Are you serious?"

"Don't you think I'd be happier if they worked?" the woman half-shouted. "Don't you think I'd be happier if I could ask the guards to look at the tapes and find out the truth of what happened here? Of course I'm serious! Now get out of here! I never want to see the likes of you again!" Margaret flung up a hand like a barrier between them, and Megan, distressed, fled the building.

Dip and Thong, who had been waiting politely outside the visitors' centre, leaped up with worried yelps when Megan darted out, and ran with her, jumping around, tangling around her feet, and nearly tripping her as she hurried back to the car and threw herself into the back seat. Both dogs bounced up with her, crawling on her belly, which no doubt left footprints all over her jumper. Megan pulled them into squirming hugs anyway, thoughts racing through a variety of useless ideas that finally ended with getting her phone out and texting Paul to say, *I know I haven't even gotten back to you about your stuff, but I could use some of your professional advice right now.*

She put the phone back on her chest, trying to decide what she *could* do, then said, "Oh," aloud and sat up. The dogs slid off her stomach and legs into the back seat's footwells and looked up at her with dark, betrayed eyes. "I know, I know, I'm the worst pet owner ever. Give me a minute." She started looking up the closest Kildare garda stations, but a vone call brightened the screen, and Paul's grinning, sunburned face came on when she answered. "Paul! You look happy. What's up?"

"Niamh's asked me to marry her, and I've said yes."

CHAPTER 19

"Holy shit, *what?*" Megan tried to stand up with shock, which would have worked better if she hadn't been in the car. She hit her head, dropped back down into the seat, and said, "*What?*" again in stunned delight. "Oh my *God*! Congratulations! Oh my God! No wonder you wanted to talk to me! How—what—Paul!" She almost shouted his name as the dogs, in full panic mode at her volume, leaped onto the seat, across Megan's lap, and then out the still-open car door. Megan lunged for the leads, barely grabbing them by dint of belly flopping halfway out of the car. The phone went flying. She snatched at it with her fingertips, breaking its fall enough that it didn't shatter when it hit the ground, then pulled it back, much too close to her face, as she righted herself again. "Tell me everything!"

Paul's smile turned to laughter as she fumbled with the phone, then settled back into a broad, shining-eyed beam. "She told you about the job in the States?"

"She did, yeah. She was terrified to tell you, Paul, she was afraid—but you tell *me* this story, what's the story, what's the *story*?"

His gaze went positively soppy, and Megan felt tears welling in her own eyes as her chest tightened with not just joy, but other emotions she didn't want to examine right then. He took a breath to start, hesitated, did it again, and finally said, "She *didn't* want to tell me, you're right, she said she was afraid to, but obviously she did. And I was thinking—well, I was thinking, this is it, wasn't I? I can't ask her to stay. I can't ask her to damage her career like that. And it was always too good to be true, Niamh O'Sullivan dating *me*. So I said—I said the first part, that I couldn't ask her to stay, and she started crying, and I started crying, and she said she knew I'd say that, and then she said, but wait, wait, and I'm thinking, what can I wait for, Nee? I'll be on the next plane home, when's the next plane home, I can't stand to stay."

Megan was crying by then, too, huge, fat tears stinging her eyes and plopping down her cheeks. Thong, worried, climbed back into the car and began to lick her face. "And?"

"And she got down on one knee, Megan." Paul's eyes widened with astonished recollection. "We were in the hotel room, and Abhaile was bouncing around because we were both crying, and she got down on one knee and picked Abhaile up under one arm because the bloody animal was going to knock her over otherwise, and she put her other hand in her pocket and I was having palpitations, I was, Megan, I literally could not believe—any of it, but people only get down on one knee for one reason, and my hands are going like this"—he put the phone down to demonstrate birdlike flutters with both hands—"like I'm a damn *ingenue*, not a grown man, and she takes this out of her pocket, Megan."

He stopped fluttering his hands and turned his left one to the camera, showing Megan a rose-gold ring with Celtic knot work and a diamond inset.

Megan said, "Holy *shit*," again, and Paul burst out with an overwhelmed laugh.

"I've never heard you swear before, and now you've done it twice."

"She didn't just find that in an afternoon in Morocco, Paul!"

"No. She found it before Christmas, she said. And bought it. Just in case. Just in case," he repeated hoarsely, and folded his right hand over the left. "I'm the luckiest man in the whole fecking *world*, Megan."

Megan shrieked gleefully and kicked her feet, which set the dogs off, but she couldn't help herself. "And? *And?* What did she say? What did you say? How did it all happen?" She yelled, "Oh my God!" at the car's ceiling, then did her best to get herself back under control so she could listen.

"Well, that's what she said, that she'd bought it before Christmas, that it made her think of me, and she hadn't had the nerve and"—his expression went slightly guilty—"also that you were so unhappy she didn't want to make it worse by rubbing an engagement in your face—"

"Oh, pshaw. I mean, that was really thoughtful, but

no, how could I not be happy for you? I love you both so much. This is wonderful. And you said?"

"I think I said 'are you sure' a dozen times before I said yes," Paul admitted. "I thought I *had* said yes. She was so nervous she had to tell me I hadn't, and ask again to see what my answer was. And she said she knew it was pressure, when she was going to leave, but she didn't want to leave without at least asking." Pure awe pulled his mouth into a smile again. "Niamh O'Sullivan didn't want to leave me without at least asking if I'd marry her first. Did I mention how lucky I am?"

"You did, but go ahead and repeat yourself if you need to." Megan beamed at him. "I'm so happy for you, Paul. For both of you. This is so exciting! Oh my God!" she yelled again, and Thong put her entire paw over Megan's mouth, clearly trying to quiet her. Laughing, she moved the dog's paw, hugged her, and put her back in the footwell. "Congratulations. I can't wait to talk to Niamh now. Oh my God! You can go on double dates with Raf and Sarah in San Francisco!"

"Ah, you're too good," Paul said happily. "First you introduce me to the woman who becomes my fiancée, and now you're giving us a starter friends group on the other side of the world. I'll miss you." Some of the joy faded from his face, and Megan's heart twisted.

"Yeah," she said more quietly. "Yeah, me too. I'm going to miss you both like crazy. But it's not forever," she added hopefully. "I mean, lifestyles of the rich and famous and all that jet-setting stuff, so even if you settle there, you can come back. I'm really happy for you, Paul. For both of you. This is way better than you coming home with a broken heart and Niamh going off to America miserable."

"It is. God, what am I going to do in America, Megan? I don't want to be a cop there!"

"No, you don't. I have no idea, but you'll figure it out. I'm sure of it." Megan smiled at him, and he beamed back before shaking himself.

"Wait, though, there was something you needed, wasn't there? My professional opinion? Better get it while I'm still a professional."

"Oh. Oh, yeah." Megan deflated, sinking into the car seat and not minding it this time when the dogs crawled on her again. "Right, so let me catch you up, or, no, maybe I'll just skip to the important part right now. The other night, after I found the bike in the hedge with you guys? I told the detective on the case, and later that night it disappeared."

There was a long pause before Paul said, "Well, that can't be good."

"Yeah." Megan rubbed a hand over her face. "So I was texting to ask what I should do now. There's no security footage. Apparently the heritage centre can't afford working cameras. So I don't know how to figure this one out. I did think, after I texted you, that I should ring the nearest garda station and ask if I could be put in contact with the kid who was shadowing Doyle on Monday. I haven't seen him since, but he's a fan. Of me. Also Niamh. But he asked for a selfie with the Murder Driver, so he might listen to me if I say something hinky might be going on with Doyle. Or he might not, because cops."

"Surely," Paul said with a broad note of grim irony, "you're not suggesting that the guards will close ranks to protect one of their own rather than pursue justice."

"Oh, definitely not," Megan said. "Not in Ireland. That's obviously not the kind of thing that happens here. Ever. There is no good ol' boys network, and furthermore, all the judges make fair, honest, reality-based rulings that only ever punish the wicked and never give a bad man a slap on the hand to let him go."

"So glad you understand that." Paul was quiet a moment, thinking. "Ringing that lad is as solid and safe an idea as any. Don't go haring off after this detective on your own, trying to get a confession out of the man. I'll ring someone in Dublin to see if I can't make sure it's at least properly looked into."

Megan made a face. "If you ring from Morocco, where you're on holiday with your fabulous girlf—*fiancée!*—about a case in Kildare, they're going to know it's got something to do with me, Paul. If you're leaving An Garda Síochána to go to America, you don't want it to be with me and one of my murder driver messes following you."

Paul breathed, "Jaysus, leaving the guards. I hadn't quite thought of it that way, though what else am I going to do?"

"There's an Irish embassy in San Francisco," Megan volunteered. "Maybe you can go be a guard for them."

He eyed her. "That'd be a different kind of guard altogether, Megan."

She grinned sheepishly. "I know, but it was a thought. Look, I'll try to get hold of Farrell first, and if I can't get anywhere with him, I'll text you and you can try Dublin, okay? I really don't want you leaving with a black mark on your name because of me."

"You're a good egg, Megan. Now, look, before I let you go, how are your friends doing? You're supposed to be on holiday."

"Raf's been all in on the murder driver holiday since the start, and Sarah insisted they stay back at the Rathballard House while I came back to the holy well to see about the bicycle, because that's where Doyle is and she reckoned they could apprehend him if necessary." Megan realized she shouldn't have said that much even before alarm shot across Paul's face, and she offered a wincing laugh. "I don't think they'll get in any actual trouble. That's usually on me."

"Megan, you are a bloody menace. What's the detective doing at Seamus Nolan's house anyway?"

"I don't know. He said he'd been called in to run Jack O'Malley—he's another environmentalist—off the land, but that'd be the estate's personal business, wouldn't it? So a guard shouldn't be doing that. And besides, then O'Malley did the big reveal on the toxic waste dump he'd found—"

"He what?" Paul stared at her, dismayed. "Megan . . . !"

"I know, I know, I don't know! The waste dump was a new one on me! I haven't had to deal with that before! But it's the worst possible thing to find on a conservation site, right? Somebody with a real vendetta against Nolan must have left it, but I haven't got a clue who or why."

"What kind of waste?"

"Farm waste, it looked like, I guess. Raf and Sarah saw it, not me, but I've got pictures if you want me to forward them on to you."

"Do." Paul looked thoughtful, then shook his head. "No, go on, never mind. There'll be a piece that fits somewhere, if you just shake it around enough. Not that you heard it from me. Go on, now. Go ring the guards and go get your friends so they're not babysitting a detective. I swear, Megan . . ."

She smiled cheekily at him. "You enjoy every minute of this. Especially when you're too far away for it to affect your career."

"Which it all will be soon." Paul gave her a nervous smile in return, then hung up to the sounds of her congratulations. She texted Niamh, too, then did ring the guards and asked for Garda Farrell to ring her back when he had the chance.

He did so about twenty minutes later, just as she pulled down the Rathballard House's long driveway, and introduced himself with a barely suppressed note of glee in his voice. Megan, grinning, said, "Hang on a minute while I park," and dropped the phone into the seat next to her so she could find a parking spot. "All right, I'm with you now."

"Ah, I could fine you, now, for talking on your mobile while driving," Farrell warned in as serious a voice as he could manage.

"I put the phone down so I wasn't talking while driving!" Megan protested, and despite his efforts to be solemn, Farrell laughed.

"Ah, sure, I know you did. What were you ringing for, Ms. Malone?"

"I saw the picture you posted," she said in her own grim tone.

Farrell squawked. "What? No! I never did! I only showed some of my own mates, and I didn't even send it on to them, they had to look at me phone!"

Megan cackled. "No, no, I'm sorry, I'm kidding. No, I'm calling because I'm in a pickle. A bind. A sticky wicket. Do people say that here?"

"Not anyone who wants to keep their teeth in their own head," Farrell said dryly. "What is it, then?"

All of Megan's good humor fled as she struggled briefly to figure out where to start. Telling a cop she suspected his partner of corruption or worse was *not* an easy conversation to have. After an awkward silence and a sigh, she said, "I told Detective Doyle about the bicycle in the hedge on Monday, and it wasn't there Tuesday morning. I don't know what happened to it, and he's up at the Rathballard House now, doing I don't know what, and I'm a little afraid that . . ."

". . . that he had something to do with Seamus Nolan's death?" Farrell picked up incredulously when her silence drew out too long.

"It's just, who else could, or would, have taken the bike? I know there *are* loads of bike thieves, but this one is just so convenient."

"Ms. Malone," Farrell said. Megan's stomach clenched: he hadn't been at all formal with her in the past, and it seemed like an extremely bad sign. After enough of a beat to make her hands start shaking with nerves, he repeated, "Ms. Malone. You told *me* about the bike in the hedge. I had it removed, and it's being checked for fingerprints."

Heat began to crawl up Megan's jaw until her whole face was so fiery with a blush that it brought actual tears to her eyes. She slumped way, way down in the driver's seat and eventually whispered, "I forgot I'd mentioned it you," in total mortification.

Farrell chuckled rather gently. "Well, you did so, and while I admire you and all, Megan, it wouldn't be your *job* to go around investigating the likes of this, so I'd say put it out of your mind and let the guards do their work."

Being put in her place by a twenty-eight-year-old was considerably more aggravating than Paul, or even Doyle, doing it. Megan sat with that a moment, then dismissed it. She hated it no matter who was doing it. Voice carefully controlled, she said, "I'll keep that in mind," and then, still embarrassed, added, "I'm glad to hear you're looking into the bike, anyway. Any luck?"

"I couldn't tell you either way," Farrell said more cheerfully. "Even if I'd like to, Doyle would have my head."

"Does he even know you're having prints run?"

Farrell whistled tunelessly in her ear, making Megan breathe laughter. "I guess not, then. All right, well . . ." If he'd been Paul, she would have said "let me know," with the hope he might actually let her know, but she doubted the young garda would. He hung up, and Megan got out of the car to slink up to the house, feeling like a complete idiot.

CHAPTER 20

"Megan!" Aisling's voice caught her just before she went into the house. Megan turned back, waved, and waited for the young woman to catch up. The hour or so she'd spent—presumably with Ian—had done her some good: she looked less stressed, if not exactly happier. "Where'd you go?"

"Investigating, which ended in total humiliation."

Aisling blinked, surprise, then disappointment settling over her face. "Oh. I hoped . . ."

"That I'd have come up with all the answers?" Megan sighed, following Aisling into the big house's foyer. "Me too. Instead I got very firmly reminded that this isn't my job. Have you seen Doyle around?"

"He was talking to Uncle Adam last I knew. I asked Ian to ask Nora—she's staff in the tearoom there—" Aisling gestured to the room, which they were passing, as if Megan hadn't been in there three times already and met Aisling herself in there at least once.

"I met Nora, yes. She's lovely." Megan peeked into the tearoom, trying to catch a glimpse of Rafael and Sarah, then waved vigorously when she caught Raf's eye.

"Oh, right, I saw you talking with her. So I asked her to bring up a cuppa to the office—" Aisling blushed as Megan started to smile. "Shut up. If I'm spying on Adam, what of it?"

"Nothing. I think it's great. Go on. Oh, wait, can we wait for my friends?" Megan pointed to Raf and Sarah, who were gathering their things and heading for the tearoom door. Aisling stopped at the foot of the grand staircase, dropping her voice as she continued her explanation.

"Sure, of course. Nora brought the tea up and she says Doyle and Uncle Adam were there, and that Adam's half-torn Da's office apart. I'm guessing it's Da's notebook he's looking for, and I've not said a word to him about where it is. I *have* looked through the computer, last night, and I don't know what he's after. There's nothing about him on it, except photographs and what he's been left in the will. I read all of that," Aisling added wearily. "He's left Adam a pittance, and I'd swear to you, the language is formal but if you read between the lines, it's like he's saying, 'and he knows why,' Megan. I'm beginning to think there was bad blood between them that I didn't know about. And my bloody *mother . . .*"

"Did he leave her anything in the will? Wait, here, I'm sorry, hi, guys." Megan smiled quickly at Sarah and Raf as they came over, saying, "Aisling, these are my best friends from the States, Rafael and Sarah Williams. They're on holiday and staying with me for a couple of weeks. Raf, Sarah, this is Aisling Nolan. I met her Tuesday afternoon . . ."

"With the hot-pink MINI Cooper," Sarah said with a smile of her own. "It's a great car. We're sorry for your loss, Miss No—"

"Aisling."

Something so sympathetic happened in Sarah's gaze that Megan's throat tightened with tears as Sarah murmured, "Aisling. Look, Raf and I have been enjoying the house, so we'll do that while you and Megan take care of whatever you were going to do, all right?"

Aisling began to nod, then took a quick breath and blurted, "No, why don't you come with us?"

"Oh, um, no, we couldn't," Rafael began, but Aisling's eyes were suddenly bright with determination.

"No, please. Partly because you can see the private part of the house that way, which would be nice for Megan's friends, but honestly, lads, it'd be doing me a favor. I've got my uncle to deal with, and he'll have a harder time pushing me around if there's a load of other people there. Especially if they're all brash Americans."

Rafael, mockingly indignant, said, "I'm not brash!"

Megan elbowed him. "You are, because you're American, but even better, you're a doctor. You're, like, *classy* brash."

Sarah snorted so loudly that even Aisling laughed, and Rafael's indignation became momentarily legitimate. "I am *too* classy!"

"Too classy," Sarah agreed, trying to hold back

laughter of her own. "That's right, babe. That's what you are. Too classy."

Rafael turned to Megan, clearly intending an appeal for help before his face fell and he muttered, "You started this," to the renewed amusement of all three women. "All right, all right, *fine*, I'll come be a classy, brash doctor in the background or something. Do I get paid an extras fee for this? What's the daily rate for extras, anyway?"

"Oooh," Sarah said brightly. "If we're filming, we need the Main Character. Where's that guy, Jack O'Malley? Otherwise, sorry, hon, I don't think we're getting our extras fee for the day."

"Rathballard House has been in some movies, but they've all been Regencies. You're wearing the wrong clothes," Aisling said, smiling as she led them up the stairs to the house's private wing. "I'll let you know next time we're filming here, though, okay? You can come be a classy background doctor then."

"I'll hold you to that," Raf said enthusiastically. He and Sarah took the stairs slowly, trailing a few steps behind Aisling to admire the paintings and furnishings of the big, old house.

Megan dropped her voice as she caught up with Aisling. "You were saying something about your mom? Did he leave her anything in the will?"

"Not even a pittance, which won't matter, will it? If they were married, it's still half hers or something." Aisling sounded worn down again, like she'd put on a quick performance for the visiting Americans and it had drained whatever extra energy she had. "I don't know how to deal with any of this. Mam, Uncle Adam, whether I even inherit anything at all . . . how do people do this?"

"With as much help as they can get," Megan said gently. "And, unfortunately, by knowing that the only way out is through."

"Well, that's horrible."

"You're not wrong." Megan put her arm around Aisling's shoulders, offering a hug, and the girl sighed and leaned in as they made their way up to the private office. The door stood half-closed, and Megan took an extra step ahead, pushing it open to expose the room.

The only reason she kept going instead of stopping in appalled shock was that there were three people behind her. Aisling stumbled past her anyway, voice lifting in horror. "Uncle Adam, what have you *done*?"

Adam Nolan stood in the midst of chaos. Half the room's shelves had been emptied, swept clear, and the books on them scattered, opened, leafed through, then dropped. Paperwork lay everywhere, piled on top of furniture that had been pulled apart, with cushions lying askew on couches that had been shoved around. The stereo system was open, vinyl records falling from their holders and CDs dumped on the floor. Every drawer on Seamus Nolan's desk gaped, some still dangling from their settings and a few upside down or leaning against the desk, leaving blank holes where they'd been. If there had been feathers from pillows still floating in the air, Megan wouldn't have been surprised, but the ransacked room had no touch of humor to it, just a livid Nolan staring desperately around the wreck he'd made of his nephew's office, Detective Sergeant Doyle leaning casually in a window as if he'd been watching the whole thing like it was a scene from a film, and Jenny Flynn standing with her arms folded, glaring at the whole mess.

Aisling, still too bewildered to have reached anger yet, said, "Uncle Adam?" again, and then, "*Mam?* Why would you let him do this? What's going on?"

"Where is it?" Adam whirled toward Aisling, who took a step back, almost running into Megan. A quick look over her shoulder assured her that Megan was there, supporting here, and reminded her that Rafael and Sarah had come to back her up, too. Color flushed her cheeks, but she stood a little straighter and set her jaw.

"Where's what? What have you done? Why are you tearing Da's office apart? Mam, why are you letting him do this?"

"Why are *you* letting him do this?" Megan asked in a lower voice, directed at Doyle.

The detective lifted an eyebrow. "It's the man's own property. Why would I stop him?"

"It's not," Aisling snarled. "Mam, tell him! If you think it's yours, why would you let him do this?"

"Where's Seamus's notebook, my love?" Jenny smiled at her daughter. "Your poor uncle has been looking for it. We only need access to your father's computer."

"Are you *mental*?" Aisling stalked farther into the room, giving Megan and the other Americans more space to spread out, too. "What in God's name do you think is on it that's worth doing this for?"

"What do you *think*?" Jenny asked incredulously. "What's the thing he might have that I couldn't let the public see?"

"I don't know!" Aisling bellowed. "*Porn?*"

Jenny's eyes popped so comically that Doyle laughed out loud and nearly bowed to the room at large. "I'll excuse myself from *this* conversation, so I will. If you'll pardon me—"

"Are you nuts?" Megan interrupted. "I'm sorry, have you never *seen* a detective show? We're in full-on revealing-of-the-secrets mode here. This is the part where your investigation bears fruit, Doyle, not that you've been doing any investigation! You can't leave!"

"He doesn't bloody care about Seamus's death!" Adam shouted. "All that matters to him is he won't get his money!"

Doyle's expression went as flat and cold as a snake's in the heartbeat-long silence that followed, before Aisling blurted, "What money?" and Adam, suddenly sickeningly pale, shook his head frantically.

"I owe him—I borrowed—it's nothing that matters, Ais, don't worry your pretty head about—"

"What money, Uncle Adam?"

Megan's phone chimed, an incongruously bright sound amidst the yelling and tension. She glanced at it, then did a double take, reading the text more carefully, and into Adam's spluttering, said, "Why have you been stealing cars and driving off the property early in the morning so often, Adam?"

Adam's face went florid again. "I'm not stealing anyth—"

"Ais, have you given your uncle permission to borrow your car?"

"What? No! He's never asked!"

"Well." Megan smiled placidly at Adam Nolan. "To be fair, I don't know the laws in Ireland exactly on this topic, but in the States, that would, in fact, be grand theft auto. A felony crime. Stealing cars is, you know."

"I didn't steal anybody's car! I brought them back!"

"Tell you what, let's not nitpick over that, then. Why are you *borrowing* people's cars at six in the morning for months on end? And why did you borrow Aisling's on Monday morning, just after Seamus left, and not long before he was murdered? I could see it as establishing an alibi," she said, mostly to Doyle, although the garda looked as if he wanted nothing more than to murder her himself, or at least escape the room. "So how long have you been planning to murder your nephew, Adam?"

"*I wasn't establishing an alibi!* I was putting money on the horses!"

"And the dogs," Doyle said into the silence that followed. "And the matches and the fights and whether a damn butterfly will land on a fence post and change the course of the world."

Jenny threw her head back and cackled like a witch as Aisling said, "Uncle Adam?" in bewilderment.

The older man turned to her, expression conniving and tone wheedling. "It's only a few bad bets, love. I'm in a little over my head, that's all. Your da meant to give me the money to pay it off, but he's dead now, and they'll be coming for me, you see . . ."

Megan, watching a thin mean smile pull at the corner of Doyle's mouth, pressed one hand to her forehead like she'd been struck with understanding. "They won't *be* coming for you, will they? They're already here for you. *That's* why you're here," she said to Doyle. "You're a collector."

Doyle's smile disappeared, leaving him looking actively dangerous. "There's a question you don't want to be asking, missy."

Rafael coughed and took a judicious step backward, which just about allowed Megan to find "missy" funny instead of infuriating. "You are," she said again. "I thought maybe Adam had hired you for private security, because there's no reason An Garda Síochána should send somebody out to the estate to run Jack O'Malley off. That's not your job. But debt collecting for a bookie, especially from a man whose income has just been cut off? I bet that makes your pension look a little healthier, doesn't it, Detective? I already know you're a thug. You wouldn't have flipped out and told me so much earlier when you knocked my scone out of my hand if you weren't actually afraid of being reported for violence."

Somehow Megan had advanced on Doyle as she spoke, although she had the presence of mind to stop out of arm's reach. The detective's face had gone nearly purple with rage as she approached, and his ears were swollen with blood flow. "It's no business of yours," he snarled. "All I want from Nolan is the forty grand."

Aisling said, "Holy fuck," and Doyle actually laughed.

"That's just the interest, a *chuisle mo chroí*. Your uncle owes hundreds of thousands."

"Seamus was paying it." Adam's entire demeanor had changed from a raging man to a whinging one. "He didn't want to see me in jail, Ais. He was paying it."

"He hadn't paid in months," Doyle said levelly. "Either your da cut him off, or he's betting it all trying to win enough to pay the debt back. It's no good having him go to jail," he added with an unpleasantly toothy smile. "He can't pay, from prison. There're a lot of ways to make him pay out here."

"I just need the safe code," Adam whined to Aisling. "I can pay the interest from what's in the safe, and that'll be enough to see me through until the land is sold."

Aisling lurched a few steps toward her father's office chair before seeing it was full of upended desk drawers. She stopped, leaning on the desk, and Jenny swooped toward her, trilling with ill-contained laughter that she was obviously trying to disguise as distress. "Aisling, my darling, what a dreadful thing for you to learn about your dreadful uncle, so soon after your dear papa's death! My dear, together we'll—"

"Oh, shove it, Mam. What is it you want?" Aisling asked wearily. "Would it be cash from the safe, too? I don't have the code."

"The password book does!" Adam howled. "Your father's damn password book! I know he kept it in here, but it's gone!"

"There's only some paperwork on the computer I'm

after," Jenny cooed. "I just need the computer pass-word for a minute, love."

"What?" Aisling said to her. "What can you possibly need? The separation papers are signed, but you didn't sign away your rights to any of your spousal inheri-tance, so what can it *possibly* be? I hope it is porn," she said to no one in particular. "I didn't look for that. I'll put it on the internet myself, I will."

Jenny gasped, "Aisling Elizabeth Nolan!" in con-vincing outrage, then darted quick looks back and forth to the others in the room before stepping even closer to Aisling. "It's nothing like that, love. Nothing for you to worry your head about. I just want copies of certain pa-pers in my own hands and no one else's."

Megan, speaking as she thought, said, "He divorced you, didn't he." She turned from Doyle in time to watch the color drain from Jenny's cheeks, then flare back in a rush of angry heat.

"I'd never say it if he did!"

"He did." Megan's fingertips went to her forehead again, like every little thought that leaped into her mind needed extra containment. "He did, and you think if you have all the copies of the divorce papers, you'll still get your share of the inheritance somehow, don't you? It's literally a matter of public record, Jenny. You can't just go sneak that off the registers. And his lawyers must know."

"Why didn't *I* know?" Aisling demanded.

Every ounce of charm stripped itself from Jenny's face, leaving her all sharp bones and flat rage. "He blindsided me on your birthday two years ago. Said you were an adult now, and he had no more reason to keep me in his own life. I needed money, and he offered me a payout, so I took it, but I wasn't thinking. I never would have left him, Ais—"

"You *literally* left him when I was *three years old*," Aisling shouted. "Oh my God! Go on with you, get out of here! There's nothing here for you!"

"You're my daughter!"

"So are my sisters, down the farm! Go be a better mother to them than you were to me, or better yet, bring the poor things here and let me take care of them, because I'll love them, at least!"

"I'm sorry," Megan said in a thin, startled voice. "Did you say 'down the farm'?"

"What?" Aisling, derailed, swung toward Megan, then calmed, blinking. "Yes, I told you that. She's got a thing for men with land, and Aoife's da has one of those big industrial farms down in Kerry."

Megan shifted her gaze to Jenny. "So how long after you signed the divorce papers did you convince Aoife's father to dump his farming waste on the Rathballard estate?"

Sarah whispered, "Oh my God," in horrified awe, drawing the attention of everyone in the room for a moment. She and Raf were standing near the door, hands clutched together and manic grins pulled across their faces. Megan nearly laughed. At least they'd have a good vacation story to tell.

Jenny, in the heartbeat that everyone's attention was off her, ran for the door. Megan bolted after her, but

Rafael let go of Sarah's hand and took the few steps that put him between Jenny and escape. She actually bounced off him, and he caught her with grace, then let her go as quickly. Jenny shrieked, throwing herself at him with clawed fingers, and as he flung himself back, hands lifted to protect his eyes, Sarah snaked a long, dancer-strong leg out and tangled it between Jenny's ankles. The woman went down with a crash.

Megan, wincing, turned to Doyle. "You know what, I have no idea what consequences you might have to deal with for being an enforcer, but I'm pretty sure you can arrest Jenny Flynn."

CHAPTER 21

"I didn't kill him!" Jenny screeched her way out of the office under Doyle's bemused arrest, writhing with anger and shouting at the top of her lungs. "I didn't kill Seamus Nolan! I never would! He was the love of my life! Aisling! *Tell them!*"

Aisling had straightened away from the desk when her mother ran, but sank back down against it, looking decades older than her nineteen years. "To be fair, I think she wouldn't," she said to the room at large. "Not out of the love of her heart for him, but for the cash. He couldn't even tell me they'd divorced." She closed her eyes, then in slow, piecemeal motions, put her face in her hands. "That's how wrapped up in her he still was. If he told me, he couldn't keep sneaking about helping her. And then *you*."

Her voice went bitter and cold as she lifted her gaze to her uncle. "You wouldn't have killed him either, would you? For the same reasons. How long did he pay your debts for, Adam? If the estate's in trouble, how much of that is on you? I need an accountant," she said to Megan. "Someone to help me figure it all out. Will you help me find one?"

"Of course." Megan nodded at Aisling, but watched Adam, who had lost color and what remained of any youthful vigor. He'd become an old man in the last minutes, instead of simply an older one. "I wonder if your father really did just slip."

Even as she wondered, she shook her head. Aisling focused on her, a question in the quirk of her eyebrows, and Megan shrugged. "The bike wouldn't have been in the hedge, if he'd slipped. I mean, Doyle could be right, it could just be that some punk wandered by and grabbed the bike because they were in the right place at the right time, but the sun doesn't rise until almost nine in the morning right now. It's dark and cold and damp, and the lights aren't good along the road there. And the bike rack is at the side of the visitors' centre. You have to actually come into the parking lot to see it. People don't usually wander country roads at half seven in the morning in the dark, looking for bikes to steal. It's more a crime of opportunity."

"Well, it wasn't me," Aisling said with a tired smile, "so if it wasn't Mam or Uncle Adam, who was it? You three were the next people to see him."

"Margaret at the visitors' centre said she'd seen the bike on her way in," Sarah said thoughtfully. "What time do they open there?"

"They were open when we arrived a little before ten," Megan said. "Which would be early for an Irish tourist attraction in the winter, but Imbolc *is* coming up."

Rafael blinked. "Imwhat?"

"St. Brigid's Day," Aisling answered. "February first, Imbolc. It's the first day of spring in the Irish calendar."

Sarah cast a dubious look outside at the gray mist. "I'm not sure you understand what 'spring' is, but okay. So Margaret could have gotten there early?"

A smattering of laughter touched Megan and the two Irish-born people, even Adam. Aisling said, "We're not known for early, we Irish," and Megan grinned.

"Not at all. But she wouldn't have had to be early. I don't think people are wandering into that parking lot looking for bikes to steal, as a rule. What matters is she saw the bike, and then it was gone. And the only person we know was there in the meantime was Father Colman."

"But the bike was gone before *we* got there," Raf objected. "And we saw Colman leaving."

"Yeah." Megan sagged. "Maybe I'm wrong. Maybe someone did just take the bike. Maybe it was just an accident. I'm sorry, Ais. I've brought all this chaos into your life for nothing."

"Not for nothing," the young woman said fiercely. "Look what you *did* turn up. My mam's dumped toxic waste on my estate, and my uncle's trying to steal it from me to pay off his gambling debts. I'd have known none of it without you—or that my inheritance was in danger at all. You," she said to Adam. "I don't know what to do with you."

"You can't do anything," he muttered. "The estate's mine anyway. I'll sell it all and walk away from this wretched wet country."

"You know they're challenging that under Brehon law," Megan said to the old man. "Seamus's lawyer has an argument drawn up for old Irish law to supersede colonizer law. Even if it doesn't work, it'll buy time, and you don't have any. Doyle's not here," she added almost cheerfully. "This might be your only chance to disappear for good, because I'm sure he's going to come back."

An actual gleam came into Aisling's eye. "I might drop a credit card on the floor that would cover the cost of a plane ticket, if I were to find that my great-uncle Adam had left a notarized letter renouncing all his rights to the Rathballard estate and title. I even might be clumsy enough to drop that card if I thought some-one would drive him to the airport and stop at my so-licitor's office in Dublin on the way to notarize that letter. Or sign over power of attorney, or whatever it was that needed to happen."

"Strangely enough," Megan said in a bright, stilted tone, "I happen to be a professional chauffeur with a Lincoln Town Car in the parking lot. Perhaps I could be of assistance, Miss Nolan."

"Oh, gosh!" Aisling clapped her hands together the-atrically. "Gosh, do you think you could, Ms. Malone? That would be sooooo helpful!"

Adam's color had come back, hot enough that Megan thought he might be risking a stroke. "You're mad. You're all mental. Are you mad?"

"Could you," Rafael asked with a sparkle in his own voice, "perhaps drop my wife and me back at St. Brigid's Well, on your way? I have some triskelions to paint on her skin, you see."

"I think that can be arranged," Megan told him cheerfully, then raised her eyebrows at Adam. "And I think you've got two bad choices here, buddy, but a quiet retirement in the Canaries sounds like a lot more fun than finding out what Doyle and his bookie employers have in store for you."

"They'll come after me," he said desperately.

Megan shrugged. "Then I'd learn to run."

It was late by the time Megan returned to Kildare; paperwork renouncing an inheritance wasn't, as it turned out, as easy as one might think. Not, she admitted to herself—because she'd left the dogs with Rafael and Sarah at the holy well—that she'd thought it would be all that easy. She wasn't even sure if it would stand up in court if Adam ever wanted to challenge it, but she'd dropped him at the departures curb at Dublin Airport, and she didn't really think she, or Aisling, would ever see him again. She had no idea where he was going, either. Hadn't asked, didn't want to know.

There was a text from Aisling when she got back to the hotel, asking if all three of them could come to the celebration of life for her father the next day. *It's not a wake, exactly*, Aisling had written. *And it's definitely not a funeral, not a Catholic one, anyway. But if you could come . . .*

Megan responded, promising she would, then dropped into bed without checking in with Sarah and Rafael. Either they were sleeping, she figured, or they weren't, and either way, they didn't need a third party involved. Although they still had the dogs, who between them qualified as considerably more than a third party. At least they rarely needed to go out in the middle of the night.

She woke earlier than she wanted to, and after trying to go back to sleep, reluctantly dragged herself down to the hotel's fitness centre, all mirrors and weight machines and an incongruous-to-her-mind cross on the wall, wrapped with a rosary. She'd lived in Ireland long enough that she thought random signs of Catholicism shouldn't still surprise her, but they did. It was less distracting than a television, at least, and she counted its beads while exercising, which was both distracting and soothing.

Which was, she supposed, the whole point of prayer beads. It made the half hour she worked out go by faster, at least, and she left all sweaty and contemplating whether she should get her own rosary just to keep her mind on something other than aching muscles while she exercised.

Rafael was taking the dogs out through the lobby when she came up from the fitness centre. Megan jogged to catch up, catching the Jack Russells' attention before Raf noticed her, and crouching to scuffle the little animals before smiling tiredly up at her friend. "Want me to walk them? You've gone beyond the call of duty already."

"We can share the burden." He offered her a leash. "You're up early. Everything okay?"

"I usually get up at half five or six to go to the gym, and habit defeated me this morning. Couldn't go back to sleep, even though I got back late. Dropped Adam to the airport, and I've got all the paperwork he signed to bring to Aisling. This has not been the holiday I wanted you guys to have."

"This has been a much better adventure than we ever could have possibly asked for." Rafael flashed a bright grin, and Megan had to admit he looked more refreshed and happier than he had when they'd arrived a few days ago. "Everything else aside, I got to shock tourists at the holy well yesterday by painting tyrannosaurs on Sarah, which was amazing."

"Triskelions! *Triskelions!*"

"Those too," Rafael said happily. "I don't believe in magic, Megs, but this whole thing has been good for us." They ducked under a black branch dripping with water as they reached the riverside, then walked down the paved path beside it in step while the dogs darted back and forth, sniffing at everything. "Did I tell you I'm studying to switch to general practice instead of working in the ER?"

"Sarah mentioned it. She was wondering if you'd actually be able to give up the high-octane ER life."

"Honestly?" Raf fell silent as they padded down the path, then shook his head. "I didn't think I could. Like, up until this week, I didn't think I could. But even though it's been a genuinely whacked week, it's also been really great. I've spent so much time with Sarah.

And I met your friends, even if it was just on the phone, and they're going to be in San Francisco, and I thought, man, if I'm working all the time, it's just gonna be Sarah and them hanging out, and I'll be the guy hearing all their great stories and wishing I'd been there. I don't know if Sarah and I will ever be lucky enough to have kids, but even if we don't, this week has kind of reminded me what it's like to have a life again. I guess it's been eye-opening? And if it's that obvious after a few days, then, yeah, the ER is going to have to figure out how to do without me, I think. I want a schedule that lets me spend time with my family." He knocked his shoulder against Megan's. "That means you, too. You're gonna visit, right?"

"Apparently all the people I love best are going to be in San Francisco, so yeah, I guess I'm gonna have to! No, seriously, I will. And if you're working less, it'll be easier, too, because I won't have to cram seeing you into the edges of your twenty-hour shifts. As if my weird life hasn't kept us from hanging out as much as I wanted so far this week." Megan made a face. "I really *didn't* want for this to happen."

"We're here for another, what, eight days? And we'll just have to come back to see more of the country, since this visit has been a little well-centered."

Megan laughed. "Well-centered. No, no, I think the whole point is that my life *isn't* well-centered, it's all, what did you say? Whacked. I don't think we say 'whacked' anymore, either, Raf. But yeah, no, I know what you mean. At least you got to see behind the scenes at the Rathballard House?"

Rafael's eyes widened. "Not just behind the scenes, but all the drama behind them, too. Is that what it's always like when you get involved in these things?"

A groan escaped Megan, loud enough that Thong stopped sniffing things and came back to make sure her human was all right. "It's not always that reveal-y. I had no idea Adam had gambling debts. But it's a little like that, yeah," she admitted. "People don't like being caught out. I just wish it—"

She broke off, and Rafael coughed in an attempt to hide a snerk of laughter. "You just wish there'd been an actual murder to solve?"

"That sounds so much worse than I mean it!" Megan wailed. "Not that I can think of a way for it to sound better! Also, I swear, Raf," she added, sobering a little, "listen to me. I still get overblown about things the way I did when I was seventeen, don't I? Aren't I supposed to sound more . . . grown-up by now?"

"You are grown-up, but people are people. We still get excited and dismayed by the same things we always did. Believe me," he said wryly. "If you spend most of your waking hours in an emergency room, it becomes really, really clear that people stay who they are through their whole lives. I think the biggest difference is that some people learn to pick their fights as they get older, and probably most of us lose some energy along the way. But that just means we save what we have for the stuff that's really important." He nudged her shoulder with his. "Like figuring out whodunit, if there's been a suspicious death. It matters to you."

Megan stopped to hug him. "When'd you get so smart, *mi amigo*?"

"I've always been smart," he replied, muffled into her hair. "This is my *wisdom* you're admiring now."

"Well, I tell you what *wasn't* wise. Falling off that tree branch backward, that wasn't wise."

Rafael let her go, offended. "*You said you'd catch me!*"

Megan burst out laughing, and they went back to the hotel bickering cheerfully, with the dogs winding around their ankles.

CHAPTER 22

Megan got a text from Aisling while they were having breakfast, a note with an access code and the explanation that the house was closed for the day, so they were welcome to come in through the back gate. *Everybody else will be*, Aisling wrote. *Even if "everybody" is gonna be weird without Mam and Uncle Adam* . . .

"No wonder she wants all of us to come," Megan said to the phone, then lifted it as if her friends could read it across the table. "There's a wake-funeral-thing for Seamus planned in a few hours. Ais asked if we'd all come. I'm going to go, because I've got this paperwork for her if nothing else, but if you'd rather not—"

"Oh, no, we're coming," Sarah said firmly. "Partly because the poor kid needs support, but also because every time we go anywhere with you, something interesting happens."

"See," Megan said to Rafael, "it turns out I need to date somebody like *her*."

Rafael's eyebrows slammed together and then shot upward in a brief wrestling match across his forehead while Megan put her face in her hands and Sarah began to laugh. Megan said, "Um," into her hands, and Sarah's laughter pealed higher, filling the hotel restaurant as Megan, to her own surprise, blushed furiously against her palms.

"I have no idea how to respond," Raf said through Sarah's unbroken giggles. "I never thought we had the same taste in women, Megs. I mean, I have to *admire* your taste, in that case, but, uh, this one's taken?"

Sarah's laughter shot upward again, and the tableware rattled slightly as she pushed her plate aside to thunk her head on her arms, laughing into the paper place mats. Megan lifted her face from her palms, caught a glimpse of Rafael's still-bemused expression, and started giggling herself, although hers was more tinged with embarrassment. Hoarsely, through laughter and self-consciousness, she said, "I swear I wasn't trying to steal your girl, Raf, I just, oh my God. I mean. She's not even—you're not even—really my type, Sarah, I'm sorry—"

"*Oh, no, that's okay!*" Sarah assured her through another gale of laughter. "No, oh my God, I'm, I cannot imagine the awkwardness of, I'm sorry, it's just Raf has told me what a disaster you two dating was, I just can't imagine you two both dating me—!"

"Also we're married!" Rafael protested. "Ideally we're not dating anybody else!"

"Sure, that too." Sarah, eyes bright with laughing

tears, tipped over to kiss her husband while Megan tried to remember how to not blush.

"I just meant, someone who came around to thinking it was *interesting* when my life got weird, instead of thinking it was awful! I didn't mean actually dating *Sarah*!"

Sarah wiped her eyes, still giggling. "I know. We know. But that was really funny."

"I'm just going to *die*," Megan informed the table, as if it was interested in her love life. "Oh, God. Thank you," she added as she looked up, face still hot even though she was regaining her equilibrium. "Thanks for understanding what I meant instead of what I said. Right, so, um, where were we? Going to Aisling's. I have no idea what's appropriate to wear to a druidic funeral, so we're gonna have to wing this one, I guess. And ask the hotel to dog sit, because I don't think anybody needs Jack Russells at a funeral."

"There's got to be somewhere at that house you can put a couple of small dogs for a while," Sarah said. "Text Aisling and ask, and we'll go figure out what to wear. Ask her about that, too."

"You're a very smart woman," Megan told her. Sarah gave a stage-worthy little bow, mostly with a flourish of her fingers, and Megan texted to ask about both of those things as they left the restaurant.

Aisling answered before they'd even made it to their rooms. "'Wear anything,' she says, and there's a dog run behind the security outbuilding they can stay in for a while. Too bad I didn't think to ask about that the other day. They could have had a much more fun afternoon than hanging out in the car."

"Ah, yes," Rafael said dryly. "That's healthy, imagining you can think of literally every possibility that could ever stand a chance of presenting itself to you."

"Saaaaaraaaaaahhhhh, he's being sarcastic at me."

"If you two don't cut it out, I'm leaving you both here and going to the funeral myself."

Megan giggled and ducked into her own room as they went into theirs, and half an hour later, they met at the car, everyone as presentable as they could be. Megan herself had defaulted to her driving uniform, which she tended to always bring with her and which was at least black. Raf had on dark-blue jeans and a deep-red button-down shirt that made his color, already improved in the days he'd been in Ireland, much better. Sarah wore a brilliant green blouse with wide sleeves and a matching wrapped skirt, enhanced with beads and necklaces, and a rich orange rectangular shawl thrown over one shoulder. The entire ensemble set off her dark-brown skin flawlessly, and Megan stopped with a whistle. "No, never mind, you *should* go without us. We're just going to make you look bad. Wow."

"And there she was telling me, don't pack a suit, it's not like I'll have anywhere to wear this anyway," Rafael said to Megan, ruefully. "Next time I'm packing a suit."

"Yeah, I think you'd better. Don't let the dogs shed on you!" She meant it to both of them, but Sarah made a fuss moving her skirt aside, as if the carrier might suddenly explode with dog fur, and sat in the front seat next to Megan for the drive to the Rathballard House's back avenue. Raf hopped out of the car to open the gate, and Megan pretended to drive off without him, "because apparently I actually am twelve again when I get to hang out with you," she told him happily when he got back in the car.

"It's great," Sarah said. "You're both idiots, but it's great."

One of the staff, someone Megan hadn't met before, took the dogs when they got to the house, and told them Aisling was waiting for them in the foyer. The three of them made their way through, not around, the mansion, to find a considerable gathering of people in the enormous open entry room. The doors stood open, too, showing that the gathering spilled out onto the broad front steps, and across the long drive. Megan, approaching Aisling to offer the paperwork her great-uncle had signed, said, "Ian told me Rathballard House employed half the village, but I didn't entirely think he meant it until now. This is wonderful, Ais. I'm glad so many people are here."

"Me too." The young woman wore a rather pretty black dress that would have been flattering if her eyes weren't so sad and tired. As it was, she looked drained, and Megan offered a hug that she accepted. "Thanks. I knew Da's pagan friends would come, but I didn't realize so many other people would be here. I've got ribbons over there to the side," she said hesitantly. "We'll be going out to the rag tree, to his altar, and I'm asking everybody if they might tie a ribbon and make a wish, even if it's just for peace," she whispered, trying not to let her voice crack.

"We'd be happy to," Megan murmured. "I'm glad this is settling down, Aisling. It's been way too much for you to deal with, but you've been a champion."

"I'd not have made it through without you. I know you only met me three days ago, but you've been a star, Megan. Thank you for everything. And thank your friends for coming too. It was such a scene yesterday, I didn't know if they would." Aisling smiled weakly, and Megan tried not to laugh.

"I think after yesterday's scene, they wouldn't have missed the rest of it for the world. Although I just thought—how far *is* your dad's, er, altar? I don't know that any of us have the shoes for a long walk through the woods."

"Oh, he paved it," Aisling said with a sniffling smile. "Big paving stones, set up out of the earth so he didn't have to slog through the muck. It's a kilometer or so, but none of it's messy. The rest of the estate is gone to wild, but not that path. Someone rang me this morning to come out to look at the waste spill, so they can figure out what damage has been done and how to clean it up. I think because it's vandalism, the estate won't be responsible for the costs, but I'm not sure yet. There's so much left to do."

"I know. But you'll manage it. And Ian and Nora and the others will help. They like you. It'll be all right." Megan gave her another encouraging hug, then stepped back to let other people talk with her, and to go get ribbons for the rag tree. The table they were laid out on had clearly been dragged in from the tearoom, and there were plates of small foods and a genuinely impressive amount of alcohol laid out on other tables around the edges of the room. With Sarah and Raf in her wake, Megan began to follow the crowd out the door, working their way toward the paved stone path that eventually led to Seamus Nolan's . . .

"Grotto," Megan said, when they arrived. It actually *was* a grotto, or a folly—a purposefully built "ruin" that had been all the rage among the aristocracy for decades in the eighteenth and early nineteenth centuries. This one had been built as a cave, a half circle that greenery had crawled over and partially destroyed over the years. Trees had broken through in places, or grown up within it, but its original shape was visible, and a small, still-running fountain sat at the back, spilling water in a quiet, pleasant burble. A Brigid's cross was affixed to the back wall of the grotto, wrapped with prayer beads, and people were walking up to those and touching them, often murmuring something before they stepped away again.

The rag tree, a hawthorn that Megan could only identify because there was a small sign posted near it with its genus and common name listed on it, sprawled gently over much of the grotto, blocking part of its open face, but making for a comfortably protected space within. Megan went inside to tie her own ribbon as high up as she could reach, hoping it would bring Aisling, if not Seamus, some measure of peace, and left again to watch other people move quietly through the same space.

"Told you," Rafael murmured as he and Sarah came to join her in watching people. "Well-centered holiday. If that counts as a well."

"I think it's a spring," Megan murmured back. A chill ran down her spine, nothing at all to do with the temperature, and she found herself staring at the little spring and the cross above it. "Well-centered."

"That's what I said. Because I'm funny."

She breathed an obliging laugh, but didn't speak, trying to grasp thoughts that were bouncing around inside her head without any particular order to them. "No, well-centered. Um. She said. Carla said. A druid I talked to yesterday. She said there had been several deaths centered around Brigid's wells, all over the country. People who worshiped Brigid, pagans, had died in a bunch of stupid accidents."

Sarah whispered, "Ooh. That's awful. That must be very hard for the community."

"She said it was, yeah. But . . ." Megan turned away from her friends, standing on her toes to see if she could find Aisling in the slowly moving gathering of mourners. Then she took her phone out, pulling up the news articles she'd first read about Seamus, immediately after finding his body. "Those aren't his prayer beads on the cross up there," she said slowly. "I mean, they probably are, but they're not the ones from this picture, not the ones he wore. He wasn't wearing them when I found the body."

"They probably fell off in the well." Rafael and Sarah both ducked their heads over Megan's phone as she expanded the picture, trying to get a better look at

Seamus's prayer beads. Raf tilted the phone toward himself. "Although . . . are they wood? They look like it. I guess they should have floated."

"Not if somebody took them." Megan's eyes were closed as she tried to bring an image to mind. "The same person who put the bike in the hedge. Crap. *Crap!* Excuse me!" She didn't know whom she was talking to, really, because Sarah and Rafael both followed her, of course, as she hurried back up the path, trying to get away from the larger group of mourners as she scrolled to the recently called numbers on her phone, and dialed.

Garda Farrell picked up with an amused, "What's the murder driver want with me now?" but Megan was already talking, trying to keep her voice down despite agitation making her want to lift it.

"Detec—Garda, Garda Farrell, did you get any prints off the bike? I don't know how long that even takes?"

"Not yet. They're going through the system, but no hits. Why?" The young man's voice sharpened. "Have you got something? Did the ex confess? Or the uncle? Doyle said it was a mess there yesterday!"

"I bet he didn't mention the part where he's working as an enforcer for some illegal bookmaker," Megan said, not quite beneath her breath. Farrell made a startled noise, but Megan barreled on. "No, it's not Jenny or Adam. It's Father Colman, Det—Garda. It's Colman, and Seamus Nolan isn't the only pagan he's killed over the past five years. Talk to Carla—*crap*, I didn't get her last name, but Healy? No, Haughey, Peader Haughey, the radio announcer, he'll have it—but I've been in Colman's house, and Seamus's prayer beads are wrapped around a cross in his living room!"

Farrell went silent a long, long moment. Long enough for Megan to look up, teeth in her lip, to find Sarah and Raf both staring at her, wide-eyed and silent themselves. Then Farrell said, "If you're right about this, I'll *be* Detective, and if you're not, I'll be laughed out of the guards, Ms. Malone."

"I'm right." Megan's heart was hammering so hard she could barely stand. "I thought it was a rosary, but it hasn't got a cross pendant. It's got a circle with a carving on it. A tree of life, like Carla's. I didn't notice, or I noticed but I didn't *notice* until I saw the one in his grotto on the estate. They're the same. And I'm betting—Colman's got other crosses, other stuff, on the wall there in the house. I bet some of them are trophies too. I'm right. I'm sure I'm right."

Another silence met her, before Farrell finally said, "I'll buy you a drink with my first pay rise if you are," and hung up.

Megan folded her phone against her chest, meeting the Williamses' gaze with her own until Rafael, audibly awed, whispered, "Is *that* how it works?"

She gave a short, high-pitched laugh. "That's more like it than yesterday, yes. Except I don't usually get to send the guards after them, I'm usually right there in the room with them, and sometimes they're trying to kill me." To her absolute horror, her voice broke on the last words, and tears suddenly burned her eyes.

Raf, without speaking, stepped forward to drag her into a hug, and a heartbeat later Sarah's arms went around both of them. Megan choked on a sob, trying to hold it back, before a rush of overwhelmed emotion dragged the tears from her, and she stood crying in her friends' arms for several ragged moments.

"Come on," Raf said eventually, as her tears started to dry up. "Let's go back up to that big house and eat all their petit fours and scones."

Megan blurted a giggle. "Okay. That sounds great. Thank you." She meant the words for more than the suggestion of food, and Raf gave her a fond look that said he understood.

"*Por supuesto, mi amiga mejor. Vamos, ándale. Necesitamos comida*, or at least sugar bombs."

Megan giggled again, leaning on Sarah as they walked back up toward the house. "I was gonna say, I'm not sure petit fours count as *food*. Tea, too, maybe. Or coffee. Coffee is better than tea. And maybe puppies to hug."

"They'll shed all over your uniform," Sarah warned. "And I'm not letting them shed all over this dress."

"No, it's too beautiful. Just like you are." Megan, still sniffling but feeling considerably better, followed them into the big house and laughed as Rafael swept down on the snack tables and started piling plates for them. "He's a good guy," she told his wife, who smiled.

"I kind of like him. You doing okay now? You're sure about Father Colman?"

"Yeah." Megan nodded. "Yeah, I am, and . . ."

"And it helps?" Sarah asked when Megan didn't finish the sentence. "With everything about your ex, I mean?"

"I think so. I think so, yeah. I'll feel better when Farrell calls me back to verify it, but . . . yeah."

Sarah chuckled. "Are you sure he's going to?"

Megan blinked, then stared at her. "Well, Paul would! Oh my God! I should text them!" She pulled her phone out to do so, but as she did, Aisling, halfway across the foyer, shrieked and sat down hard on the marble floors.

Everyone nearby rushed toward her, but cleared a path as she said, "Megan? Megan, are you here? Megan, go to RTÉ News! No, you're here! Look! Here! You were right! Oh my *God*!" As Megan had done a little while earlier, Aisling burst into tears, then threw herself into Megan's arms as she knelt next to her. Aisling's phone played a live feed from Naas, County Kildare, in Megan's ear, a news reporter saying this was mobile phone footage from a local in Naas capturing the moment when Father Richard Colman was arrested on suspicion of murdering Seamus Nolan, the "Irish Druid."

After a minute, Aisling, still in tears, fumbled the phone around so she and Megan—and thirty other people, although they were turning to their own phones for ease—could actually watch the footage through a mixture of hugs and tears. Garda Shane Farrell, who should have said "no comment"—Megan knew that much by now—told the amateur reporter that the guards had received a tip from a concerned citizen, which sent Rafael and Sarah into a spasm of slightly hysterical glee, whispering, "That's Megan, that's her, she's the 'concerned citizen,'" to each other, and behind him, a flush-cheeked, visibly furious Colman was escorted away.

"He loves Brigid," Megan said almost sadly, watching the priest's arrest. "The Catholic version of her, anyway. So much that he couldn't stand people drawing so much attention to the old goddess idea. What a waste. How stupid and sad."

She nearly jerked out of her skin as her own phone rang, and answered, completely stunned to hear Farrell's voice on the other end of the line. "You were right. I asked about the bicycle. He saw it and knew Seamus was there, he said. He put it into the hedge and went to kill the man, malice aforethought. I think he might have been half out of his mind with some kind of religious fervor, but it's what he did. You saw him leaving the second time, after he'd thrown the bicycle away and shoved Seamus into the well."

"Oh my God," Megan said faintly. "I didn't think of that. That was the part I couldn't make work. But oh my God. Thank you for telling me."

"Don't tell anybody I did," Farrell said with sour amusement. He hung up, and Megan gave another little shrill laugh, then looked up at Sarah and Raf.

"We heard." Raf plunked down on the floor with Megan and Aisling, pulling them both into a hug, then adjusting to include Sarah in it when she knelt with a dancer's grace. "We heard. You did it, Megs. You figured it out."

"You did everything," Aisling said through tears. "You saved my whole life here."

"Well." Megan shrugged uncomfortably. "I'm not sure about *that*."

Aisling, stubbornly, said, "Did too," and Raf leaned like he would knock his shoulder against Megan's if they weren't all tangled up in a hug.

"Take the win, Megs. You earned it."

"Yeah. Okay. I'll try." Megan unwound from the hug, helping Aisling to her feet. "It's gonna be okay, Ais. Now, go talk to Ian, all right, sweetie? He's over there trying not to explode from wanting to check in on you."

The girl glanced toward the gardener, smiled through her sniffles, and hugged Megan one more time before going to get a hug from Ian, too. The young man put his arm around her shoulders protectively, and Megan, helping Sarah to her feet, said, "I think she'll be okay."

"She will," Raf said as he got up. "And as for us, how about we get through the rest of our vacation without any more murder mysteries, huh?"

Megan laughed. "All right. Well. I make no promises, but I'll think about it. And maybe we'll just stay away from any holy wells."

"Or golf courses," Sarah said.

"Or restaurants, or churches, or big, old manor houses," Rafael suggested. "Or whiskey distilleries, for that matter."

"Right, so basically we're going back to my house and not leaving it for the next eight days, is that what you're saying? And then we'll end up killing each other because we'll have gone stir-crazy, so that won't work out at all."

"Okay, fine. In that case," Sarah said, "I propose that Raf and I go into everywhere *first*, in order to prevent you from being the person who walks in and finds a body."

"I'm not sure that's how it works . . ."

"Oh, I am. If somebody else takes the lead, nobody dies. That's pretty clear."

Megan held up her hands, conceding. "All right. Okay, come on, then. Let's go find more adventures, but you guys go first."

Rafael took Sarah's hand, kissed it, and led her out of the manor house, Megan trailing behind with a smile.

ACKNOWLEDGMENTS

I would particularly like to thank @TheIrishFor on Twitter for a bit of Irish-language pronunciation guidance, as well as Kate Sheehy, Ruth Long, Susan Connolly, and Sarah Rees Brennan for a broad spectrum of answers to random questions. I'd also like to thank Antony Johnston for allowing me the shout-out to Gwinny Tuffel, star of The Dog Sitter Detective mysteries, which are a delight!

In the instances where I've taken some liberties with actual geography, well, that's on me, not on Ireland, if you happen to visit anywhere I wrote about. :)

-Catie

Visit our website at
KensingtonBooks.com
to sign up for our newsletters, read
more from your favorite authors, see
books by series, view reading group
guides, and more!

BOOK **CLUB**
BETWEEN THE CHAPTERS

Become a Part of Our
Between the Chapters Book Club
Community and Join the Conversation

Betweenthechapters.net